THE PROMISE

J.S DONOVAN

❀ Created with Vellum

1

HARTWELL

The wood in the firepit snapped and popped. Like fireflies, cinders drifted into the air. The flame reflected in Elizabeth's gorgeous eyes. She was a small-town girl with unabashed beauty, a brilliant mind, and rare parents who'd understood the balance between consequence and grace. Despite all that, she had a hole inside her. An emptiness only destiny could fill. She glanced up from the flame, dark dots seared in her vision like film grain. Tommy, John, and Gena sat on lawn chairs around the campfire. They laughed at one of Tommy's jokes. He was always quick on a pun. John scooted closer to Gena. A sheen of sweat glistened on his forehead as he tried to find the right time to hold Gena's hand. Like Elizabeth, they were all young, beautiful, with minds clouded with big dreams.

"You good?" Tommy asked.

It took Elizabeth a second to realize he was talking to her. She tucked her hair behind her ear. "I'm great."

"You don't look very *fired* up about summer semester." A wry smile grew on Tommy's face.

Elizabeth cringed at his joke. "I'm just a little *burnt out.*"

Tommy replied, "I know a few ways to *rekindle* that flame."

Elizabeth's face glowed cherry red.

Gena's jaw dropped before becoming an open-mouthed smile. John was impressed by his friend's courage.

Elizabeth cleared her throat. She looked down at her feet. "Wow. When did, uh, you become so bold?"

Tommy said, "It's our last week in Hartwell. I want to leave on a good note."

Elizabeth's heart hammered in her chest. "Well, if you want to talk, um, scoot your chair over here."

Tommy seemed surprised by Elizabeth's response. He quickly put on a nonchalant expression. He picked up his chair and walked it next to Elizabeth, then sat down to her right so close, their armrests touching.

Elizabeth's heart fluttered.

Tommy said, "I've waited a stupid long time to tell you how beautiful you are."

Elizabeth blushed and asked jokingly, "Oh yeah? What part?"

Tommy studied her face. "Your smile."

"Gosh, you're corny."

"Would you rather have me say your breasts? They're awesome by the way."

Too embarrassed to look at him, Elizabeth scanned the dark woods. Trees extended endlessly in every direction. Night critters chirped.

Watching the budding chemistry between his two best friends, John swallowed his nervousness and gently held Gena's hand.

She quickly slipped out from his grasp.

Emotionally stricken, John drew back his hand and put it in his pocket.

Gena kept her eyes to herself, her tongue rolling on the inside of her cheek, the awkwardness bearing down on her.

Tommy said to Elizabeth, "I want to be with you, Lizzy."

"Tom, I—" Elizabeth stopped herself. College started in two weeks. All four of them would be splitting up. Chasing a fleeting romance with a childhood friend was foolishness. Heart pounding, she thought, *It's time you lived a little.*

She turned to Tommy. They gazed deep into each other's eyes. All the romantic movies Elizabeth watched made the moment feel surreal and comical.

"What were you saying?" Tommy asked.

"Oh, nothing." Elizabeth kept herself from laughing at the textbook romance and leaned in for a kiss. *Out of all people, she was with Tommy friggin' Demko. Who would've thunk?"*

Bam!

The loud noise caused Elizabeth to recoil and look over her shoulder.

In front of her, John fell backward and scurried away from the fire. Gena was out of her seat, screaming.

Elizabeth wiped her face. Something smeared her hand red. Tommy was slumped in the seat next to her, a hole in the back of his head.

Gasping, Elizabeth fell from her seat, her shoulder hitting the dewy grass.

Another gunshot sounded.

The bullet blew chunks of bark off a nearby tree.

"Run!" John grabbed Gena's hand and dashed into the darkness.

"Wait up!" Elizabeth ran after them.

Bam!

Bam!

She heard the wind cut near her head. The bullet missed her by inches. She zig-zagged, making it harder for the shooter. She ran blindly in the darkness. The wind pushed against her. Her heart was going to explode. Her mind turned off. Instinct guided her. She rolled her ankle. Screaming, she tumbled down a hill. She rolled head first, hitting rough dirt and small rocks. She slammed into an oak tree, coming to a harsh stop.

Elizabeth lingered there for a moment, pain coursing through her body. She grabbed the tree and used it to stand. Torn leaves and broken twigs clung to her hair. Dirt painted her pretty face. She wanted to yell for John and Gena, but that would betray her location. Skull throbbing, she jogged deeper into the woods.

Gunshots echoed in the distance.

Elizabeth breathed heavily. The wind felt like splinters lodging her throat. *Tommy is dead,* she thought. Tears streamed down her dirty cheeks. Her jog became a walk. Using the bottom of her shirt, she rubbed the dirt away from her face. She propped herself up against a tree and turned her eyes to the starry heavens. She shut her eyes for a second, trying to calm herself.

A twig broke in the distance.

Elizabeth gasped and cowered behind a nearby tree. She scooted on her bottom and pulled her knees to her chest. Her back pressed against the rough bark. Nervously, she rubbed the leaves from her hair.

Another twig broke.

Terror kept Elizabeth from turning back. She focused herself and did her best to steady her breathing. She knew she had to make a choice: run or hide.

Elizabeth battled her fear.

Footsteps approached her.

She got to her feet, her hand covering her mouth. She had made her choice.

2

THE STAIN

Wearing a cheap suit and tie, Clyde Barker drove his black 1982 Cadillac to the small town of Hartwell, Georgia. He kept one hand on the steering wheel. Dollar store sunglasses rested on the bridge of his nose. He stood over six and a half feet tall. His muscles were long and strong. The smell of jailhouse sanitizer clung to his large hands, but working pro bono for druggies, hookers, and juvenile screws-ups left another stench on him. Bitterness. His clients' lack of respect made him question why his father ever chose this career.

Clyde turned the radio dial. Guitar riffs from ZZ-Top filled the car. His large foot teased the accelerator. The Caddy's engine growled. The boxy four-door car whipped through Georgia's back roads. Going from Atlanta to Hart County wasn't more than a few hours northeast. Clyde stayed off interstates the whole way. Even without traffic, he never enjoyed long strips of straight pavement. Twists and turns kept him breathing. It reminded him that he was alive.

His cell phone on the front seat dinged. He lifted it off the manila folder and checked the text.

You almost here? the sender asked.

Soon, Clyde replied. He tossed the phone back on the folder.

Trees and farmlands flanked the road. Captivated by nature, Clyde needed to remind himself why he chose the concrete jungle of inner-city Atlanta over the rural beauty throughout the rest of Georgia. Money would've been the simplest answer, but Clyde's bank account was a joke. He hoped that he'd land that one big gig that would rapture him from his dingy attorney's office into a renowned law firm at the heart of downtown. As of now, he was chasing the wind. The part of Atlanta he inhabited was grimy and crippled by vices. As an upstart attorney, the work opportunities were endless, but the clientele were poverty-stricken and debased users. He enjoyed the idea of helping people more than the act itself. That's what righteous suffering was: doing the right thing even if it meant personal torment. He imagined his father was that way.

Clyde turned down the forested road and followed the cracked asphalt driveway. A cop car was parked in front of the ugly yellow house. Unmowed grass sprouted around the single-story building. Old grime clung to the walls and its paint reminded him of greenish urine. Dozens of roof shingles were missing. Broken window blinds dangled loosely on the other side of dusty windows. A bowling ball-sized hole had rotted into the off-kilter front porch.

Clyde rolled to a stop beside the cop car. The decal on the Impala sedan read *Hartwell Police Department*.

The redhead stepped out and put her hand on her hip. Amber-tinted sunglasses covered her amber eyes. Freckles spotted her cheekbones. Though she had a hardened expression common among many law enforcement women, Officer Sarah Sullivan was gorgeous.

Clyde grabbed his phone and folder and stepped out. "You could've told me it was a dump."

"I thought you'd like to see for yourself," Sarah teased. She smiled, revealing the two front teeth on her bottom jaw that slightly overlapped. Somehow the imperfection made her look more beautiful. More human.

Clyde hugged her. She squeezed back.

"You make me feel like a midget," Sarah said, her face against his chest.

Nearly a foot and half taller, Clyde snickered. He pulled away from her, and his reflection stared back in her sunglasses. "I've missed you," Clyde said.

"When did you become such a sap?" Sarah asked, grinning widely.

Clyde shrugged.

Sarah squeezed his bicep. "No longer noodle boy, huh?"

It was hard to believe that the last time they saw each other was fifteen years ago. Clyde had changed from the tenth-grade lanky giant into a mountain, but Sarah was always lovely. She just had a few more freckles and little laugh lines beside her naked smile.

She walked her fingers up Clyde's chest. "With arms like that, you could pick me up and toss me wherever you wanted."

Clyde opted for an awkward smile over a verbal response. Sarah always had a way of making him feel uncomfortable. Half of what she said was a tease. That was her personality, and it hadn't changed in the last decade and a half.

Clyde opened up the folder and grabbed the key from beside the land deed. "Shall we?"

Sarah nodded.

Walking together, Clyde opened the screen door and let Sarah have the honors.

"You do it," Sarah said. "It ain't my house."

They traded spots. Sarah held the screen door while Clyde unlocked the front door. He immediately noticed the shag carpet on the living room floor, calling to mind all the little board game figurines it consumed many summers ago. Sarah's nose crinkled at the strange, sour stench. It wasn't that anything had gone bad. Certain houses had certain smells, and this one was one of the worst. Its atmosphere was damp and mildewy despite the outside air being warm and dry. Clyde stepped aside, letting Sarah enter first.

Clyde followed her in, shutting the screen door but not the front door. Shafts of light streamed into the dusty house. The furniture was old and worn-down. A few stuffed trout trophies hung on the walls, but there were very few pictures.

Sarah approached the fist-sized holes on one wall. She knelt slightly and peered inside. "You got a rat's nest."

Clyde lingered behind her, looking at the chewed-up blue, green, and red electrical cables all jumbled up. "Add it to the list along with spackle."

A DVD shelf contained dozens of horror movies and true crime documentaries. Clyde walked to the lounge and stopped at the old wooden desk. There were scratches on the top where a pencil had pressed too hard through a page. A 1990s desktop monitor and computer sat on it. It still had a floppy disk reader. Clyde turned it on. A DOS program loaded. The green cursor blinked on the black screen. The document was waiting for a letter never written.

Sarah tested the kitchen sink. The faucet violently spat water. Sucking air through her teeth, she quickly turned it off. Little water droplets spattered her waist. She stood silently, looking at the small kitchen table. It was made for two people. Like an exploded tomato, crusty blood spatter stained the unsightly wallpaper. The removed bullet left a hole at the center of the maroon blot. It had been shot at a 45-degree angle above one of the seats.

Clyde entered. His stomach turned. A frown sank his face.

"Sorry," Sarah said quietly.

Clyde grabbed a washrag hanging on the silverware drawer's knob. He wet it, wrung out the excess water, and approached the stain. Using a waxing motion, he washed the wall. The blood turned from a deep maroon to a rich red. Pink water trickled down the wall. Sarah grabbed her own rag. Kneeling down, she worked underneath Clyde. They cleaned most of it, but the stain was deep. Clyde got what he could. He planned on replacing the wallpaper anyway.

Leaving the rags in the sink, Clyde and Sarah went out the front door. They sat on the rocking chairs on the front porch.

"Oh," Sarah said, remembering something. She got up and jogged to her cop car, then bent over and grabbed a cooler from the trunk. She carried it over to Clyde, popped it open, and sat down. A twelve-pack of PBRs rested on a bed of half-melted ice cubes.

Clyde ripped a can from the plastic net, feeling the cold on his fingertips. He put his fingernail beneath the opener tab.

"Hold on," Sarah said, getting her own beer.

She smiled mischievously.

Clyde understood her intentions. "You can't be serious."

"Come on. You can't say you haven't been thinking about it since the moment you called," Sarah tempted him.

Clyde said, "Alright. Have it your way."

They held out their beer cans and shook them furiously. When they finished, they quickly opened their cans and drank.

Sarah started laughing as beer fizz rolled down Clyde's chin. Her laugh caused her to spit up her beer as well. Looking into each other's eyes, they kept drinking until both cans were finished. Clyde beat her by a second. He crushed the beer in his hand and tossed it aside.

Sarah wiped her chin with her sleeve. "You've gotten better."

"I haven't done it since high school," Clyde replied. "*Ack.* That taste."

"You don't drink it for the flavor." Sarah grabbed two more cans, giving one to Clyde.

Clouds painted the perfect indigo sky. It was only a little past 4 pm.

Clyde smirked and opened the can.

Nursing their beers, the two of them looked out at the front lawn. Tall weeds with green, wheat-like husks and dandelions at different stages of life grew among the ankle-high grass. Chigger bugs hopped from plant to plant. The fields extended out to acres of woods. The house wasn't much to look at, but the twelve acres of untapped land would fetch a pretty penny.

Sarah removed her aviators and set them aside. She stretched her arms above her head and arched her back, then yawned.

"Long day?" Clyde asked.

"Slow," Sarah replied. "You?"

He replied, "I'm staying busy."

"You're a lawyer. I'm a cop. Who would've guessed it? Do you like the job?"

It was a hard question to answer. Clyde replied, "Sure."

"You're not very convincing," Sarah said.

Clyde stayed silent. His career would make his father proud. That's what mattered.

Sarah teetered in the rocker. "When was the last time you saw him?"

Clyde snapped out of his train of thought. "Who?"

"Your uncle."

"Oh, the last summer you and I were together," Clyde said. "He dropped me off at the foster home and that was that."

"Did the two of you ever talk?" Sarah asked.

"He'd call me on my birthday," Clyde replied, realizing just how depressing it sounded.

Sarah said, "I'm sorry he's gone."

"Uncle Andrew always kept his cards close to his chest. I didn't find out I was in his will until after he was gone," Clyde admitted. He didn't know what to do with the house and land he now owned.

"Hey," Sarah said, getting Clyde's attention.

Clyde waited for her to speak.

"Thank you for reaching out," Sarah said.

"Anytime," Clyde said.

"Why did you wait so long to call me?" Sarah asked.

"Life got in the way," Clyde replied.

"That's not what a girl wants to hear." The lusty fire was evident in her amber eyes.

"Sorry," Clyde apologized.

Sarah leaned over, her pretty face nearing his own. "What are you going to do to make it up to me?"

"Nothing." Clyde casually sipped his beer.

Sarah pulled away. "*Nothing?*" She repeated, offense in her voice. "Where's the fun in that?"

Clyde didn't answer.

"You came all this way and you don't want to be properly reacquainted?" Sarah asked.

"We were never acquainted in the first place," Clyde replied.

"I remember when you used to drool every time you saw me," Sarah said.

"You're attractive, Sarah," Clyde admitted.

"And?" Sarah asked.

"I like us—" he gestured between the both of them. "Like this."

Sarah leaned back in her chair and sipped her beer.

Clyde could see the cogs turning in her mind.

The two of them sat in awkward silence.

Birds sang in nearby trees. Crickets chirped. The calming southern breeze washed over them.

Clyde said, "So… what else is new with you?"

They decided to discuss trivial life things. After a while, the small talk and reminiscing of yesteryear replaced the quiet. Sarah left before sundown. Her cop car drove down the road. Clyde returned inside and locked the door. He sighed. His heart was torn. Part of him wanted to call her back over. He fought the urge. He wasn't going to be in Hartwell forever. He needed to keep things simple.

He turned on the TV and sank to the couch. His uncle's last saved channel was the Antique Road Show. With nothing else to watch, he lay on his side and stared lifelessly at the screen. His mind raced. He thought about court dates, arguments, legalese, and ways to defend his guilty clients. *Innocent until proven guilty,* he told himself, but most of the time, Clyde could sense the truth. He knew how to read lies and picked up on tics. He felt a little bit of his soul die each time he fought on behalf of a guilty man. He felt even worse when he succeeded to trick the entire jury.

Clyde awoke a few hours later. The lights were still on. The TV played a cheap infomercial. He got up and dragged himself to the bedroom. The bed was unmade and still had the same sheets Andrew had used when he was alive. Clyde kicked off his shoes and fell face-first on the mattress. He shut his eyes, falling quickly back to sleep.

A loud crash jolted him awake.

Clyde sat upright. He rubbed his hand down his face and listened. The wind whistled inside his house. Heart pounding, he stepped forward and nearly tripped on a baseball bat. Clyde picked it up. Choking the grip, he walked into the hallway. His hair was messy and his eyes were bloodshot. He walked quietly and peered around the hall's corner.

The front door was wide open. The wind bumped the screen door against the threshold. *Thump. Thump. Thump.*

He remembered locking it.

Someone was in his house.

3

INTRUDER

The shag carpet brushed against the soles of Clyde's black socks. He moved carefully, keeping the baseball bat near his shoulder. He glanced out the screen door. Only his Cadillac was visible. He moved to the kitchen. The room was undisturbed. Clyde reached the back door and opened it quickly, ready to strike whoever was on the other side. There was no one.

Instead of checking every room, he grabbed his cellphone from the couch and stepped out to the front porch. He dialed Sarah.

It rang and rang.

"Come on, pick up," Clyde mumbled, making his way to his car.

He unlocked the door and sat on the driver's side, then locked himself inside.

"Hello?" Sarah answered, sleep still in her voice.

"It's Clyde." He looked around nervously. "I think someone broke into the house."

"Hmm," Sarah mumbled.

"I'm serious," Clyde said. "Get over here."

"Did you call the police?" she asked.

"You are the police."

He heard Sarah lift up from the bed. "Hang tight. I'll be there in ten."

"I'll stay on the line just in case," Clyde said. He put the phone in the cup holder and had a pensive look on his square face. The bat rested on his lap. He tapped his leg. He watched the open front door, expecting the intruder to come out at any moment.

Red and blue lights flashing, Sarah's cruiser pulled up beside Clyde. Keeping the lights on, she got out. Clyde exited also. Her layered ginger hair was down to her shoulders. The red and blue lights flashed over her face. Her hand stayed on her gun.

"This better not be an elaborate booty call," Sarah said.

"I haven't seen anyone leave," Clyde said, ignoring her comment.

"Did you see what they looked like?" Sarah asked.

"No," Clyde replied.

"Wait here." Sarah walked up the steps and to the screen door. "Hartwell PD. Open up."

Getting no response, she moved inside.

Clyde stayed out. He watched the sides of the house, expecting the intruder to show up.

He waited a few minutes.

Worry squeezed his chest. He thought about Sarah. He wanted to move inside but stopped himself. She told him to wait, he'd have to wait.

The screen door opened, and Sarah stepped out.

"Anything?" Clyde asked.

Sarah marched down the stairs and approached him.

"Well?" Clyde asked.

"You sure someone broke inside?" Sarah asked.

"I locked the door right after you left."

"Maybe the wind blew it open," Sarah replied.

"A gust that strong? No. That's impossible. I swear I locked it, Sarah," Clyde replied.

"Relax," Sarah said directly. "You want to sleep at the station tonight or a hotel?"

"I'd prefer neither," Clyde answered.

"Okay. Well, there's no one in your house, Clyde. No damage to the door either," Sarah said. "Is it possible you were dreaming?"

"I wouldn't have called you if I thought it was nothing," Clyde said.

"I understand," Sarah said, not believing him. "I have a shift tomorrow at 7 am. I'll have to get up at 5 so if you don't mind, I'm going to head home."

"Right, yeah, do what you got to do," Clyde said. "What would you like me to do if something like this happens again?"

"Call 911," Sarah answered and got into her cop car.

"Thank you," Clyde said.

Sarah slammed the door shut and sped into the darkness.

Embarrassed, Clyde returned inside. He locked the door and double-checked it this time. He peered into various rooms and closets, making sure there was no one inside. Lastly, he checked his room. The master bedroom was rather typical. It had a queen-sized bed, nightstands, a tall lamp in the corner of the room, a dresser, and a closet. Clyde got on the bed and shut his eyes.

He woke up before sunrise. Clyde put his suitcase on his bed and took out running shorts and a tee-shirt. He packed light. Three of everything. He jogged in place as he reached the front door. He set his timer and ran outside, embracing the chilly morning as he ran up the driveway and onto the single-lane road.

He jogged. His long legs gave him amazing distance. The crimson sunrise rose across the horizon. He completed his first mile in six minutes and forty seconds. It was just a second slower than the top one percent in his age bracket. Taking a short moment to rest, he looked out at the cows grazing on the fields. A bull with large horns turned to him, munching with its lopsided jaw.

Clyde reset his watch and continued his run. From his calves to his thighs, his muscles burned. He pushed himself. He kept alongside the barb-wire fence, then went two and a half miles before turning back. Morning fog hovered over a stretch of woods that didn't appear to be owned by anyone. Clyde headed back to his house.

Drenched in perspiration, he went inside, stripped off his sweaty clothes, and did a hundred sit-ups and a hundred push-ups while wearing his boxers. He finished his final push-up and rested on his belly, winded. Pain surged through every muscle. It took him a long minute before he decided to drag himself to the shower.

The scalding hot water splashed on him. He gasped and turned the dial, but the water turned freezing cold. He tried to find a balance but had to settle on one or the other. He chose cold. Chill bumps dotted his body. He recalled his run times per mile: 6:40, 6:44, 6:50, 7:01, 7:17. *Could be better,* he thought.

After getting dry and dressed, he checked Andrew's pantry and found a box of multigrain cereal. The milk in the fridge was a day past its best-by date. Clyde finished it, eating two bowls of cereal. Stuffed, he found a notepad on Andrew's desk and jotted down everything he needed to repair in the house. The first thing was the bloodstain. He also found a blotch of black mold near the ceiling vent that needed fixing. He wasn't the best handyman in the world, but he'd much rather work for free than have to pay someone else.

He searched the closet and basement but didn't find any of Andrew's tools. Clyde checked the decrepit shed behind the house. He shouldered his way through the jammed door. Inside the dusty room, he found a claw hammer that had a giant crack on the handle resting on a plywood shelf. Other tools sat in the wooden crate. Rust coated their metal so much that they were brittle and dangerous. Clyde jotted down the tools he needed on his list. Wearing shorts, a work tee-shirt that had a stretched-out neck, and a Chicago Cubs hat, he got into his car and drove to town.

Hartwell was an old southern town. There were around four thousand residents, but most were scattered on the outskirts. A faded Pepsi logo painted the side wall of one of many historic brick buildings lining Main Street. Clyde parallel parked outside of the hardware store.

He grabbed a basket on the way inside. The cashier—an old man with a bald head, bushy mustache, and face like an old dog—eyed Clyde. Clyde grabbed a claw hammer, drywall saw, paint, spackle, nails, and a dozen other tools he needed to fix the house. He paid in credit, hoping to flip the house the moment it was livable.

"I like the hat," the cashier said in his deep Southern drawl.

"Yeah, I'm hoping we get another win at the World Series," Clyde replied.

"Keep praying, friend."

Clyde chuckled.

"You look familiar," the cashier said.

"I'm Andrew Barker's nephew," Clyde admitted.

"Oh." the cashier's friendly countenance turned sour.

Clyde sensed the man's animosity toward Andrew but chose not to investigate. Andrew's business was no business of his.

A receipt printed out of an outdated receipt machine.

Clyde put it into one of the bags.

"Clyde? Is that you?" a man said behind Clyde.

He turned around, facing the six-foot two man. He wore a frilled fishing hat and had grey stubble on his cheeks and neck. His kind blue eyes were friendly and trusting. The man wore a fleece. A small fly-fishing hook was embroidered above the right breast. "You've gotten big, boy."

Clyde shook his hand, still unsure of the man's identity.

"I'm Don Fegan. One of Andrew's fishing buddies," the man said. "I was there that summer when you caught your first trout. You were smiling ear-to-ear."

"I remember," Clyde said, still a little fuzzy.

"I'm guessing you're here to repair his place."

"Yep." Clyde lifted his bags a little. "It's a real fixer-upper."

"If you ever need to let off some steam, I go fishing Sundays and Fridays," Don said. He opened his wallet and fished out a business card. Clyde noticed the large stack of hundred-dollar bills inside.

Clyde put one bag on the counter and slipped the card in his back pocket. He shook Don's hand again. "We'll see what happens."

"I look forward to it," Don replied.

Clyde took what he needed and left.

Don rested his elbows on the counter. "How's the shop, Tim?"

"You know how it is," the cashier replied. "There's always something."

Clyde returned to his car. He texted Sarah an apology for

last night and asked if she wanted to come over and hang out.

Only if I can help fix up that house of yours, Sarah replied.

He smiled. *Be my guest.*

Clyde returned home. He brought his heavy bags and put them on the kitchen table. Using a razor, he cut a line across the wallpaper and pulled it down. Still feeling the burn from his morning workout, he wadded the paper and tossed it into the trash can. As a kid, he was never much of an athlete, but now he was pretty decent. Some people reached their peak in high school. Clyde thought that was his low point. He had been skinny, shy, and weak. But once he realized the need for personal goals in his life, bodybuilding, exercising, and cardio activities became a temple to him. *If a shark stops swimming, it dies,* his law professor told him. Clyde tried to live by that saying.

He pulled out the refrigerator and placed plastic sheeting over the ground and countertops. He popped the top off the beige paint and uses his fresh paint roller to work on the walls.

Sarah arrived in the late afternoon. She drove her civilian vehicle. Her hair was in a loose ponytail. She'd tucked her white tee into paint-stained cargo pants. She waved, then grabbed her tool belt from the back seat.

Stepping out the front door, Clyde said, "I just bought new tools."

"I hope you kept the receipt," Sarah said, bringing her tools inside.

Clyde gave her a quick hug. "Thanks for coming over."

Sarah stayed quiet and walked past him.

Clyde said, "You're mad."

"You woke me up at 3 am," Sarah said.

"I'm sorry I overreacted," Clyde apologized.

"Whatever," Sarah said. She sniffled. "You've been painting."

"Uh-huh," Clyde said.

"Unless you plan on getting a buzz, open some windows," Sarah said.

A half-smile grew on Clyde's face. "Yes, ma'am."

They pushed all the furniture into the middle of the room and focused on the walls. It would take days, maybe weeks to get the house all fixed up, but the two of them worked well together. Sarah followed Clyde's lead most of the time, but when there was a problem that she couldn't fix, she pointed it out directly. She would brush up against Clyde at certain points when they were beside each other and seemed to position herself in a provocative manner when she bent over or grabbed tool. Clyde's head spun, trying to figure out if she was doing it intentionally or not.

At dark, they were patching up drywall when Clyde noticed something outside the window. A hundred and fifty feet away, a figure was silhouetted in the dark. While using his forearm to wipe the sweat from his forehead, Clyde approached the window. Listening to crickets chirping, he put his hands on the windowsill and stared at the stranger. The person was just far enough out of the light that Clyde could barely make out their body shape. A mask covered their face, but darkness concealed the details.

"Sarah," Clyde said.

"Hmm?" she replied, rubbing spackle on a few small holes.

"There is someone outside."

Sarah put aside her tools and walked up next to him.

The figure stepped back into the darkness.

Clyde pointed. "There."

Sarah looked perplexed.

Clyde stepped outside the front door. "Hello!"

His voice carried. The silhouette moved in the darkness, sprinting away on the single-lane road.

"See him?" Clyde asked.

"Nah," Sarah replied.

"Let's go after them." Clyde checked his pockets. He didn't have his cars keys on him. The clutter in the living room and kitchen discouraged him from looking. At least he had the house key.

"Clyde, what are you—"

"You drive," Clyde said and hurried out the door.

Reluctant, Sarah followed after him. He locked the door behind her and hurried along to her car. A neutral expression on her face, Sarah started her Impala.

"To the right," Clyde said.

Sarah drove that way.

Clyde kept an eye out for the runner. Sarah drove slowly. Her headlights reflected off the evening fog.

Sarah glanced over to Clyde. He was too busy looking at the road to notice. He said, "It might've been the same person who broke inside last night."

"Sure," Sarah mumbled.

Clyde didn't see the man for two miles. He was tempted to turn back, but then he saw the figure dart into the woods.

"There," Clyde said.

"How did he get ahead of us?" Sarah asked.

Sarah pulled over to the side of the road. Clyde got out. Sarah grabbed her flashlight and followed him into the forest. Trees casts long shadows as the beam of light crossed over them.

Clyde saw the figure run up ahead. He jogged after him. "Hey! Hey!"

Clyde raced after the figure.

"Wait up!" Sarah shouted.

Clyde weaved between trees. The guy in front of him was fast. He must've been a runner, too, and young. The light got farther away as Clyde outpaced Sarah. He stopped in a clearing. His foot crunched old wood. He lifted his foot, seeing an old fire pit.

Winded, Sarah jogged up behind him. "What the hell, Clyde? If he was armed, I couldn't have helped you if you kept getting ahead of me."

Clyde scanned the trees surrounding him. "Come out!"

Only the wind replied.

Chills danced up Clyde's right arm. He felt inclined to walk that way.

Suddenly, Sarah grabbed his left forearm. "We won't find him out here."

"Did you see his mask? What was up with that?" Clyde asked.

A twig snapped in the darkness.

Clyde turned toward the noise. He listened.

Sarah shined her light over a bush.

4

THE PIT

Sarah drove Clyde back to the house.

"That was a colossal waste of time," Sarah said exasperatedly.

Clyde said, "Hopefully, he won't come back."

"You own a gun, Clyde?" Sarah asked, parking the car but leaving the engine running.

Clyde shook his head.

"Start thinking about it," Sarah said. "Hartwell is a nice town, but it ain't without its crazies."

Her hand stayed on the shifter.

"Are you heading out?" Clyde asked.

"I think so," Sarah said. "I'll stop by again soon."

Clyde smiled at her. "Thank you for your help... with everything."

"Yeah, well, someone has got to look out for you," Sarah said.

Clyde got out of the car. He asked if she left anything inside. She said no and drove away.

Clyde stepped into the messy living room. Open paint

cans, plastic sheeting, and tools covered the floor. Clyde worked on a way to seal the fist-sized holes in the walls.

His phone rang. He answered, realizing it was one of his clients. Pacing back and forth, Clyde talked to the man about how the case would change now that he had violated parole. The client was out of money and begged Clyde to keep representing him. Clyde's compassion pulled at him, but he declined. He didn't plan on leaving Hartwell until Andrew's house was on the market. The client was upset, called Clyde some interesting names, and hung up.

That night, Clyde woke up, hearing the television playing on max volume.

Taking his baseball bat, he walked through the living room and pressed the TV's off button. The ceiling fan was the only noise that remained. Clyde walked back to the hall when the TV turned on again, playing static.

"What's wrong with you?" Clyde grumbled as he turned off the TV and unplugged it.

Feeling unsettled, he double-checked all the locks on the doors and windows. The broken blinds made it easier for someone to look inside. Clyde hated that. He took a bedsheet and tape and spent thirty minutes covering the windows. Accomplished, he slept until his alarm got him up at 5:30. He forced himself to rise and stretched. After relieving himself in the bathroom, he studied the stubble on his neck. He opened his toiletry bag and removed his straight razor and shaving oil. He sharpened the blade on a leather strap then touched the razor to his skin. Chill bumps rose and his hairs stood. Careful, he glided the blade up to his jaw. He watched himself in the mirror.

When he finished, he set the blade aside, washed his face, and proceeded to start his morning run. His mind raced with his feet. Who was stalking him? Why? Clyde had few connections to Hartwell. He was only around for one summer and a few other holidays. Andrew's home wasn't much to behold. Was there something inside he was missing? Something someone wanted to steal? Clyde didn't know his uncle very well. Maybe he pissed off the wrong people.

Clyde took a breather. He rested his palms on his knee and concentrated on breathing. He glanced to his right. The woods stood on the other side of the road. It was the same place where the silhouette ran. Roughly fifty feet into the woods, a young woman stood. She couldn't have been over twenty. Powdery dirt stained the front of her black overalls and the shoulder of her white tee. A few broken leaves snagged at the tips of her long hair. Her blue eyes were vacant. Her expression lacked emotion.

Clyde watched at her, feeling off-kilter by the way she watched him. The strange girl just stood there, staring at him. Clyde felt something was wrong. He couldn't explain it, but it was as if he had stumbled upon a bad omen.

A pick-up truck pulled to a stop in front of Clyde, blocking the view of the young woman.

Clyde was so caught up with the young woman that he didn't hear the rumbling vehicle pull up.

The window lowered. A woman with a round face and short brown hair smiled lopsidedly at Clyde. She was in her late thirties and wore a plaid blouse. The top four buttons were undone, revealing a gap in her flat chest. "Hey, stranger."

Clyde tried to get a look past her but couldn't. "Uh, hi."

"I've never seen you around before. Are you new to Hartwell?"

"Just visiting," Clyde replied anxiously.

"You got family here?" the woman asked.

"Not anymore."

"It's a strange place to visit without knowing anyone," the woman remarked.

Clyde didn't understand why this woman was bothering him right now. "I'm fixing my uncle's house." He hiked his thumb back to the way he came.

"Oh, you're related to Mr. Barker," the woman said. "My condolences."

"Thanks," Clyde replied.

"You look tired," the woman said. "You want a ride back?"

"I'm okay," Clyde answered. "I should finish my morning run."

"Right. See you around." The woman drove off.

The young woman in the woods wasn't there anymore.

Trying to figure out what just happened, Clyde continued his run.

He spent the rest of the day consumed by work, both on the house and over the phone. Sarah was on patrol the whole afternoon and couldn't help him. She wasn't exactly happy that Clyde had cried wolf on her twice. He believed that there was someone stalking him, but until he had proof to show Sarah, he didn't want to bug her again.

That night, after Clyde had reached his work limit, he got into his Cadillac and cruised through town. Hartwell was alive on Saturday night. Families dined out. Groups of teenagers walked the sidewalks. A large line of kids funneled into the local skate-in. They carried their roller skates and told stories of past triumphs. Clyde stopped at a traffic light. The light's red hue shined over him. He watched the skate-in. Amid the crowd, he saw the mysterious blonde woman. She stared at Clyde as the crowd moved by her like the flow of moving water. She was unfazed by the crowd. Though blue, her eyes were like pits.

Clyde turned away. He glanced to the other side of the

road. Standing in a record and music store, Clyde saw a young man. He glared at Clyde from the other side of the store's glass. He wore a sports jacket and dirty slacks. He had nicely-trimmed brown hair and watched Clyde as well. Did these two kids know him? Why were they watching him? Questions swirled in Clyde's mind.

A car honked its horn.

Clyde realized the light had turned green. He drove through town, grabbed dinner to-go, and followed a skinny two-lane to the local lake. He parked in the empty parking lot and hiked the grassy knolls surrounding the body of water. Clyde plopped down on one of the hills. Stars and the crescent moon reflected on the still black waters. Clyde ate his dinner.

He remembered the first time he came out here. It was one of his oldest memories. His mother, father, Andrew, and him had sat on this very hill and shared a picnic. He didn't remember the nature of the conversation, but there was laughter. When Clyde returned to the spot later in his life, it was just him and Andrew. There was no laughter. His uncle barely said anything at all. At one point, he invited Clyde to take a walk around the water.

Clyde recalled Andrew's words as they walked by the shallow end. *"You'll get through this. Situations like this strengthen you. It keeps your perspective healthy."*

Clyde kept silent as he had most of that year. He didn't care about perspective. He wanted his family back.

A dog barked in the distance, snapping Clyde out of his memory. He listened for the dog bark. It was an angry noise but sounded more like a cry for help. Clyde saw no one else around. The barking came from the nearby woods. He set his to-go box aside, turned on the flashlight on his phone, and listened for the dog.

The moment he stepped into the woods, the barking stopped. Clyde continued deeper. "Hello?"

Fifty yards deep, Clyde heard the dog whimpering. He shined the light, seeing a pit in the ground up ahead.

Concerned, he slowly approached. Fallen leaves and twigs snapped beneath his feet. The dog stopped crying. Clyde reached the edge of the pit. His light shined upon the full-grown husky trapped at the bottom of the five-foot-deep hole. Clumps of dirt and mud clung to the dog's white fur coat. The dog tilted its head up to him. Its spotted tongue dangled out of the side of its black lips. It smiled at the sight of Clyde.

"Hey, bud," Clyde said softly. "Where's your owner?"

The woods appeared to be empty of people.

Clyde pursed his lips. He lowered to the edge of the pit.

The husky scratched on the dirt walls, attempting to reach Clyde. She whimpered as dirt rained down upon her.

"Don't bite me," Clyde said as he slipped into the four-foot-wide hole with the large dog. The husky jumped on him, resting her front paws on Clyde's chest and attempting to lick his face.

"Okay, okay," Clyde chuckled. "That's enough."

He grabbed the dog's torso. "Up and over."

He lifted the husky and placed her on the edge of the pit. The dog lapped at his face as he climbed out. Her breath was atrocious.

Clyde climbed out and took a knee. He checked the dog's neck but didn't find a collar. Unable to find the owner, Clyde put the dirty dog in his back seat and returned home. He brought the dog into the bathroom and put her in the tub. While the tub filled up, Clyde squeezed his shampoo into his hand.

"Sorry, pup. I only got the human stuff." He rubbed the

shampoo deep against the dog's fur. The bathwater darkened.

The first layer on the dog was dirt. Clyde found the second layer of muck to be blood. Lots of blood. The dog was free of open sores. Wherever the blood came from, it was most definitely dead.

5

SAFE

Clyde opened his eyes. He was curled up in a dark pit, resting on a bed of loose dirt. He rose, alarmed by his surroundings. Looking up, he saw a starry sky. He got to his feet, but the hole was over twelve feet deep.

"Help!" he called.

Not even the wind replied.

He clawed at the walls of the pit, trying to climb his way out. His fingernails shaved loose dirt before hitting the cold packed earth behind the first layer. A fingernail broke. The pain antagonized him.

He cried for help.

His mind spun, trying to remember how he got here. He set the dog outside after its bath and headed right to bed.

Did I sleepwalk? Clyde asked himself. A greater fear scratched the back of his mind. *Someone dragged me here.*

He tried desperately to climb out, resting his back against one wall of the pit and using his feet to walk up the other. He managed to make it four feet before a large chunk of dirt broke away from his feet and slid to the pit's bottom. Clyde lost his grip and landed on his bottom. He tried to climb again, making it farther this time before more of the wall crumbled under his hands.

He brushed his hand across the dirt wall, feeling for any root or something else he could hold. The results were fruitless.

Groaning, Clyde craned back his neck. Beat down by feelings of defeat, he opened his eyes and saw the silhouetted figure standing at the pit's top edge.

The man wore a mask made of red cloth. It was crudely stitched together from the crown of his head, down the bridge of his nose, and to the loose flap of cloth dangling below his chin. Two large, crude eye holes were cut in the fabric. The man had used black make-up around his eyes to hide his skin tone.

"What do you want with me?" Clyde shouted, angry and terrified.

The man lifted a hunting rifle, aimed at Clyde, and pulled the trigger.

Clyde jolted out of bed, covered in a cold sweat. He dragged his feet to the bathroom and washed his face. He checked himself for dirt or wounds. He was clean and unharmed. He knew it was only a dream, but it felt so real. He could close his eyes and remember the pit vividly. The image of the red mask was forever branded into his mind. He returned to the bedroom, seeing it was only a little past 3:20 am. He crawled under the covers. His racing heart prevented him from stealing any sleep.

He forced himself to rise just before dawn. Tired, he put on his running shorts, running shoes, and a tee-shirt. He stepped out the front door.

The husky was curled up on the welcome mat. Her ear twitched. She awoke and stood the moment she saw Clyde.

"Hey, girl. Want to go running?" Clyde asked.

The husky followed him.

Clyde's running time for his first mile was six minutes and fifty seconds, and his second mile was seven minutes and thirty-one seconds. He took a little break, disappointed in himself. Once again, he found himself beside the woods. Instead of the blonde young woman staring at him, he saw a brunette. She wore a long-sleeved shirt and baggy pants. Blood caked the side of her hair.

"You okay?" Clyde asked.

The brunette stayed silent.

"Whatever you and your friends got going on, it isn't funny," Clyde said.

The brunette walked back into the woods.

"Finally," Clyde mumbled under his breath. He rubbed the husky's soft head. "Sarah was right. There are a lot of crazies out here."

After running the last half of a mile, they turned back. Clyde refused to record the times for his last two miles. It was too depressing. At the house, he kept the husky outside while he went into the kitchen and poured her a bowl of cereal.

He brought it out and set it near the front door. "It's the closest thing I got to dog food."

The husky was in the front yard, leaping after an injured bird. The little bird dipped low at just the wrong time and was snapped inside of the dog's jaw. The husky shook her head back and forth, her blood-stained teeth burrowing into the little animal. Clyde watched a puff of feathers flutter in the air.

There was always the knowledge of violence surrounding Clyde's profession, but to see it played out before his eyes sickened him. The animal kingdom was often brutal and unforgiving to the helpless. Mankind was similar, but sometimes compassion ruled the day. *Discipline and restraint. Just two qualities that separate us from the rest of creation,* he thought. Granted, animals could be trained, but mankind had perfected lawfulness. Some chose to avoid it or actively fight against it, but Clyde was thoroughly convinced that nearly every challenge could be overcome through practice and dedication.

When the dog finished, it turned to Clyde, looking innocent. The dead bird dropped from its blood-soaked jaw and plopped on the dewy grass. The husky pranced up the steps. She dipped her face in the cereal bowl and lapped up the milk.

Clyde left the husky alone and returned inside. He turned on the kitchen sink. Water spurted out in every direction. He opened the cabinet below the sink and examined the piping. Duct tape wrapped the center pipe. It appeared to be loose and near snapping. Clyde grabbed his tools from the kitchen table and moved the dish soap bottle and other outdated cleaning products out of his way. He got his head and shoulders under the sink. Trying to avoid replacing the entire pipe at the moment, he went to tighten the fastener that connected the duct-taped pipe to another. Using a crescent wrench, he gave it a twist. The fastener tightened too much.

Snap.

The top of the duct-taped pipe snapped and water spewed over Clyde. He grabbed the pipe, trying to keep it from flooding, but the crank behind the duct tape bent in and water shot through the cranks. A dirty jet smacked Clyde in the eye. Cursing up a storm, he pulled himself out from under the sink. The entire pipe broke off and water flooded all through the cabinet and across the floor.

Clyde ran to the bathroom and grabbed a handful of towels. The dirty water spread across the floor. Dead beetles and spiders floated on the surface. Clyde shut the doors and used the towels to guard the gap beneath the door. He used his last towel to cover the pipe under the sink. He grabbed a broom and swept the rest of the water to the center of the room. Using his shirt, he soaked up the water. He spent the next five minutes running through the house, trying to find the water valve. He discovered it above the washer and dryer in the basement.

He turned it off and returned to the kitchen. He took the towels from beneath the doors and used them to clean up the floor, then went to his room and changed out of his dirty clothes. Pissed that he never got a chance to work out, he sat on the edge of the bed and considered the day. Spending one more minute inside of this house was going to drive him crazy. He searched his dirty pants and found Don Fegan's business card in his back pocket. He gave the man a call.

Don answered.

Clyde said. "You still up for fishing today?"

"I'm already on the water," Don said proudly.

"Mind if I join?"

"I can't say no to good company."

Clyde glanced out the window, seeing the husky walking through the front lawn, sniffing something. "Can I bring a plus one?"

AS CLEAR AS GLASS, the racing river snaked through the valley. The water came up to the middle of Clyde's thighs. He wore Don's extra pair of waders. Both of them were tall guys and the waders were a close fit. The husky explored the bank. She jumped in the water and swam upstream.

"I ain't never seen a dog like water as much as that one," Don said. He was dressed in a frilled fishing hat and vest with many pockets. Polaroid sunglasses hugged his stubbled face. "She's likely to scare away the trout."

"I'm still getting used to her myself." Clyde cast his line. The insect-shaped hook landed on the top of the water. "She was trapped in a pit near the lake."

"You don't say?" Don replied curiously.

"Yep. A five-foot hole. I don't know if she fell in or someone put her there. I want to find the owner, but I don't know where to start," Clyde replied.

"Keep her," Don said.

Clyde gave him a look like he was crazy. "I haven't had a dog in years."

"If the owner wanted her that bad, he wouldn't have been so careless," Don said.

Clyde reeled in his line. They moved farther up the river. He let the husky roam. The dog was smart enough to stay within Clyde's field of vision.

Don pointed to a section of rapids up ahead. "Andrew caught a rainbow up there. Sixteen inches. One of those lucky casts."

"Did he get a lot of trout?" Clyde asked.

"He was good. Not as good as me." Don flicked his wrist. His line gently landed on the water.

"He took me out here a few times," Clyde said.

"It's a good spot. There's a better one a quarter-mile north if you don't mind the hike," Don said.

"I wish I got the chance to say goodbye to him," Clyde said.

Don snagged a fish. He fought it for a moment before it got away. Don's disappointment was palpable. "He was quiet to the end. He became a shut-in, you know? I'd try to rouse him up to go fishing, but he started ignoring my calls. I knew he was depressed, but, uh, I thought he'd just get over it."

Clyde lowered his rod. "Did he say anything to you before he..."

"Not really," Don replied. "The last time we talked, he called me a two-faced liar."

"What? Why?" Clyde asked.

Don shrugged. "He was slipping. Living alone like that for so long, you get angry and resentful even against those who want to help you. One day, he'd had enough, grabbed his old gun and... sorry, that wasn't a nice thing to say."

Clyde tried not to imagine his uncle taking his own life.

Don kept fishing. "I'd say his depression went all the way back to the death of your folks. After twenty-five years, he never let it go."

Clyde blinked. He was back in his childhood home again, but only for a second. He saw the blood leaking out from his mother's gaping wound. She opened and closed her mouth like a fish struggling to breathe. Like a lantern slowly dimming out, the light in her eyes faded. She stared blankly at Clyde. Father was a few feet away. He passed away a few minutes before.

"Got one," Don exclaimed.

Clyde returned to reality.

Don battled the fish and reeled it in. He held the thirteen-inch rainbow trout. "Quick. Get a pic."

Clyde pulled out his phone and snapped a picture of Don and the fish.

Don took his pliers out of his vest's front pocket and removed the hook from the fish's lip. He gently lowered the trout back in the water. He held it for a moment, letting it catch its breath before sending it on its way.

"Send that pic to me when you get a chance," Don said as he reset his hook. "Yeah, uh, Andrew really went through the wringer these last few months."

"That's rough," Clyde said, guilty he didn't reach out more.

"Last month was the worst. He was given a restraining order," Don said.

"For what?" Clyde asked, casting his line.

"Following this guy. He got fed up and eventually called the cops," Don explained.

"Do you know the guy's name?" Clyde asked.

Don gave him a strange look.

"So I know to avoid him," Clyde replied.

"Roland Alcott," Don said.

The next few hours were peaceful. Clyde enjoyed the water, the sights, the sounds of nature, and the simple pleasure of fishing. It took him a while to get the hang of it again, but by the end of the afternoon, he caught four little trout and one nine-incher.

Don and Clyde walked along the bank on the way back. Upon reaching Don's new truck, Clyde stripped off his waders and returned the vest.

On the way home, Clyde bought piping for the sink and a large bag of dog food. The husky sat on the front seat. Her beautiful white and black face looked like a Rorschach painting. She smiled and stuck her head out the window, her tongue flopping in the wind. They arrived at Andrew's house. Clyde let the husky run around the lawn while he went inside.

The house had a rancid stench. He probably should've bought some air fresheners while he was out. Using the new piping, he looked on the Internet for the best way to fix the sink. He was always a fast learner, especially if he was doing hands-on activities. He replaced the pipe. Anxious, he turned the sink valve. The water flowed smoothly and clean. Before he celebrated his small victory, he picked up the dried but dirty towels from the floor and headed to the basement.

Stacks of cardboard boxes and old metal filing cabinets lined the concrete walls. The washer and dryer were in the back. The heater system was on the other side. Old clothes and blankets piled in a large mound nearby. Clyde didn't know why his uncle didn't take this stuff to the homeless shelter. Most of the blankets had moth holes or were stained. Clyde looked above the mound and saw a damp spot on the ceiling. He felt the top of the blanket. It was wet. He must be below the kitchen.

He put the blankets in the washer, unintentionally revealing a black safe. It was three feet tall and two-and-a-half feet wide. Clyde stopped what he was doing and knelt before the cold metal box. He brushed his fingertips around the door, hoping it would be open. No luck. Getting a professional to bust the safe would break his budget. He twisted the dial, putting in his uncle's birthday. The door remained shut. Clyde thought for a minute before putting in the Star Wars release date, Andrew's favorite movie. Wrong.

Clyde moved to one of the metal cabinets and searched the files, hoping to discover a Post-It note with the code. He found receipts. Andrew was a freelance journalist. Tax write-offs were a common part of his job. Clyde removed a dusty graduation certificate from the University of Georgia. Clyde tried the graduation date for the code. Nothing.

Clyde pulled out the notepad app on his phone and wrote down every number of combinations that failed so far. He tried release dates of Andrew's favorite movies, significant events in the family, and random combinations commonly used by most people. An hour went by slowly. Clyde tried failure after failure. He sat cross-legged in front of the safe, frustrated but too stubborn to quit. A date swirled in the back of his mind since he started, but it was so ludicrous he refused to use it. Until now.

Clyde put in a September date from twenty-five years ago. As Clyde turned the dial for the final number, he thought about his mother's dying breath and the pool of blood growing across the floor.

Click.

The safe opened.

Clyde stayed still. Why would his uncle use the day of his own brother's death? Part of him didn't want to look inside. He opened the safe door carefully, revealing two shelves. A stack of cash, a few outdated bank bonds, and a snub-nosed revolver rested on the top shelf.

Clyde grabbed the cash. It was all hundreds. Clyde brushed his thumb down the side of the stack. It must've been between five and eight grand. He pocketed it, planning on counting it later. He lifted the bank bonds. They were dated to back to the 1950s. They must've belonged to Andrew's father. Clyde kept them in the safe, planning to wait a few years before cashing them. He lifted the revolver and opened the chamber. An empty shell casing fell out and rolled on the floor. The rest of the five bullets were loaded. Obviously, it wasn't the gun that killed Andrew, but Clyde was curious why one shot was fired. Leaving that in the vault as well, Clyde explored the bottom shelf.

Apart from a sentimental class ring, Clyde saw two folders. The first was titled *Dean and Lisa Barker.* Reading his parents' names caused Clyde to hesitate. Afraid to touch his parents' folder, he reached for the second. It was a labeled *The Massacre of Hartwell.*

6

THE GIRL

Clyde opened the folder, seeing pictures of strangers and a crime scene. *Why would Andrew have this?* he asked himself. Curiosity prompted him to dig deeper. Suddenly, the lights cut off.

Clyde sat silently in the dark. He wouldn't be able to see his hand even if it was an inch from his face. Chill bumps rose on his back from right to left as if someone had crossed behind him. He set the folder aside and fished out his cellphone, then turned on the screen. The sudden flash of light blinded him for a millisecond. He turned the flashlight on his phone and shone the light through the basement. The small cone of light had little impact on the overall darkness. A rat scurried across the far end of the basement.

Clyde stood up and walked through the darkness. He stubbed his toes on the corner of an old table. The pain shot up through his foot. He grunted and limped on his way to the breaker box. He popped it open. None of the switches were flipped. There was no reason why the light should cut off. He toggled the switches off and then on again.

Light returned to the basement. Clyde put away his cellphone, discouraged that he'd have to fix the electric too.

Upon returning to the safe, he shut the door. The stack of Benjamins weighed down his pants pocket. The rest of the items were stowed away. As he turned to leave, he noticed the folder on the floor. He grabbed it and hiked the steps. He stepped out of the basement, struck by a breeze. The front door was open. The wind gently tapped the screen against the threshold. Clyde put the file on a nearby lampstand and approached. He stepped onto the porch. Nighttime shrouded the front yard.

"Hello?"

No reply.

Lying on the front porch, the husky lifted her head, her blue eyes begging Clyde. Clyde petted her behind the ears and invited her inside. "Come on. It's not like the house could get any messier."

He locked the door and closed the window blinds. He walked through the house, making sure no one had gotten inside. The place appeared empty. Clyde kept his guard up.

After grabbing the folder, he headed for the lounge. He took a seat on the comfy recliner. Before he could open the folder, the husky jumped on his lap.

"Off," Clyde said.

The large dog stretched its body across his thighs like a blanket. Its front and hind legs hung off the sides of the recliner. Clyde had never seen a dog stretch out like that.

"Come on, girl. I need space." Clyde gently pushed her.

The dog yawned loudly and didn't budge.

"Oh, so that's how you want to play this?" Clyde asked.

The husky had no intention of moving.

Clyde left her there. He rested the folder on the dog's back and opened it. The windows shook. Clyde listened to the howling wind. He had the suspicion that someone was watching him, but the house was empty. He lifted a stack of photographs and sifted through them. The first showed a balding man between the ages of fifty and sixty-five. He had a square jaw and symmetrical face that probably made him very handsome in his youth. He wore a golf polo, shorts, and expensive white shoes. The photos were taken with a long lens at the local golf course. Foliage in the foreground of the shot led Clyde to conclude that the photographer was hiding. There were other photos of the man getting into a luxury Audi sedan, and eating outside at an upscale restaurant with men in suits.

Clyde moved those dozen and a half blurry photos to the back of the stack and looked at photos of another man. He was also Caucasian and between his fifties and sixties as well. He wore a camouflage hunting jacket, had a receding hairline, and a greasy grey ponytail. Salt and pepper stubble painted his pointed chin, scarred upper lip, and neck. The photographs of him were taken in a bar. He sipped a beer bottle. More pictures of him were taken outside a trailer mobile home where the man fed dry corn to the chickens in his coop. In the last photo, the man looked directly at the cameraman. His mug was mean and his eyes were bloodshot.

The next set of pictures showed a black man with white curly hair. He was ten years older than the two men before him. He wore an old plaid shirt unbuttoned to reveal his dirty muscle shirt. Despite his age, he was fit enough to run a marathon. He had an oval-shaped face and dark eyes. Every wrinkle was a scar from his hard life. The photos of him were taken in an aisle at the local hardware store, at the side of a creek where he fished, and at a tacky strip club.

Clyde moved his pictures to the back of the list. The final set of photos were of Dan Fegan. Clyde lowered them, his mind racing. There were photos of Don eating dinner with his plump wife, fishing, and talking to people from various stores around town. Clyde didn't know the exact context of the pictures, but he had to assume they were people Andrew had suspected of something.

Clyde wondered which one of these men, if any, was the one who filed the restraining order on Andrew. He rested the stack of photos aside and looked through printouts from a crime scene in a woods. There was a yellow marker next to a .223 Remington rifle cartridge, a picture of a recent campfire, blood spatter by a lawn chair, bullet holes in trees, and footsteps running in different directions. There were no pictures of the victims. Clyde was unsure how Andrew even got the photos from the police. Two folded maps were the last items in the folder. Clyde unfolded one of them, but it was too large to get a decent look at sitting down. He moved the husky. The dog moaned before walking a few feet and napping on the floor.

Clyde opened the first map, displaying Hart County, GA. Multiple locales had small holes in them from push pins. The second map was smaller and showed the town of Hartwell. Clyde found a box of push pins in a nearby drawer and tacked both maps to the wall. It took a few moments to fill every existing little hole with a pin. When he finished, he stepped back from the two maps. A few landmarks and random parts of the woods were marked on the county map. The local town map had a bar marked, the skate-in marked, and a few houses.

Clyde didn't know their exact connection, but they must've been pretty important for Andrew to hide in his safe. His phone rang, breaking his concentration. He answered. "Hello?"

"Clyde, it's Sarah. I need you to come over," Sarah said, urgency in her voice.

"What happened?" Clyde asked.

"I can't talk right now. Just get over to my place as fast as you can."

"Sarah—"

She hung up.

A second later, Clyde received a text containing her address.

Clyde said to the husky, "Guard the house, girl."

He slung on a thin jacket and hurried out the door.

The husky stayed inside.

Clyde called Sarah while he got into the car. She didn't answer. Clyde rested his phone on his lap, put on his seat belt, and started the car. Part of him thought about getting the revolver from downstairs, but he didn't have a weapon permit. Unarmed, he reversed out the driveway and raced through town.

Driving through a cul-de-sac, he pulled up in front of a single-story house. Ten cars packed the roadside and driveway. Clyde found a spot in the back. He jogged down the sidewalk and reached the front door. He pressed on the doorbell and waited anxiously. The neighborhood was quiet. There were a few street lights casting yellow blobs of light on the sidewalks.

The door opened.

Sarah stood on the other side. She wore a low-cut tee-shirt and yoga pants. Her red hair was down and she had a wide smile on her freckled face. "About time you showed up."

People holding drinks and laughing walked by behind her. Faint music could be heard in the background.

"What's going on?" Clyde asked.

Sarah stepped aside and allowed him to enter.

Hesitant, Clyde walked in. Sarah shut the door behind him.

"I thought you could use a night off," Sarah replied.

"I'm not big on parties," Clyde said, eying the other guests.

Sarah's lips curled into a wry smile. "I know."

Clyde figured out quickly that he had been duped. "Look, I should really get going."

"Stay." Her command was softened by a smile.

Clyde pursed his lips.

Sarah walked ahead of him. "What can I get you to drink?"

"Water is fine," Clyde replied.

He stepped into the living room. Couples in their thirties gathered, drank, and chuckled. It was a relatively quiet party; not like you'd see at a college frat house. Nevertheless, the guests were of the sort that clung to their youthful ways. A few people glanced at Clyde, but no one approached him. His tall stature put him a head above everyone else.

Sarah brought over a wine glass and a cup of water. Clyde followed her into the fenced-in backyard. They sat in comfy outside chairs. Sarah gave Clyde his water.

"With all the house repairs, we haven't had some time to really catch up," Sarah said, nursing her wine glass.

Clyde was unsure if this was another one of her *lines.* He felt awkward, not wanting to reject her twice.

Sarah said, "And no, the first day doesn't count. You barely said anything."

"It's been busy. I want to put the property on the market ASAP."

"Weak excuse," Sarah replied.

"Maybe, but it's the truth. I'm not staying in Hartwell forever," Clyde said.

"Big city calling your name?" Sarah asked.

Clyde never really had much pride in Atlanta. It was just the place he needed to be to make money. "No, but my landlord might be. You'd like the city. There are a lot of parties like this."

"I'm sure they do, but do they have mudding, hunting, fishing, and skinny dipping in the spring? Nah, I don't think so. I'm a Hartwell girl through and through. We should have some fun before you get going."

"Yeah," Clyde replied.

"Okay, what sounds best to you?" Sarah asked.

"I dunno," Clyde replied. His crazy work schedule consumed most of his time.

"Don't be so boring."

"I usually don't get out much," Clyde admitted.

"I could tell," Sarah said dryly. "Come on. There has to be something you do apart from work."

"I like running," Clyde replied.

"That's a start," Sarah said.

"Working out, too."

"That's alright, but what about something that gets your blood pumping?"

"It's mostly cardio," Clyde explained.

"That's not what I meant," Sarah said. "Geez. Don't you do something that's a little risky?"

"I, uh, I like to drive fast," Clyde said, embarrassed.

"And I'm good at collecting tickets. I knew we were going to be good friends," Sarah said.

"So, what's the party all about?" Clyde asked.

"It's just something I do every now and again. I don't like it when the house gets dull," Sarah said. "I guess I never grew out of my college days."

She said it as a joke, but Clyde could see some truth in her statement.

The conversation fizzled into silence after a little more small talk.

Sarah broke down the invisible wall of conversational impotence when she asked, "You ever feel like you're missing something?"

"What do you mean?" Clyde asked.

"I've been a beat cop for the good part of the last decade, and Hartwell ain't as quiet as it looks, which is exciting. But I have this nagging feeling like... It's like life is passing me by. You ever get that?" Sarah sipped her wine.

"We're all after something that'll last," Clyde replied. "My uncle Andrew used to say I was destined for great things. I'm thirty years old, unmarried, and live in a studio apartment. Every month is a struggle to pay my rent. If he's right, I have to believe the best is yet to come. Even if he's wrong, at least I have the idea of hope keeping me going."

Sarah had a glassy-eyed stare. "Life is running away every day. I just want to seize the moment. Waste no opportunity."

"That's not a bad way to live," Clyde said.

"Darn right it ain't," Sarah replied. "I only wish there was some way for me to get a promotion. Traffic is getting boring. I'm the only woman on the police force, you know. Well, there's Margery, but she's the clerk. All the good ol' boys like to keep their position, just like their papaws before 'em. It's taking a while to climb the ladder."

"Have you ever looked into the Hartwell Massacre?" Clyde asked.

Sarah glared at him.

"You've heard of it," Clyde said.

"Everybody here lived it, Clyde," Sarah replied. "You should know. You showed up a few years after."

"I don't remember much from when I was fifteen," Clyde said. "Apart from you, that is."

"Aww, you're a sweetheart." Sarah pinched his cheek.

"Was it ever solved?" Clyde asked.

"No, and it probably won't be."

"Why's that?" Clyde asked.

"That case has been cold for decades," Sarah explained.

"But if you figured it out, I'm sure there would be a nice promotion for you," Clyde said.

"The chances that my boss will sign off on reviewing a twenty-year-old case is unlikely without new info," Sarah said. "That event ain't widely discussed in Hartwell. Frankly, it's a black stain on the town's history."

"All the better to solve it," Clyde said. "Before all the suspects grow old."

"I was twelve when it happened. I have no stake in that," Sarah said.

"If someone doesn't solve it soon, the murderer dies and no one learns the truth," Clyde said.

"Clyde, there are some skeletons you don't want to go digging up," Sarah said.

Clyde ignored her warning. "Tell me about what happened."

Sarah stood up. "I'm going to get another drink."

"Did I do something to offend you?" Clyde asked.

"If you keep asking questions like that, you'll offend everyone." Sarah headed inside.

Clyde stayed put. He listened to the night critters and reflected. This talk of fate and murder left him feeling angsty. When he finally fulfilled his role as a successful lawyer, he'd hoped to never have to question in his place in the world. The last thing he wanted was to end up like Andrew, alone and bitter.

Sarah was gone for a long time. Clyde got the idea that she was ghosting him, but didn't intend to go inside. Parties were never his thing. Sitting outside on the quiet summer evening was much more appealing. An uneventful thirty minutes prompted Clyde to leave. He returned inside, seeing the men and women drinking and talking. A few said hello to Clyde. He mumbled a generic reply and kept walking. He spotted Sarah on the living room couch. She sat next to a handsome fellow. She laughed at his corny joke and rested her hand on his thigh. She clearly demanded attention and wasn't getting enough from Clyde. He didn't know many men who could turn down Sarah.

Clyde headed out the front door and drove away without looking back.

A late-night fog obscured his path. He slowed down as he traveled the winding, single-lane road. Without roadside lights, the fat moon was his only beacon outside his car. Out of the corner of his eyes, he spotted a woman standing at the corner of the road. Seeing dark blood pouring out of her mouth, Clyde slammed on the brakes.

7

REVELATION

The tires skidded to a stop, leaving two long tracks in their wake. The woman stood in Clyde's rearview. She had long blonde hair and overalls. Clyde recognized her. Heart racing, he reversed the car. He stopped, but the young woman was running into the woods. A bloody gash stained her back.

Clyde got out of the car. Leaving the door open, he shouted. "Hey, ma'am! Are you okay? Hey!"

She ran out of his sight.

Cold chills raced over Clyde's body. Seeing the trail of blood on the grass and leaves, Clyde raced after her.

It was like his legs were carrying him. Instinct took control. If this woman was injured, he wasn't going to let her run off and die.

"Wait up!" he shouted.

He weaved through the trees and jumped over fallen trunks. The girl seemed to always stay thirty feet ahead no matter how fast he ran. Clyde made the mistake of not bringing a flashlight. The woman vanished down a hill. Clyde descended. His feet slid on fallen leaves and old dirt, but he kept his balance. He stopped at the bottom and glanced around.

Chill bumps covered his flesh and all the hair on his arms stood. He controlled his breathing, though he was not even close to being winded. In the dark, all he could see were the shapes of trees. The trail of blood had stopped.

"Ma'am! Hello? I'm trying to help you! Can you hear me?"

Without a reply, he felt his pockets, looking for his cellphone. It was gone, along with his stack of cash. The phone was probably on the front seat. The cash, on the other hand, was gone for no good reason.

"Are you kidding me?" Clyde mumbled. His fear turned to anger. He hiked up the slope, looking for his money but not having any luck. He tried to find his route back to the road, but he was at the heart of the woods.

"What is this? A way to rob me? Is that it?" Clyde shouted, frustration in his voice.

The blood was fake, he knew. The blonde was probably in cahoots with the masked man and the brunette girl. Maybe even that boy in the sports jacket he saw the other night. They could have snuck up on him while he was distracted and took the money or collected it after it fell out of his pocket.

Clyde marched his way in the direction he thought he'd come from, but twenty minutes of walking proved that he had miscalculated. Clyde boxed his shoulders and started in a different direction. An hour and forty minutes of walking in circles had left him sweaty, bug-bitten, and pissed off. He saw headlights through the tree line.

"Finally," Clyde grumbled.

He pushed aside bush leaves and low-hanging branches and stepped out to the road. His Cadillac's front door was left open, the engine running. Clyde brushed off leaves and spiky seeds from his legs and took a seat. He pinched the bridge of his nose. Unable to end his frustration, he grabbed his cellphone. He opened Sarah's contact info but stopped himself. The bloody girl, no matter how much of a crafty thief she was, deserved a chance. He put his cellphone aside and drove home.

He checked around the lounge and basement for the stack of cash, but it was gone. He went to bed angry. Skipping his morning run, Clyde donned his suit and tie. He arrived at Hartwell's high school and waited patiently by the front desk.

The principal, a short and plump female, smiled falsely at him. She had little stud earrings and brown hair that looked like a globe around her head. "Yes?"

Clyde showed her his attorney's license. "I was hoping you could help me out."

"What seems to be the issue, *Mr. Barker*," she read his name.

"I believe a couple of your students took something from me," Clyde said. "I thought it would be more polite to speak to them or their guardians before taking this to court."

"Have you contacted the authorities?" the principal asked.

"I'm hoping to avoid that," Clyde said.

"See, Mr. Barker, it's against school policy to do as you asked."

"I'm aware," Clyde said, "But I'd rather not ruin these kids' lives over a stupid mistake. Can I at least give you their description?"

The principal eyed him, unsure if she should trust him.

Clyde spoke reasonably. "We've all done things we wish we didn't. Let's give mercy a victory for once."

"Alright, Mr. Barker. I'll see what I can do," the principal compromised.

"Thank you," Clyde replied, humbly bowing his head. "The first one I'm interested in is a blonde..." Clyde went on to describe the girl's overalls, her brunette friend, and the guy in the sports jacket.

The principal glared at Clyde. Mouth closed, her jaw set to one side.

"Something the matter?" Clyde asked.

"You're a sick man, Mr. Barker," the principal said, disgust in her voice.

"Excuse me?" Clyde replied, confused.

"Don't play dumb," the principal barked. "You get on out of here before I call the police."

"I seriously don't know what you're talking about," Clyde said.

"Fine, you need me to show you, I'll show you." Face glowing red, the principal stormed into another room.

Clyde stood by the desk. A few students seated nearby stared at him. Clyde tried his best to ignore them.

The principal returned, holding a yearbook. She flipped through a few pages before stopping and turning the book to Clyde. Her face contorted into an angry expression, she pointed at a picture on the bottom of the page. It was captioned. "*Most likely to succeed.*"

The picture showed four students seated at a cafeteria table. The one to the right had auburn hair, a collared shirt, slacks, and nice shoes. The one next to him was a handsome young man wearing a sports jacket. The last two were young ladies Clyde recognized. One blonde. One brunette.

"Who are they?" Clyde asked.

The principal said, "You can read."

Clyde skimmed the captions. The blonde was Elizabeth Mara, the brunette was Gena Cobbs, the one in the sports jacket was Tommy Demko, and the auburn-haired man was John Roth.

"That's them, but I don't get what I'm looking at," said Clyde.

The principal looked at him like he was insane. "You don't know? Elizabeth and Tommy are dead. Gena and John have been missing for two decades."

8

WHAT SHE CRIED

Clyde sat in the driver seat of his car. He grabbed the steering wheel but didn't start the engine. He blinked, re-imagining the girls he'd seen running. *It's all fake. It has to be fake.* He turned the key and returned home quickly.

The husky sat patiently on the other side of the front door, waiting for food. He locked the door. His heart raced. The dog barked at him. He poured her a bowl of dry food and stood in the messy kitchen. Something pulled at the front of the shirt. At least it felt that way, but there was nothing. A cold chill grew up from his fingertips to his elbows, eventually going up to his neck.

You're just tired. You need to rest, he thought but still followed the tingling feeling. It took him to the living room window. He parted the blinds.

The four young people stood on the front lawn. Elizabeth, Tommy, Gena, and lastly John. The top third of John's face was blown open. Blood oozed down his jaw and chin. They all glared at Clyde. Their blank eyes and neutral expressions were uncanny.

Clyde backed away from the window. He tripped over his heel and hit the floor.

His heart pounded in his chest. A cold sweat doused his trembling body. He sat unmoving and terrified, then shut his eyes and steadied his breathing. *None of it is real.* Chill bumps rose all over his flesh. He sensed the presence of people nearby. He balled his fists and opened his eyes.

The four dead teenagers loomed over him.

The droplet of blood from John's obliterated face dripped off his chin and splattered on Clyde's right eye.

Clyde flinched, blinking out the cold blood.

John opened his mouth to speak, but only a ghastly rattle escaped his mouth.

Dark circles under the young women's eyes. Their lips were pale. Broken leaves and twigs clung in their hair. Gena the brunette had two bullet holes in her torso. The blood on the side of her head must've been from one of the other victims, probably John.

Breaking his gaze, Clyde scurried to his feet and darted to the front door. He grabbed the knob and gave it a twist.

Suddenly, a cold hand fell on his shoulder.

Clyde froze.

His breathing quickened.

Out of the corner of his eye, he saw Elizabeth lean in. She kept her face forward and her expression lifeless. Her mouth hovered an inch from Clyde's ear, but he felt no breath.

She spoke softly. "Justice."

Clyde kept his hand on the knob. His fingers were hardened in place, as if he had rigor mortis. Choppy breath escaped his lips.

"Justice," she repeated.

The word nailed into his heart. Buried in fear, a fire

burned within him that he couldn't explain. His entire being trembled. Even his soul stirred.

Elizabeth retracted her hand. Slowly and cautiously, he turned back to the dead.

Elizabeth stood in front. The beautiful young lass locked eyes with Clyde. Her gaze crawled into the depths of Clyde's soul. It seemed to brand his innermost being. She had marked him. He didn't know how he knew that or what it meant, but something strange and profound had happened. His fear remained, but he felt an invisible cord connecting himself to Elizabeth.

He blinked.

Elizabeth was now standing beside the others.

One at a time, their gaze locked onto Clyde. And every time, he felt a deep, unexplained connection. The process only took thirty seconds, but it felt an hour.

In an almost ritualistic manner, the dead turned their backs to Clyde and funneled through the hallway before vanishing as they turned the corner. The chills across Clyde's body faded away.

The house was silent.

Seated, the husky tilted her head in confusion.

Clyde rested his back against the door and slid down to the floor. He only had two thoughts. The first was that he was a raving madman and his mind was broken. The second was he had stepped into a hidden reality shrouded by his own, and everything he knew about life and death was a lie. Either way, the experience transformed him. Nothing would ever be the same. How could it be?

At some point in the five minutes after, he managed to find his way into Uncle Andrew's whiskey cabinet. He broke the seal on one and drank straight from the bottle. The liquid went down like fire. Its taste clung to his tongue. He took another swig.

He shuffled his feet to the bedroom and crashed on the bed. The husky jumped on the bed and curled up next to him. Her warm fur brushed gently against Clyde's side. Her breathing was steady and calm. The midmorning sun shone in, breached the window blinds, and cast jail bars across Clyde's face. Eyes half-open, he took a long swig and rested.

He opened his eyes.

The husky was still curled up beside him.

It was dark outside.

The digital clock read 3 am.

Clyde swiveled his feet out of bed.

A headache pounded on the inside of his skull.

He rested his face in his palm.

A pulling sensation caused him to lift his head.

Elizabeth stood two feet away. Her pale skin seemed to glow in the moonlight.

Clyde stared her in the eyes. "It's you again."

Silent, the specter turned around and walked out of the room.

Clyde stood up, feeling a strange sensation drawing him to her.

"Come, girl." He rubbed his hand on the husky's side.

The dog yawned and followed him out the front door.

Elizabeth continued down the road.

Using the flashlight on his phone, Clyde followed. The husky stayed faithfully by his side. Though still at the early stages of their friendship, he couldn't ask for a better companion to follow him into the unknown.

Clyde walked the path he always ran.

The ghost stayed thirty paces ahead. The wound in her back leaked with every step.

It was a long trek. Clyde didn't know if he was dreaming or awake. A part of him knew that he had to follow her, but part of him told him to flee. Two miles later, and Elizabeth was leading him into the woods where he had chased her the night before. *I'm going to be slaughtered,* Clyde thought. Having never experienced anything supernatural, he had to assume the girl had evil intent. That didn't deter him. He was ready to see where this ended... as ready as one could be, at least.

Clyde shined his light on Tommy. The young man sat on the dirt, back to Clyde. Tears of blood leaked out of a bullet hole in the back of his skull. Clyde walked by Tommy, shining the light on charred wood and the circle of stones in front him.

Clyde continued deeper. Night bugs nipped at his skin. He smashed them, leaving behind their guts. Clyde swatted aside tree branches and forced his way through thorns. An owl watched him from a tree branch, its face twisted upside down.

The pulling sensation on Clyde's body grew stronger. Clyde continued his walk. He sweated out his booze. A small rock cave appeared in the distance. The entrance was like a jagged mouth turned on its side. Elizabeth slipped through easily.

Clyde stopped at the mouth of the cave, questioning his life choices.

The husky whimpered.

"It's okay, girl." Clyde scratched her behind the ear.

The dog barked at the entrance.

Clyde turned sideways and slipped inside. Spiders with long legs scurried across the low ceiling.

Beetles burrowed into the rough dirt under his feet.

Without entering, the husky paced back and forth and

whimpered as Clyde got farther out of her sight.

The cave branched into different directions. A human-sized tunnel seemed like the appropriate direction, but Clyde heard Elizabeth shuffling inside of one hole the size of a crawl space. The dead girl faced out to Clyde. Only her face was visible. Blonde hair rolled over her face as she tilted her head. She backed into the hole.

Trembling, Clyde squatted before the small gap.

Elizabeth was gone.

The husky barked louder and whimpered.

Clyde dropped to his hands and knees and entered the gap. Dirt stained his knees and palms. The rock walls and ceiling were coarse and had sharp bumps. The tunnel got tighter and more constricting around him. The air inside was cold and dry. It was impossible to turn around. The ceiling gradually got so low that Clyde lowered to his belly. A small millipede raced up his hand and up to his shoulder. He tried to shake it off but could not twist his body. He knocked his head against the rock roof and grunted through his teeth.

He continued. The gap was not made for someone of his stature. Despite the cold, droplets of sweat poured down his face. Getting out was what he feared more what he'd find inside. He moved, barely, his chin inches from dragging on the floor. He kept an eye on his low phone battery. The light shined ahead, reaching the mouth of the tunnel. It appeared to open up into a natural chamber.

Clyde quickened his pace. He squeezed through, rubbing his broad shoulders against the edges of the exit point. The natural chamber was about ten feet by six feet wide and about nine feet tall. Clyde stood. He didn't bother brushing off the dirt caking the front half of his body. Elizabeth stood by two skeletons dressed in decaying clothes. The skulls smiled at Clyde. Patches of dry skin and thin hair clung to dry scalps. The left upper third of one of the skulls was shattered. The small skeleton had two bullet holes in her shirt.

John and Gena lingered behind Clyde. They stared blankly at their old remains.

"Is this why you brought me here?" Clyde asked Elizabeth.

The ghost stayed silent. Clyde shined the light across the room, seeing rifle shell casings on the dirt. He finally shined the light on the skeleton's hands, seeing that they were holding each other when they died. Clyde felt fear, sorrow, and anger.

Clyde checked his phone service. He had zero bars, unsurprisingly. He snapped a few pictures of the skeletons. His phone battery was down to the last three percent. He got back to his belly and squeezed his way through the hole. The journey back took much longer. The phone dropped to one percent. He crawled swiftly, knocking the sides of the tunnel. He reached the mouth of the crawl space. Able to breathe again, he bushed his way out and scurried out the cave.

The husky jumped him when he exited. He rubbed the dog's sides. When the dog jumped down, Clyde sent a quick text just as his battery died.

9

GUNNER

Sarah stood at the cave's crevasse. One hand rested on her hip. The other held the massive torch flashlight. Caked in dirt, Clyde stood beside her.

"Clyde, what is this?"

"They're in there, Sarah," Clyde replied.

"You called me out here at 4 am for this crap."

"I would've told you more details over the phone, but…" He lifted his dead phone.

"Why didn't you call the police?" Sarah asked.

"It would look suspicious."

"Because it is," Sarah exclaimed. She crinkled his nose. "Have you been drinking?"

"Not recently," Clyde replied.

Sarah pinched the bridge of her nose. "Clyde, I… Ah, never mind."

"Say it."

Sarah turned to him. "You're not okay."

"How long did it take you to figure that out?" Clyde answered sarcastically.

Sarah glared at him.

Clyde gestured to the cave. "The bones are there. You need to bring a forensic team to fish them out."

"This is Hartwell PD, not CSI. We have five officers, myself included. We have a hard time keeping an eye on the drunk tank as it is," Sarah answered.

"That promotion you want is waiting in there," Clyde replied.

His words caused Sarah to think. She asked, "What made you want to go in that cave anyway?"

"I can't tell you," Clyde replied.

"That's not the right answer," Sarah replied.

"Sarah, you just have to trust me," Clyde replied.

"I haven't seen you in fifteen years," Sarah said.

"I would've been ten years old when these people died. I was in an orphanage at the time, okay?" Clyde explained. "I have nothing to do with those kids in there."

"What about your uncle?" Sarah asked.

"I don't know," Clyde answered honestly. "I'd say he's a suspect, just like everyone else."

"You have a suspect list now?"

Clyde had said too much. He redirected the conversation. "Call it in, Sarah. You can say I found the bones if you want. It doesn't matter to me. Either way, I don't have the answers you're looking for."

Sarah turned back to the cave. "You understand that if I don't find any skeletons in there, I'm going to make your life a living hell."

"I wouldn't expect anything less," Clyde replied.

"The crawl space you said?"

"Yep, it runs pretty deep. Someone your size won't have too much of an issue navigating it," Clyde said.

Sarah's shoulders went slack. "All right. Take your dog and run on home."

"Thank you, Sarah," Clyde said.

He called the husky over to him while Sarah lifted her radio.

Before she pressed the button, she said, "There better be some darn fine bones in there."

Clyde and the husky traveled back through the woods. The path wasn't hard to travel this time. He had acclimated to landmarks and the husky was a good navigator. Thinking it was about time he named her, Clyde called her Pathfinder.

Her smile and dangling tongue showed her approval. He got home and stripped off his clothes. He took a cold shower, getting the dirt out his hair. Towel wrapped around his waist, he stepped out and heard a knock on his door. Putting on his running shorts and crumpled tee-shirt he found on the floor, he answered the door, seeing two officers. One was a black man with a long face. The other was a white man with square glasses.

"Mr. Barker, we'd like to talk to you," the black cop said. His name tag read *Haze.*

Sarah must've ratted him out. Clyde asked. "Can I make you a cup of coffee?"

"We meant down at the station," the white cop corrected. He was named *Pickman.*

"I see," Clyde said. The sun had just started to rise, but the world was still in darkness.

Clyde entered the back of their cop car.

"You're new in town, huh?" Officer Haze asked him.

Clyde looked out the window. His eyes had dark circles much like the dead.

"He's not much of a talker," Pickman said, hoping to bait Clyde.

He kept quiet. When they arrived at the station, they put

him in one of two interrogation rooms. He sat in the chair and rested face down on the table.

The hours ticked by, but it felt more like days. Clyde waited, albeit frustratedly.

The door unlocked.

A man stepped into the room. He was balding, between the ages of fifty and sixty-five. He had a square jaw and symmetrical face that probably made him very handsome in his youth. Clyde recognized him as the rich golfer from Andrew's folder. The man wore a black police uniform and patch that signified him as the police chief.

"Hey, Mr. Barker. I'm Robert Hawkins. My friends call me Bob," the police chief introduced himself.

"Clyde."

"I hear you made a significant discovery last night. Care to explain a little more?" Hawkins asked.

Why was the police chief questioning him and not an officer? Clyde wondered. He replied, "I'm not sure what you want to know."

"Two unidentified bodies were discovered. An officer of mine said you're the one who provided the tip," Hawkins explained.

"I did," Clyde replied.

Hawkins waited for him to further explain. Clyde did not.

"Look, Mr. Barker. Clyde. I'm in a very interesting predicament here. On one hand, I want to thank you for your discovery. On the other, I want to find out how you learned about the location of those skeletons."

"A guess really," Clyde replied.

"A guess?" Hawkins asked, not believing a word.

Clyde locked his fingers on the tabletop. "I knew about the massacre as a kid. My uncle told me all about it. I always wondered where the other two missing victims went. I mean someone would've had to have seen them. I got to thinking. If I was running away from a killer, where would I go? The cave seemed like a logical place to hide. I sent my tip to Officer Sullivan. I didn't really expect it to pan out, but I guess she thought the theory was worthwhile," Clyde lied seamlessly.

Hawkins scrutinized him for a long moment.

"Is there anything else?" Clyde asked, sounding polite and cooperative.

"Your uncle was a curious guy, you know."

"Is that right?" Clyde asked.

"Yeah. A guilty conscience really tore him up. I'm sorry for your loss."

Clyde nodded soberly.

After a few more rudimentary questions, Hawkins sent Clyde away.

He didn't have to comply with the police. He could've represented himself and saved some time and trouble, but cooperating would get the cops off his back. They had nothing on him and he had nothing to hide. His inside sources wouldn't hold up in court.

The first thing Clyde did when he got home was feed Pathfinder. He spent a few minutes petting the dog. He sat on the lounge chair. Pathfinder curled up at his feet, chewing on an unused paint roller. Clyde flipped through the folder. He re-examined the photos of the police chief. Had the dead talked to Andrew as well? What made him suspect Bob Hawkins and the other three men? Hearing the word *Justice* in his mind, Clyde wanted to turn in the file as evidence, but if Hawkins was the killer, he could easily bury it. If the dead wanted the police to solve the case, they would've come to Sarah or another officer. They had waited twenty years for Clyde. He had to be the one to uncover the truth.

He didn't know why he had such a drive. Looking Elizabeth in the eyes that sparked something. He had question upon question as to what had happened to him and the limitations of his powers. As a lawyer, he wanted to know how and what ways he could communicate with the dead. Did it only apply to those who were murdered? Did he have to find them or did they come to him? Were they bound to a geographical terrain? If so, how far must Clyde go if he needed to escape them?

All of these questions and more were only distractions from the case at hand. He looked at the picture of Don.

"Why you?" Clyde asked. He tended to think out loud when he got little sleep. He called Don but didn't get a response. Clyde checked the date. Don should be out fishing. Clyde changed, put Pathfinder in the car, and drove to the river.

He arrived at the riverbank but did not see Don. He walked a while, recalling the good fishing spot Don said was a ways up the river. Pathfinder raced ahead of Clyde, jumping from rock to rock as they walked alongside the rushing waters. Its sound soothed Clyde. The trees and foliage were deep green and the air was fresh.

Don stood at the center of a dead-end in the river. Submerged up to his knees, he flicked his wrist and gracefully cast his line. He gently tugged on his fly-like hook, giving it a lifelike movement. Trees grew out of the walls of the riverside. A small waterfall poured nearby, creating a rainbow. Don enjoyed his own private paradise. His pocket-covered vest was unbuttoned today. A Glock 22 was strapped to his ribs.

Clyde lingered at the water's edge. He waited until Don had a cast few more times before making himself known.

Don waved at him. "Clyde, good to see you. If I'd known you were coming, I would've brought a set of waders."

"I'm fine watching," Clyde replied. "Honestly, I was just looking for an excuse to get out of the house."

"I hear ya. Business has been way too *business-y* for me this week," Don replied.

Clyde took a seat. He watched the surrounding woods. His eyes caught on Gena, standing near the top of the waterfall and slightly concealed by a moss-covered tree trunk. The brunette watched Clyde. He wasn't sure what to do to appease her. He wasn't sure why he even wanted to.

Pathfinder sat at his side. Her ear twitched to the sound of an unseen bird.

"You want to talk about something," Don said, casting his line.

"I do," Clyde replied.

"Shoot," Don said.

Clyde said, "I, uh, I've been digging into Hartwell's history, and I found out about that massacre a couple of decades ago."

Don listened intently as he tugged on the line.

Clyde said, "That must've been hard for you."

"Nah," Don replied. "I never knew the girls or their folks. I was more shocked than anything else."

"It must've hurt the businesses," Clyde said.

Don shrugged. "I own a small flower shop alongside the hardware store and grocer. The little flower shop actually turned made out really well for the vigil."

"I thought you'd be a little more beat up by the whole ordeal."

Don lowered his rod. "We all mourned, Clyde, but after so many years, you learn to let go. Yeah, it broke a lot of people's spirits, but at the end of the day, death is death. We all have to go sometime. When I see God, I'll figure out the reason for whys and hows. Until then, it isn't my wheelhouse."

"I guess that's one way of saying it," Clyde replied.

"It's the only way. Otherwise, you'll drive yourself crazy," Don replied. "No offense, but I think it was those murders that drove Andrew off the deep end."

"Did he talk about them a lot?" Clyde asked.

"For a time, yeah, and then he just shut up about it." Don cast his line. "I could tell it was on his mind." He caught a trout, fought it, and reeled it in. "Get a pic."

Clyde snapped a photo using his phone and texted it to Don.

Clyde asked, "If you don't mind me asking, where were you when the massacre happened?"

Don lowered the fish back in the water. He started to talk to land. "And why would you ask me that?"

"Just curious," Clyde said.

"I was out of town," Don said firmly.

"With your wife?"

"It was a business trip," Don replied. "Just me."

Clyde could tell he was lying. About what or why, he did not know.

Don hiked out of the bank. Water dripped from the legs. He put his rod aside, put his hands on his hips, and bent his back as he stretched. The sunlight captured the black hilt of his loaded gun.

10

ON TARGET

The map of Hartwell and Hart County started to make sense. The woods marked by a pin on the county map was the place where the massacre happened. Marked homes, skate-in, and other places around town followed the route the kids took that fateful night. At least that was Clyde's theory. At some point, they got together, started a campfire, and were mercilessly gunned down by a hunting rifle. Judging by the shell casing, it was a fairly common model.

He went to bed early that night and got up the next morning, only having a few hours of sleep. He ironed his suit and tie, packed his briefcase and shined his shoes. He watched the news as he brushed his teeth. No one reported on the skeletons being found. Bob Hawkins wanted to keep the case under wraps. What made Hartwell so appealing was its quietness. News of murder could scare away the right people and attract the wrong ones.

Dressed the part of a lawyer, Clyde got into his Cadillac. He turned on his classic rock-and-roll radio station and cruised through Hartwell. He followed a few backroads to a street lined with several houses. Using the picture of the map on his phone, Clyde stopped in front of a house. He dropped down the mirror, fixed his tie, and checked his teeth. All set, he exited the vehicle and approached the first home on his list. He knocked on the door. He recited his sales pitch in his head. The goal was to just get the people talking. Hopefully, Elizabeth and the others would help from there. *You realize you're insane, right?* Clyde told himself. *Maybe, but results don't lie.* He noticed that he was talking to himself in his mind and stopped.

A small Asian lady answered the door.

Clyde smiled politely. He told over the woman. "Hi, ma'am. I was wondering if I could speak to Mr. or Mrs. Roth?"

"No Roth here," The woman replied.

"Do you know where I can find them?"

The woman shook her head.

"Were you around twenty years ago?" Clyde asked.

The woman replied. "Eighteen. Owners sold the house for cheap. They wanted to get away quickly."

"Do you have their number?"

"I'm sorry, no."

Clyde thanked the woman for her time. John Roth stood on the roof of the house. The sun glistened on his bloody head wound.

Clyde got into his car and crossed off the first name on his list. *Off to a good start,* he thought cynically. Two streets over, he arrived at Tommy Demko's house.

The roof was missing a dozen shingles. Grass grew wildly in the front yard. The paint peeled. The homeowners must've taken a page out of Andrew's book. The minivan in the driveway was about as old as the murders. A large dent dinged its side. The dirty headlights had an unnatural beige tint.

The homeowner answered at Clyde's second knock.

Clyde faced an average height, middle-aged man. His large beer belly bulged under his NASCAR tee-shirt. A large hole was in the armpit, revealing the stretch marks at the back of meat-as-a-muttonchop biceps. He unashamedly wore whitie-tightie underwear. He had thin hair on top of his round face.

"Hi, are you Mr. Demko?"

The man looked at Clyde's suit like he was a pretentious A-hole. "You'll have better luck selling to someone else, buddy."

"I'm not a salesman. I'm a lawyer," Clyde replied.

The man cursed under his breath. "I thought we didn't have a HOA here? Did those screwballs in county vote for it?"

"Not at all, sir," Clyde said. "I'm actually here to talk about Tommy's passing. Some new evidence has arisen in the case, and –"

"And the court thinks I killed my boy," the man lashed out.

"Not at all, sir."

"You are here to protect me? I was here that whole night. My wife, my dog, I have witnesses and alibis," the man said.

"I understand," Clyde said calmly.

"Then why the hell are you here?"

"Can we talk inside?" Clyde asked.

Grumbling, the man stepped back and allowed Clyde to enter. Two large pit bulls charged him the moment he stepped inside. They jumped on Clyde. He swiftly lifted his briefcase to protect himself from their slobbery bites.

"You get down from there!" the man shouted. "Get!"

The dogs scattered at the sound of his thundering voice.

Using his sleeve, Clyde wiped the drool off the corner of his briefcase. The dog's fangs left little notches in the black leather. Clyde wasn't happy.

The man gestured Clyde to sit down at the tiny kitchen table. Dog fur and powdery insect pesticide ran around the edges of the room like a salt circle. Large chunks of foam had been ripped out of the couch, probably from the dogs. Dirty plates rested on a TV tray. The carpeted floor had urine and beer stains. The house's stench reflected its appearance.

"I'm Clyde, by the way."

Clyde shook the man's sweaty hand.

"I'm Howie. Tommy is… was my son." Howie took a seat next to Clyde and turned it at an angle to face Clyde. He sipped from an open can of Pepsi on the table and man-spread. Clyde saw a little more than he had bargained for. He kept his eyes on Howie's less-than-appealing face.

"My condolences," Clyde replied.

Howie frowned and sniffled. "He was a good kid. He got the good looks from his mother but his throwing arm from me. I tell you what, Tommy could play." Howie said, fire in his eyes. "He was a quarterback for that school just down the road. He broke records that still ain't been touched. The kid was smart too. Straight As. Advance placement. He got all his smart from his mother's side. At his age, I was the biggest screw-up you could be." Howie chuckled at his own expense.

"Can you walk me through what happened that night?" Clyde asked.

Howie eyed him suspiciously.

"I'm on your side, Howie," Clyde said.

"You're a lawyer. The only better liar is the devil."

Clyde smirked. "I'm more interested in the truth than you know. It's personal."

"You weren't even alive back then," Howie remarked.

"My uncle killed himself looking into this case," Clyde said. "Twenty years or twenty days old, I'm getting to the bottom of it."

Howie heard the sincerity in Clyde's voice.

"I'll tell you about that night," Howie replied. "I was working down at Evergreen—it's a lumber yard thirty miles west of here. I got home late. Tammie was cooking dinner. Tammie is my wife."

Clyde nodded, easily drawing the connection, as he listened to the man speak.

"I remember she made pasta. The surgery on her broken knee a few months ago had eaten at our funds, and we'd been living on a shoe-string budget. Anyway, I noticed Tom wasn't home. Tammie said that he went camping with friends and would not be joining us for dinner. That was that. The next afternoon, we got a knock on the door. It was a police officer and Chief Hawkins himself. He told us what happened."

Howie went quiet for a moment. His eyes glossed over.

Clyde said, "How was Hawkins that day?"

"Distraught like the rest of us," Howie replied. "Nothing like that has ever happened in Hartwell, and nothing like it has happened since."

"Hawkins didn't seem strange to you?"

"Everything and everyone felt strange that day," Howie replied.

"Is Tammie still around?" Clyde asked.

Howie set his jaw. He shook his head. "She decided to live *free* a few years back. We haven't talked since."

Clyde asked, "Is there any way I can reach her?"

"Her phones don't work no more. I called her many times," Howie said, refusing to give up her information.

"Last question," Clyde said. "Was there anyone you suspected?"

"Yeah," Howie's expression darkened. "The nigger."

"I'm not familiar," Clyde replied.

"I don't know his name, but the man is a killer." Clyde jammed his finger on the table. "I don't think the shooting was ever about Tommy."

"What do you mean?"

"Those girls he was with were pretty and bright. They never found one of them," Howie said. "She's probably locked in some basement somewhere. The blonde was killed for sport."

"This, uh, black gentlemen you mentioned. Do you know where I can find him?"

"He lives up by Payne Creek. I can't say where. The man hides out," Howie said. "I've seen him before at the bars around here, but he steers clear of me. He knows he's not welcome."

Clyde opened the briefcase and showed Howie a picture of the black man from Andrew's collection. "Is this him?"

"That's the one," Howie said bitterly.

Clyde gave his phone number to Howie. "Call me if you remember anything else."

Howie eyed the number as he scratched the stretch marks on his bare inner thigh. Clyde showed himself out.

Once in his car, he jotted down notes. He pulled Google Maps and found Payne Creek. It stretched for a few miles before crossing into South Carolina. That wasn't too far north. Hartwell was near the western corner of Georgia. Clyde could cross state lines easily. He wanted to get more information before visiting the man. There were two more houses on the list.

He traveled down a long driveway. Pretty white fences

flanked both sides of the road. The grass had a fine checked pattern. The landscaping crew must've worked wonders. The house at the end of the road looked like a two-story red barn. It had a large tin star on it and an American flag sat at an angle above its door. Three farmhands tended to the horses in the field beside the house. One horse had a cast on its leg, another stallion had ugly spots, and a thoroughbred was so skinny its bone could be seen through its skin. There were a few others, but none of them would win any beauty pageants.

In his early forties, a man wearing a white cowboy hat oversaw the horses and farmhands. He opened a packet of nicotine gum and put two sticks in his mouth. He had a dimpled chin and strong jaw like John Wayne. Wearing denim from head to toe, he looked like the model on the front of a rancher's magazine.

Clyde got out of the car and waved him down.

The man shouted to the farmhands, "Keep cleaning 'em. Teeth, too."

He walked to the fence and rested his forearms on the top beam. Chewing his gum, he looked Clyde up and down. "You aren't from around here, are you?"

"I'm from Atlanta," Clyde said.

"It's looking more and more like California over there every day, I hear."

"More or less," Clyde agreed.

"I'm Terrence Cobbs. It's a pleasure to make your acquaintance."

Clyde introduced himself as well. He stood on the other side of the fence. "Nice farm. It yours?"

"Family-owned," Terrence said. "I know what you're thinking: why the broken horses?"

"I'm sure you have a good reason," Clyde said.

Terrence pointed to the horse with the leg cast. "That beauty won't run again. The one with spots had a strange skin disease. I reckon she'll be bald in a year's time. I'd tell you the sickness's name if I knew how to pronounce it. The rest are discards from the derby."

"Horse rehab?" Clyde asked.

"Sort of. More like a new home," Terrence replied. "My ma and I never liked the idea of putting a horse down. We take them up and give them a new life. Every few weeks, we invite over the local special needs kids to be their buddy. It'd melt your heart seeing them kids with them horses." Terrence's eyes teared up.

Clyde said, "It's good work."

"You got that right," Filled with pride and achievement, Terrence gazed at his farm.

"Are you related to Gena Cobb?" Clyde asked.

Terrence's smile faded. "I'm her older brother. Why?"

Clyde nodded soberly. "I have some information about her case."

"You FBI?"

"No, sir," Clyde replied. "I'm just an interested party."

"What did you find?" Terrence asked.

"Gena's gone, Terrence."

"She's been gone for years. That doesn't mean we're going to stop looking," Terrence said defensively.

"She's *gone* gone," Clyde said, hating being the bearer of bad news.

Terrence waved his comment off. "Sure. What proof you got?"

"Their identities have not been confirmed yet, but my source in the local PD said that recently two skeletons were recently discovered in the same woods where the shooting happened," Clyde explained. "I suspect you'll be receiving a visit from the police sometime soon."

Terrence took off his hat and rested it against his chest. He shut his eyes and inhaled through his nose.

Clyde waited for him to process the information.

Terrence said, "You telling the truth?"

"I wouldn't come all the way out here if I were lying," Clyde said.

Terrence said, "Pa had a stroke all those years ago. Ma and I have been taking care of him ever since. We put our fortune into this place. We wanted to do something that would make Gena proud. You think she'd like it?"

"I believe so," Clyde replied.

Terrence sniffled.

"Where were you when it all happened?" Clyde asked softly.

"Partying," Terrence said, trying to fight back tears. He put another piece of nicotine gum in his mouth. "I was at Wilber's house. Do you know him? James Wilber?"

"Never heard of him," Clyde replied.

"That's where I was," Terrence said. "I was twenty-three at the time. I just finished community college but I was still doing all the stupid late-night stuff. Gena was eighteen. She was planning on going to the University of Georgia. She got the scholarship and everything. I was hungover when Ma told me what happened. Pa collapsed soon after he heard the news."

Clyde said, "I'm sorry, man."

Terrence wiped his eyes. "Her vanishing turned me around real quick. I cleaned myself up and took over the ranch. It's been a journey."

Clyde asked, "During that time or since, has there ever been anyone you suspected of taking her?"

Terrence thought for a moment. "I suspected a lot of people. None of them ever found their way to the police. There were a few people that stalked Gena. Old boyfriends mostly."

"Do you remember their names?"

Terrence said. "I remembered everything about them, and how the police cleared them all. There was one freak that was worse than the rest."

"Who is that?"

"His name was Glen. He was a tall, lengthy fellow. He was expelled from high school for disorderly conduct a few years before the killings. He would've been in his early twenties when the murder happened."

"Where can I find him?" Clyde asked.

"No one knows. He left two to four years after the killings. Poof. Just gone. No one knows where he went. He claimed to have an alibi, but I didn't believe it. If there was anyone that could've attacked them, it would've been Glen."

"Thank you, Terrence," Clyde said. "Did your mother know anything about killings?"

"Nothing, but I'll talk to her about it. If there's anything worth saying, I'll give you a call," Terrence replied.

"Thank you," Clyde said, telling him his phone number.

"By the way, what organization are you a part of?" Terrence asked.

"I'm a lawyer. I have my own office in Atlanta. If things get hairy, I have your back," Clyde said.

"I hope I don't ever need you," Terrence said.

Clyde replied, "Me either."

The last stop was located on Lake Hartwell. Clyde kept this Glen character filed away in his mind. He was too young to a part of Andrew's suspect list, though. Elizabeth's house overlooked the lake. It had a beautiful wooden dock. The water captured globs of sunlight and shimmered. Clyde double-checked his attire. The last parent shouldn't be that bad. The daughter had been gone from twenty years. Hopefully, that would be enough time for the wounds to heal. Clyde thought back to the night his parents died. That was twenty-five years ago, and he still felt disconnected from the world because of it.

He knocked on the door.

A woman in her fifties answered. She wore a colorful flowing shirt and airy pants that caught the wind like white sails. Her grey hair hovered above her shoulders. She had multiple rings on her fingers. One had a black onyx the size of a penny. One of her eyes was the color of the ocean. The other was milky white. She gazed into Clyde's eyes. He could almost see part of Elizabeth in her.

"Mrs. Mara," Clyde said. "I'm Clyde Barker, practicing attorney."

"Call me Jasmine. Why have you stopped by today?"

"I have information about your daughter," Clyde replied.

Jasmine's expression turned bitter. "You found the man who killed her?"

"Not yet, but new developments in the case could lead to new revelations," Clyde said. "I'm here to get the facts straight, not like most people in my profession."

The joke brought a smile to Jasmine's face. "Come." She stepped out and closed the door. "The house is a mess. We can talk by the dock."

Clyde followed her down the descending driveway. The wooden dock groaned beneath their feet. A canoe was tied to the final post. It bobbed gently. Jasmine stood at the edge. "Lizzy used to love coming out here."

"It's beautiful," Clyde remarked.

Jasmine kept her gaze forward. "I'm sure you have questions."

"A few, yes," Clyde replied.

"Ask away."

"Tell me about Elizabeth," Clyde said.

"She had such a brilliant mind. She won multiple scholarships to different colleges and had a hard time choosing. She planned on being a surgeon. I felt horrible knowing a beautiful girl wasted all her youth locked away in a classroom, but then the incident happened."

"Was there anyone who wanted to hurt her?" Clyde asked.

"No one sane," Jasmine asked. "She had such a kind heart. Never hurt anyone."

"Anyone insane you suspected?" Clyde asked.

Jasmine said, "No one I could name, but justice will come for my little girl. Evil doesn't go unpunished for long."

"Did she act different days before it happened?" Clyde asked.

"She was nervous," Jasmine admitted. "Her life was about to change. Moving out of Hartwell was a big step. The camping trip was the last fun time with her friends before they left."

"Did she ever feel like there was someone following her?" Clyde asked. "Someone named Glen, perhaps."

"I knew a Glen back when I taught tenth grade. Glen Iving. He was a quiet boy. He skipped most classes and failed others. He was suspended from school for sneaking into the girls' bathroom. After that, I heard nothing about him. Does he have something to do with Lizzy's passing?"

"It's all just hearsay at the moment," Clyde admitted. "Where were you during that night?"

"Dance classes. There was a small studio on Main. I'm sure you've seen it. It's called Little Dancer."

Clyde jotted down that name. "Was it busy that night?"

"No worse than usual," Jasmine replied. "Am I a suspect now?"

"I'm just here to get the facts straight," Clyde replied.

Jasmine gave him a harsh look.

"When did you hear about her death?"

"The next afternoon. I was the first person Chief Hawkins visited," Jasmine said. "You know, my daughter was going to change the world."

"I'm sure she would've," Clyde politely agreed.

"You don't understand. She had brains, beauty, and a rare dose of common sense. Some people get one of those three. Rarely does anyone get them all," Jasmine said.

Clyde replied, "I'm truly sorry for your loss."

"Oh, Lizzy," Jasmine said, suddenly crying. "Why won't you come home to me?"

Tears and snot rolled down Jasmine's face. Clyde gave her a hug. She cried, holding him closely. Standing on a nearby pier, Elizabeth watched them. Her face was completely devoid of emotions. If she felt anything as a reaction to her mother's tears, it would be beneath her blank exterior.

"Tell me something, what vile, jealous, spiteful person would take my daughter away?" Elizabeth cried.

Clyde calmly stroked her back. He felt rigid. Close, intimate, relational connections were foreign to him. Most of the time, he ran away from them.

Eventually, Jasmine stopped crying and pulled away from Clyde. "I wish I could see her one last time."

I'm looking at her right now. Clyde thought, staring at the dead girl. A droplet of blood trickled out of the corner of her mouth.

Jasmine rubbed Clyde's shoulder. "Oh my, look at the mess I've made on your nice suit."

"It'll wash out," Clyde replied. He lifted his briefcase and showed her the bite marks. "A pit bull got this one this morning."

He popped open the tabs and drew out the pictures of Andrew's three suspects. He deliberately withheld the picture of Chief Hawkins. It was far too controversial. "Do you recognize these men?"

Jasmine sifted through the photos. "This one is Don. He owns the hardware store and flower shop. Some other business too, but I can't remember." She pointed at the picture of the black man. "That's Curtis. He lives on Payne. He's a very misunderstood man." She studied the picture of the man with the ponytail. "I've never seen this person."

Clyde put the photos back. "Were there any rumors surrounding those three during the initial investigation?"

"Gosh." Jasmine rubbed her forehead. "It's so long ago and things were so crazy, I can't remember."

"Do you know where on Payne?"

"I can't say."

Clyde and Jasmine returned from the dock.

"Thank you for talking to me," Jasmine said.

"Next time we can talk about something a little less heavy," Clyde said.

"I'd like that." Jasmine waved at him as he drove away.

A mile away, Clyde pulled over to the shoulder of the road. He opened the photos of his phone. He had one saved of the maps on his wall. He zoomed into Payne Creek. It looked like Andrew already had Curtis's home marked. Clyde checked the dashboard clock. It was 6 pm. It would be the last stop he made for the day.

"Any time you guys want to help me, that would be great," Clyde said to no one.

He was hoping the dead would show up. They did not. If

he found out they knew the killer's identity all along, he would be pissed off. Granted, if they knew the killer, they would probably haunt him instead of Clyde. The situation still felt surreal. He drove to Curtis's house.

The back road had many twists and turns. Black birds watched him from lichen-covered branches. The falling sun cut through the canopy of woods. Rusty nails pinned a "No Trespassing" sign to a tree. It sprouted beside the dirt road and tilted at an angle, as if it was about to fall on any vehicle crossing under.

Clyde followed the dirt road. Rocks bounced in the wheel well of his car. A grassy stripe ran between two deep tire marks. At the end of the road was a second "No Trespassing" sign and an old cabin. Dense woods enclosed the front and back yard. The cabin dated back to the nineteen fifties. An A-frame roof topped its simple design. Wooden window shutters covered the dusty glass.

A tarp covered a motorcycle. Clyde concluded it was a hog by the shape of it. He kept his phone close and headed to the front door.

He knocked a few times, quickly becoming discouraged. He opened a set of blinds and cupped his hands around the glass. The minimalist interior design was much more organized than he'd anticipated. Books packed a shelf. A box TV faced the recliner. A work desk sat nearby. Tools and dismantled gun parts rested on the top. An AR-15, AK-47, and two modified semi-automatic rifles Clyde didn't recognize stood upright in the glass door gun cabinet. An American flag in a triangle sat on top of the cabinet. Curtis was a soldier.

Clyde closed the shutter. He treaded along the side of the cabin. The shed in the back had a protruding roof that covered a workstation outside the side door. A large buck dangled from a rope. A black man with curly white hair carved out its torso. With gloved hands, he grabbed handfuls of its colorful innards and dropped them in a tin bucket nearby. The man wore the top of military fatigues and washout jeans rolled up around his boots. His back was turned to Clyde.

"Do you know how to read?" The man's voice seemed like only the human sound for miles.

Clyde took a step forward. "Sorry to intrude—"

Curtis twisted around. "You ain't sorry about nothin'."

His unbuttoned shirt revealed his lean torso. The seventy-two-year-old was as fit as a fiddle. There were burn scars up and down his chest. His man boobs sagged slightly as a sign of his age. His rubber gloves extended halfway up his forearms. Blood stained them crimson. He held blue and violet organs at his waist and unceremoniously dropped them in the tin bucket.

Splat.

The severed end of ropey large intestines dangled on the other side of the rim.

"What you want, man?" Curtis asked. "Speak quick before I pin this knife between your eyes."

"I want to talk about those young men and women who died twenty years ago."

"You're asking the wrong man," Curtis replied and carved out the buck's stomach cavity.

"I'm an attorney," Clyde said.

"And who you representing?"

"You, maybe."

Curtis chuckled. "Go home, boy."

"New evidence has surfaced in the Hartwell Massacre. There's a good chance the case is going to reopen. From what I hear, you are a lead suspect."

Curtis stopped carving. Keeping his face to the gutted deer, he said. "Who told you that?"

"Sources," Clyde replied. "You need to lawyer up, Curtis."

"Does it look like I got money for that?"

"Relax. My rates are reasonable," Clyde replied. He crossed his arms. "And you need an ally."

"Why do you care so much anyway?" Curtis asked.

"Let's just say I have too much free time on my hands," Clyde replied.

Curtis chuckled. He pulled off his gloves and set them on the table beside him. "You want to talk, we'll talk. But I'm not paying you nothing right now."

"I wasn't planning on charging. Maybe you'll learn one day that I'm a man of the people."

"You're a BS-er," Curtis replied. "Don't lie to me."

Curtis told him to wait outside. Clyde did so. He squinted, seeing someone behind the shed. He looked closer. It was a female mannequin. There were dozens he could see scattered throughout the woods. They faced the house. Bullet holes peppered their featureless faces and naked bodies.

"There ain't much to do out here but shoot," Curtis said.

Clyde's heart jumped in his chest. He hadn't heard the man approach. Curtis held two glasses of ice tea. "Peach flavor."

"I'm fine," Clyde said, suspicious of drinks from a stranger.

"You're not a trusting man," Curtis remarked.

"Just not a thirsty one," Clyde replied.

Curtis took a gulp from the cup he was going to give Clyde.

Clyde turned to the mannequins. "You got your own private range."

"I got targets all up and down the woods. Some even in the trees," Curtis replied. "Just like 'Nam."

"You must've been young," Clyde remarked.

"We were all young and stuck in that green hellhole. You can get out of a place like that, but it doesn't get out of you."

Clyde thought about his parents. He nodded soberly.

"What happened that night, Curtis?" Clyde asked.

The black man got lost in his own mind. He returned after a few seconds. "I can't tell you."

"There is a world of difference between can't and won't," said Clyde.

"Those girls were pretty. Real pretty. The kind of pretty that's dangerous," Curtis said.

"You knew them?" Clyde asked.

"Everybody knew everybody back then," Curtis said.

"You know anyone that wanted to hurt them or the guys?"

"There are a lot of creeps around here. They may hide behind pretty smiles, but they got hearts of darkness."

"Can you give me a name?" Clyde asked.

Curtis blinked. He glanced around, as if not knowing where he was for a second.

"You okay?" Clyde asked.

"I've got to go," Curtis said, sounding confused and terrified.

"Hey," Clyde said.

Curtis backed away from him. "You go home now. It's almost dark."

The man wasn't mentally well. Clyde gave him his business card and left him in peace. "We'll talk again soon."

Clyde drove back home, watching the sun go down. He got a lot of information today, but nothing got him the answers he needed. Granted, if it had been as easy as talking to a few folks, the police would've closed the case years ago. His list of suspects was growing. The sun had fallen by the time he pulled up to his uncle's house.

A cop car was parked in the driveway.

Clyde grunted.

He stopped, turned off the ignition, and exited his vehicle.

Sarah stepped out of the cop car. Her face was as red as her hair. "What do you think you're doing?"

"Rough day at work?" Clyde asked.

"Screw you, Clyde." She punched him in the chest.

The little woman packed a punch.

"Ow." Clyde rubbed his peck.

"Going around to victim's families? That's low."

"The case is twenty years old," Clyde replied.

"After you found those bones, everyone is interested again," Sarah said. "But you knew that and still went on to play detective."

"I have the right to the truth like everyone else," Clyde replied.

"Everyone at the station knows we're friends. They already know you're interfering with the investigation. It's going to backfire on me," Sarah said.

"How did they find out so fast?" Clyde asked.

"Terrence Cobbs called the station this afternoon, asking about new information surrounding the case. There's only one other person outside of the police department who knew about the skeletons, and that's you. I need you to drop your little charade before it harms the investigation."

"My uncle died trying to solve this case," Clyde said. "What if he learned something that drove him to suicide?"

"Is that why you came all this way? To give him some eternal rest?" Sarah asked angrily.

Not him exactly. "It's complicated."

"Then un-complicate it." Sarah swatted at a mosquito. "Can we talk inside? I'm getting eaten alive out here."

Clyde hesitated. He didn't want to show her the map yet. Elizabeth had chosen him. She wanted him to solve this. "I have a lot of repairs going on inside. I'd feel better staying out here."

"Ugh. Whatever," Sarah replied.

"My uncle had a few suspects in mind."

"He was running his own investigation?" Sarah asked. "Why?"

"I don't know," Clyde admitted.

Sarah tried to stay angry, but her intrigue was showing. "Who did he suspect?"

"One of them was Curtis. He lives on Payne Creek."

"Mr. Lowry, I know him," Sarah said.

"I visited him today," Clyde said.

"You what?" Sarah replied. "That man has enough firepower to kill this whole town, and you waltzed up to his front door. At least tell me you were armed."

Clyde kept his mouth shut.

Sarah shook her head. "Did you at least learn anything from him?"

"Nothing much, but I can tell he's not all there," Clyde replied.

"You're right about that much. Curtis killed his wife when he was twenty-two," Sarah said. "That was fifty years ago."

"What happened?"

"He got home from his tour of duty. He and his wife went hunting. She got shot by his gun. He claimed it was an accident. He claimed that they split up and he didn't realize it was her," Sarah explained. "The judge barely bought it, but his lawyer found a technicality during the arrest and was able to get his sentence reduced. He served fifteen years for involuntary manslaughter. He got out and hid away in his cabin, shooting his mannequins every morning. The massacre happened a little over a decade later."

"Why didn't the police arrest him?"

"I looked through the old files this morning. They tried, but there was no evidence pointing to him. He didn't own the same rifle. From what we know, at least," said Sarah.

"You think he'd go after those kids?"

Sarah replied, "You can't change a killer."

11

SUSPECTS

Sarah leaned her bottom against her cop car. She crossed her arms. Her freckled face was as hard as stone. "Who else did your uncle suspect?"

Clyde was unsure about how much to share with Sarah. He trusted her, but he didn't want to see his targets getting whisked away by the police before he could learn the truth. He only gave her one other name. "Bob Hawkins."

Sarah blinked as if she didn't hear him right. "My boss?"

"That's who," Clyde replied. "Andrew could be wrong, but Hawkins was undoubtedly on the list."

Sarah took a deep breath. "You realize I can't just launch an investigation on my boss."

"You'd have to do it secretly," Clyde said.

Sarah shook her head. A frustrated smile formed on her lips. "This is insanity."

"I can't look into him myself," Clyde replied.

"You're not supposed to be doing any of this," Sarah sternly reminded him.

Clyde said, "I'm not backing off, Sarah. I made a deal with myself that I'm going to see this to the end."

"When did you become so bullheaded?" Sarah asked.

"I've always been this way," Clyde replied. "We can work together. I have time. You have the ability to make arrests. You can see me as your informant. If I find something on Curtis or someone, I'll let you know directly."

"What if you find something you're not supposed to and get killed?" Sarah asked.

"Then you'll know to start looking into my suspect list," Clyde replied.

Sarah put her hand on her hip. "You're impossible, Clyde."

"Does that mean we're in this together?" Clyde asked.

Sarah glared at him. The croak of frogs interrupted the long silence. "Yeah, fine. We're in this together."

Clyde extended his hand.

Sarah reluctantly shook it.

"This is going to be good," Clyde replied. "I can just feel it."

Sarah gave him a look like he was crazy. "We'll talk later, Clyde."

"Give me updates on the chief. If he starts giving you trouble, let him know that you have a good lawyer."

The joke softened Sarah's expression. "Whatever."

Clyde smiled at her.

She drove away.

Clyde felt his heart racing. Knowing that he wasn't alone lightened his stress. He opened the front door, and Pathfinder leapt on him. Clyde fell back. The dog stood on his chest and licked his face. "Okay, okay, you win. I'm sorry I'm late."

He slipped out from under the dog and sat on the broken porch, then rubbed the husky behind the ears. "I don't know about you, but I'm starving."

Clyde went inside. The house was an accident waiting to

happen. The amount of work left to do discouraged him. He poured Pathfinder a bowl of dry food, cleaned up her droppings, and opened a dusty can of soup from Andrew's cupboard. He poured it in a bowl and heated it in the microwave. The broth was too hot and the chunks of beef were too cold. Clyde kept waiting for the ghosts to visit him, but the house was silent. He lay in bed. Pathfinder curled up next to him. Using the light on the lampstand, he reviewed his notes. People tend to retain what they read before they got to bed. If the case was the last thing he put into his mind before bedtime, it would be the first thing he'd think of when he awoke.

The problem was that Clyde didn't sleep. His eyes were shut, sure, but his mind wouldn't shut off. He wanted answers to the case, but more importantly to the supernatural realm. Could he talk to his parents again? Could he learn the truth behind their murders? What about Andrew? Why hadn't he revealed himself?

Rays of sun breached the window blinds. Clyde got out of bed, somehow both excited and exhausted. Having missed his run yesterday, he ran an extra mile. His body hated him for it, but it woke him quicker than expresso. Going by the woods, he didn't see any of the victims. He went back to the house, did a hundred sits up and push-ups on the bedroom floor, and took a cold shower. He donned his suit despite how unclean it was getting. If he wanted to be taken seriously, he had to dress accordingly.

He reviewed Andrew's map, seeing locations he'd yet to travel. One was ten miles out of town, isolated in farm fields and wooded areas. Pathfinder stuck her head out the window as Clyde drove. Her tongue flopped in the wind. She smiled. The dog seemed so free.

Clyde grinned just looking at her. God had brought her to

Clyde as well. He followed the road, enjoying the rural Georgia landscape. There were hills but a few great mountains. Fields stretched far and wide separated by walls of trees. The road took Clyde through plots of undeveloped land. Puffy white clouds cruised across the blue sky.

He turned onto a gravel driveway and followed it to a doublewide trailer. Patches of weeds sprouted in the dead grass around the property. A chicken coop stood off beside the house. Feathers and hardened chicken feces collected at the bottom, but there were no chickens. Clyde kept the window down for the husky and stepped out. The moment he shut the door behind him, the owner of the trailer burst out.

His receding hairline turned into a ponytail that rested on his shoulder. He wore a yellow jumpsuit and boots without socks. The wiry man matched Andrew's picture. He had a name tag above his breast. His name was Roland.

Clyde said. "Good to see you. I'm Clyde Barker, attorney--"

A vein bulged in the man's forehead. He drew out his pistol.

"Hold on," Clyde put out his hands.

"You get back in your car," the man threatened.

"I just want to talk."

"Talk? Is that why you brought that mutt over here?" Roland barked.

Pathfinder snarled at him.

"Her?" Clyde hiked back his thumb. "What does she have to do with anything?"

"You get back in your car and drive on out of here!" Roland shouted. "Get!"

He fired two shots in the air.

Clyde ducked his head and scurried into his car. He reversed out of the driveway.

The rumble of the engine muted Roland's slew of obscenities. He fired two more shots in the air. Clyde raced down the street, adrenaline pumping.

"What did you do to him?" Clyde asked.

Pathfinder lowered her head in shame.

Her pouting eyes melted Clyde's frustration. "That's okay. We'll have to rethink our strategy, that's all."

On his drive through town, he spotted a man in a dark red mask standing in an alley, concealed by the shadows. The man watched him. Clyde went by too fast to get a good look. Seeing that the road was only lightly trafficked, he made a U-turn at the first traffic light and drove by the alley. The man was gone. All four of the ghosts were accounted for. This wasn't one of them. Clyde pulled over and called Sarah, and told her about the man in the mask.

"I'll keep an eye out," Sarah replied.

"Hey, if it's not too much, can you get me the address for someone named Don Fegan?"

"I'm not allowed to do that for citizens," Sarah replied.

"Live on the edge a little," Clyde said.

"Clyde," Sarah said plainly.

"Pretty please."

Sarah sighed. "Give me a minute."

"Have you had a good morning?"

"Slow," Sarah replied. "I'm on traffic duty."

"Did you see Hawkins?"

"He was rushing around this morning. He's still waiting on the lab results for the bones," Sarah explained.

"It's pretty obvious who it is," Clyde replied.

"He wants to draw out the discovery. Hartwell is a quiet,

uneventful town. He wants to keep it that way... I got the address. You want to write it down?"

Clyde put it directly into his phone's GPS. "Thanks, Sarah."

"You want to have a drink tonight?" She asked.

"I'd like that," Clyde answered.

He headed to Don's house. Just how he expected, Don's car wasn't there, but his wife's car was parked in the driveway.

"Let's see if we can't learn something new," Clyde told Pathfinder.

The husky followed him out his door.

"Don's not here," the plump woman yelled from the open upstairs window.

"That's a shame," Clyde replied. "When will he be back?"

"Late this evening. You'll have better luck talking to him over the phone," the woman said.

"I drove all this way. Is it okay if I have a glass of water before I head back?" Clyde asked.

The woman gave him a curious look. "I'll be right down."

Clyde eyed the nice white house and square bushes outside. A few yellow flowers grew in front of them. Don was a wealthy man. What would cause him to kill someone?

The woman answered the door. Make-up caked her plump face. She had a kind smile and large eyes. She extended the glass of water.

Clyde nursed the cup. "Are you Mrs. Fegan?"

"I am," the woman replied. "Call me Mary."

"Clyde. It's a pleasure. Don and I went finishing the other day," Clyde said.

"Did you now? He never told me, but Don is always one to keep things to himself."

"Oh yeah?" Clyde said.

"It's just who he is. A lot of businessmen are like that, I heard," Mary said.

"That must be hard for you."

Mary replied, "I didn't think we'd survive our first few decades, but now we've come to an understanding that there are some things about each other we can't fix."

Clyde took another sip. The husky sat calmly by his side. "I've been hearing rumors about the woods on Fairbanks. People say it's haunted."

Mary shook her head. "Who has been telling you those tall tales?"

"It's just the word on the street," Clyde replied. "There must be some truth behind it, right?"

Mary sighed. "Many years ago, a few young men and women were attacked on their camping trip out there."

"What happened?"

"Two died. Two went missing," Mary said. "It was Hartwell's darkest hour."

"Were you around during that time?" Clyde asked.

"Yep. I was in our old home back then. I remember watching the news on TV. Even the reporter was crying. Poor girl," Mary said.

"Was Don with you?" Clyde asked.

"No. He was on a business trip. It was so many years ago, I don't remember where he went. I just know that I called and called him but he didn't pick up. Apparently, he was negotiating a very important deal. As I said, the first twenty years were the hardest," Mary said.

Clyde finished his glass and thanked her.

"Have a good day, Clyde. I'll tell him you stopped by."

"No need. I'll call him myself," Clyde said politely.

He drove away.

Clyde rested one hand on the steering wheel. "What do

you think, pup? Was it business or was he on clean-up duty?"

Pathfinder bowed her head.

"We'll figure it out."

Clyde slid into the hardware store. He let the husky follow him inside. Clyde small-talked with the man inside. He was suspicious of the dog, but the husky was extremely well-behaved. Eventually, Clyde got around to talking to the cashier about Don. He was a nice guy and a reasonable boss, apparently.

Clyde got a list of shops Don owned. He had a stake in a lot of places around town. Clyde made a point to get to each one. He shared friendly banter with the employees and talked about Don. One of the older employees told Clyde that he had a lady friend around the time of the killings. The employee didn't know the woman's name or how to find her. There was a good chance it was just a rumor. He continued gathering information until he was able to get the name of the mysterious woman. It was rumored that she still lived in town. Clyde spent the afternoon asking about her at different restaurants and shops. It took most of the day but he eventually discovered that she worked at a diner just outside of town.

Clyde drove there. He had to leave the husky in the car, but he kept the window down. He specifically asked the server if Hannah Granger could serve him. The young lady obliged.

Hannah, an attractive middle-aged woman who had sun-kissed hair and was dressed in a yellow waitress uniform, stood by Clyde's table. She held a pen and notepad, ready to write. Clyde ordered breakfast for dinner. Running around so much, he had forgotten to eat. He waited until after he finished his meal before asking if Hannah had a moment to talk.

The woman lowered her eyebrows. Clyde used a napkin to wipe the corner of his lip and gestured for her to sit.

Hesitant, Hannah did so. Clyde realized that she didn't have a wedding ring. "You know Don Fegan?"

Hannah nodded slowly.

"I don't mean to alarm you, but," Clyde leaned in and spoke in a quiet tone. "New evidence has surfaced in the Hartwell Massacre. The police are going through old suspects. Don is on the list."

Worry reflected in Hannah's pretty eyes.

"I can help get him out of his mess, but I need to know where he was during the day of the killings."

Hannah stared at him, eyes watering.

"Please, Hannah," Clyde said. "If he wasn't on a business trip, I need to know."

Hannah lifted out of her seat. "I can't talk about this."

"I'm on his side, Hannah. Help me help him," Clyde replied.

Distraught, Hannah shook her head. She went into the kitchen. Clyde waited five minutes. She didn't come out. He left her a nice tip and his business card before exiting the diner.

Sarah called Clyde on his way to the car. "What's up?" he answered.

"I got off early. You want to hang?" Sarah replied.

"I haven't committed any crime."

"Funny," Sarah said. "Meet me at Cosmic Lanes. I have some information you might find interesting."

"On my way," Clyde dropped Pathfinder back at the house and changed into something casual.

Cosmic Lanes was a typical small-town bowling alley. It had tacky neon lights, dirty floors, and was completely flooded by locals on two-dollar lane night. Clyde collected his size fourteen bowling shoes from the long-necked man at the counter and spotted Sarah at Lane 9.

Clyde took a seat and tied on his shoes.

Sarah was wearing a short-sleeved shirt and dark jeans. "I have to warn you, I'm pretty sucky at this game."

"That makes two of us," Clyde said. "Use the guards if it makes it easier."

His remark offended Sarah. "I still have some dignity."

She grabbed an eight-pound ball.

Clyde went for the fifteen pounder. It was the only thing that fit his fingers. "What's this information you wanted to share?"

Sarah lined up her shot. "Shh. Let me concentrate."

Clyde watched her.

With perfect form, she cast the ball. It raced down the side of the lane before curving at the last three feet and striking all pins.

Clyde gawked.

Sarah shrugged. "Beginner's luck, I guess. Your turn." She winked.

Clyde kept his eye on the middle pin. He rolled the ball. It cut down the center and scattered all ten pins.

Sarah crossed her arms.

Clyde fought hard to hide his little smile. "Must be contagious."

"It's on now," Sarah replied.

Despite being such a hard-edged woman, Sarah bowled gracefully. Strikes and spares followed her every toss. Clyde's shots packed a heavy punch. In the middle of the first game, he was down by a handful of points. In the last two brackets, he scored two strikes and took home the victory.

Sarah glared at him. "You teased me."

"It wouldn't be as much fun if I didn't." Clyde grinned.

"I have the power to arrest you, you know?"

"And I have the power to BS my way out of it," Clyde answered.

"Next game," Sarah replied.

"You had information for me first," Clyde said.

"It's always business with you," Sarah said.

Clyde sipped his water cup.

Seeing that he wasn't relenting, Sarah said, "I talked to Curtis's sister."

"What did she have to say?" Clyde asked. He watched her bowl another strike.

Sarah returned, walking smugly. "Ever since Curtis got back from the war, he's been prone to blackouts."

Clyde thought back to Curtis's distant expression at the end of their conversation. He wondered if the man was having an episode. "Are the blackouts violent?"

Sarah nodded, "And they are usually triggered by stress. Sometimes, the blackouts last for seconds. Other times, Curtis could lose hours."

Clyde grabbed his bowling ball. He refocused on the game and scored a spare.

"Yes," Sarah cheered at his defeat.

They sat down across from one another.

"Tell me about Roland Alcott," Clyde said.

"He's a local A-hole. I swear that man has spent more time in the drunk tank than anyone else in Hartwell. He's violent too. He even tried to get handsy with me a few times," Sarah said. "Is he on your suspect list?"

"For now," Clyde replied. "I tried talking to him. He's not the most welcoming person in the world. Maybe you can warm up to him?"

"What type of woman do you take me for?" Sarah asked, gently spreading her legs.

Clyde didn't know if she was doing so intentionally. He quickly averted his eyes.

"Let's keep playing," Sarah said. "I want to kick your butt."

They played two more games. Sarah won one and Clyde won the other. He walked Sarah to her civilian car, where she gave him a hug. Her hands hung behind his neck. She looked into his eyes. "Thanks for tonight. I like seeing you have fun."

"Maybe when this case is solved, we can get back to fixing up the house," Clyde replied.

"Always business," Sarah remarked. She drew away from him. "Goodnight, Clyde."

"See ya," Clyde stayed put until she was out of the parking lot.

He got back home and waited for Elizabeth. He sat at the kitchen table. Hours ticked by. He paced and did intermediary push-ups and crunches. His biceps and abs ached.

At 12:37 am, the hairs on his arms stood up. Clyde lifted his head from the table and faced the four pale cadavers standing before him. Their ghastly visages and leaking wounds sickened Clyde. He could sense their impatience.

"I've been asking around town," Clyde said. "But it's not getting me anywhere. There are too many variables. Too many suspects."

They glared.

Clyde spelled it out for them. "If you know something, please tell me. Even if it's just a witness."

Clyde heard a scratching sound on the wall behind him. He glanced up at the exact spot where Andrew's blood spatter had been. The words "*Catherine Barnes*" were carved into the fresh layer of paint.

Clyde turned back to the ghosts. They were gone. He twisted back to the wall. The writing had vanished as well.

12

OLD FRIENDS

Clyde waited on the front porch, watching the sunrise. The hole near the front door nagged him. He grabbed a few 2x4s, the nail packet and claw hammer, then headed inside. The wood around the hole was heavily rotted. Clyde stepped into the hole. The rot spread through the entire porch. Much to his dismay, covering the hole would be of little use. He put back the supplies. When he exited, Sarah's squad car arrived in the driveway.

He locked the front door and sat shotgun in the cop car. Sarah wore her dark blue uniform. Her hair was pulled back into a tight ponytail. "You want to tell me how you got this woman's name?"

"It was in my uncle's stuff," Clyde lied. "I'm not sure how Catherine fits into all this yet."

Sarah eyed him. Clyde sensed her suspicion.

Sarah said, "I don't see why you couldn't find her yourself."

"I don't have access to her address and phone number like you do." Clyde gestured to the laptop mounted to the dashboard.

"So you're using me for my assets?" Sarah teased.

"You know your way around a gun, too. If this Catherine chick is crazy, I need you watching my back," Clyde replied, half-joking.

Sarah smirked. She took Clyde beyond the outskirts of Hartwell and into the backwoods of Georgia. Following the address listed, Sarah drove down a road lined by trees. Each tree was evenly placed and their thick canopy arched over the single-lane street. A plantation mansion stood at the end. Rectangular in design, the two-story mammoth had tall colonnades, an expensive second-story porch, and truncated roof. Trimmed rose bushes sprouted out the front of the house. The property was old but expertly maintained.

Sarah looked at the house in awe. "I lived in this town my whole life and I never knew this was here."

Clyde recognized the woman who answered the door. In her late thirties, the skinny woman had a round face and short brown hair. She wore a blouse over her flat torso and shorts over her toned legs. The woman worked out.

"Catherine Barnes?" Sarah asked.

"I'm her. Has something happened, Officer?" Catherine asked.

"We're just looking to chat," Sarah said. "You have a moment?"

"I suppose I do," Catherine said. She glanced at Clyde. "I never knew you worked for the police."

"I'm a tagalong," Clyde said. "This isn't actual police business."

"A social visit, then," Catherine said. "Please. Come in."

They stepped into the gorgeously furnished house. Expensive china filled a display cabinet. Piano music played softly through the house.

"Nice place, Ms. Barnes," Sarah remarked.

"Thank you, the house has belonged to the family since after the Civil War." She glanced back at them with a half-smile on her face. "The real owners were lynched. Bigots, you know? My family purchased it at a modest price and restored it back to its former glory."

"You have any family still around here?" Clyde asked.

"I'm afraid it's just me now."

She showed them through the house and into the kitchen. "Anything you would like to eat or drink? I can make tea."

"We're okay," Sarah replied. "We wanted to ask you a few questions."

"Would it be okay if we talked in the gardens? I wouldn't want to waste this lovely morning," said Catherine.

Sarah gestured for her to lead the way.

Catherine took them out the back door. They followed a stone path into a garden that was as impressive enough to be its conservatory. Plants grew tall and vibrant. Flowers of all types swayed in the wind. Catherine walked proudly through the snaking path. "I have all sorts of flora here, from the exotic to the medicinal. It's like my own little Eden." It was clear that she loved showing off her garden. "Anyway, ask away, Officer."

Sarah turned to Clyde.

"Thank you, Miss Barnes—"

"Call me Cathy," the woman replied. She smiled. It was naturally lopsided.

"Cathy, we wanted to talk to you about the Hartland Massacre," Clyde said.

Cathy froze for a moment. Clyde could see the horror in her eyes. "It was the worst time of my life."

"Tell us what happened the day of the attack."

"Glen and I spent the whole day out here."

"Glen who?"

"Iving. He moved away many years ago," Cathy said.

"Was there anyone else with you apart from Glen?" Clyde asked.

"No. Just the two of us. My father was having one of his drinking days," Cathy said. "Long story short, I knew those kids that were murdered, and when I heard the news about their deaths, I locked myself away for weeks, horrified that the killer might come after me next."

"Why you?" Sarah asked.

"The killer targeted them because those kids were one of a kind. It seemed logical he would come after me," Cathy replied. "No one trusted anyone back then."

Clyde asked, "What was your relationship with the deceased?"

Cathy brushed her hand through her hair. "I was a few years younger than them, and although I never talked to them myself, everyone in the school knew who they were. Even my father and his friends said that those four kids would change Hartwell forever. I envied those kids for their bold ambitions. I was the heiress of this *lovely* estate. Father forbade me to leave Hartwell." Talking about the inheritance made her bitter.

"Was Glen their classmate?" Clyde asked.

"He was already a graduate at the time. We were just friends. He was misunderstood. I felt the same way. It seemed like we were a good match," Cathy explained.

Sarah and Clyde traded looks.

"And what grade were you in?" Clyde asked.

"I was a sophomore at the time," Cathy said. "I turned sixteen a few months before."

Sarah remarked. "That's a little young to be hanging out with someone Glen's age."

Cathy glared at her.

"Do you have any guesses as to who might've killed those kids?" Clyde asked, quickly changing the subject.

"I'm still asking myself that," Cathy replied. "I will say this. Everyone loved them, and they knew it. In some twisted way, it's poetic that they were humbled."

Sarah asked. "Where is Glen now?"

"I haven't seen him for years," Cathy replied. "I believe he left Hartwell."

"Do you know why?"

Cathy shook her head. "He was a loner."

This had to have been the same Glen who was rumored to have stalked the girls prior to the murders. Clyde wasn't going to reveal that information yet. If Cathy was his friend, she might want to defend him or point Clyde in the wrong direction. He decided to ask her about the other suspects.

He opened his mouth to speak but stopped himself. He saw Elizabeth Mara and Gena Cobbs amidst the tall plants. They glared at him. *What do you want?* Clyde asked silently. He stood before Cathy but was still unsure how she fit into this whole ordeal.

"You look like you're about to say something," Cathy said, smiling.

"No, I'm…" Clyde thought for a second. "What are your thoughts on Don Fegan?"

"I don't know him," Cathy replied.

"What about Curtis Lowry?" Clyde asked.

"I feel bad for the guy. I think he gets a bad rep for no reason," Cathy replied.

"Roland Alcott?" Clyde asked.

Cathy nodded. "Roland? I've known him since I was a little girl. He is my landscaper."

That was the lead Clyde needed. "Is there any way you could help me talk to him?"

"Is he a suspect?" Cathy asked, hungry for gossip.

Clyde said, "No one is an official suspect."

Sarah added, "And we'd like to keep any rumors about such things quiet."

"It's Hartwell, sweetie. Dirty laundry is going to get out," Cathy replied.

Sarah said, "I'm asking politely."

Cathy turned to Clyde. "I can take you to Roland. He might be suspicious of Officer Sullivan, but I'll be able to ease his mind."

Clyde asked Sarah. "What do you think?"

Sarah checked her watch. "My shift starts in an hour. How soon can you contact Roland?"

"We can go there now," Cathy replied. "Roland knows me. He'll open up."

"There's no time like the present," Clyde said.

"Awesome. I'll get my truck," Cathy said, excitement in her voice.

Clyde and Sarah returned to the cop car. They trailed Sarah's large pick-up truck.

"I don't like her," Sarah said, both hands on the steering wheel.

"Tell me how you really feel," Clyde remarked.

"You see the way she looked at me? She was totally judging me," Sarah said. "She may have said that she never heard of me, but that was a lie. I'm kind of a hot topic around here. And no, that's not boasting."

"In what way?" Clyde asked.

Sarah tightened her hold on the steering wheel. "My lifestyle isn't agreeable to everyone. People talk."

"Since when does petty stuff like that affect you?" Clyde asked.

"Ugh. There's a reason why I don't hang out with other

women. It's always sidelong glances and lying," Sarah vented.

Clyde said, "She had good information."

"I saw you looking at her *information*," Sarah said.

Clyde chuckled.

Sarah's expression hardened.

Clyde's laughter died down. "You really think I was checking her out?"

"Please, Clyde. For every disgusting glance she sent my way, she sent a sultry gaze to you," Sarah said. "Besides, she's clearly your type."

"My type? What do you know about my type?" Clyde asked.

Sarah kept her eyes on the road and her mouth shut.

"Did I do something to offend you?" Clyde asked.

"Just drop it, okay," Sarah replied.

Clyde wanted to apologize but stopped himself. Maybe Sarah was mad because he turned down her advances. Sleeping with her the first day he arrived would've ended in an awkward disaster. Maybe not on her end, but definitely on Clyde's. *Simple. You have to keep things simple,* he told himself.

Sarah broke the silence. "You mentioned Don Fegan. Why?"

"He was on my uncle's list," Clyde admitted.

"Don's been known for some shady stuff in the past. He is always looking for a way to expand his monopoly. There's a little joke going around town that he'll own Hartwell one day."

"He seems like a relaxed guy most of the time," Clyde said.

"Around his friends, he's the humblest man you'll ever meet, but he's a shark in the business world," Sarah said.

"I sensed he's secretive," Clyde replied. "I'm not convinced he's a killer though."

"Neither am I, but if your uncle didn't trust him, he's worth watching at least," said Sarah.

"My thoughts exactly."

Clyde asked. "Were you on duty when they found my uncle?"

"I dodged that bullet, thank the Lord," Sarah said.

They arrived at Roland's doublewide trailer and joined Cathy at the front door. Roland answered Cathy's knock. He opened the door five inches, the length of the taut door chain. He lit up seeing Cathy, but quickly snarled when he saw Clyde. "What is he doing here?"

"Relax, Roland," Cathy said. "They're friends." Cathy gestured to Sarah. "This is Officer Sullivan."

"I know her! Why did you bring a cop here?" Roland asked, turning red with rage.

"They just want to talk. Will you do that for me? Please?"

The way she said it calmed Roland. He closed the door, unlocked the chain, and reopened it for his visitors. The trailer was dirty and horribly maintained. He stood in the living room and slipped his hand in his back pockets. He fidgeted.

"Nice place you got here, Roland," Sarah said, looking at the clutter.

Roland clenched his jaw.

Cathy said, "They want to know about the night of the killings."

"What killings?" Roland asked.

"The shooting twenty years ago," Clyde clarified.

Roland said, "Those kids... they were doomed from the start."

"You sound confident of that," Sarah said.

Roland replied. "Woman, I don't care if you're a cop or

not. There are things that happen in this town that you can't begin to understand."

"Try me," Sarah challenged him.

"Your boss---the *good* Chief Hawkins—likes to diddle little kids," Roland said.

The blatant accusation shocked them all.

"You got proof to back that up?" Sarah asked.

"None I'm showing you," Roland said. "You'll put me back in the tank."

"You don't want to get on the wrong side of the law," Sarah said.

"I've never been on the right side and don't plan to start now," Roland said, getting heated. "Your boss is a pedo. He knows I know and finds ways to keep me locked away every chance he gets."

Sarah said, "You get locked away because you're drunk and disorderly."

"It's a personal attack against me. It always is," Roland replied.

"So you're the victim?" Sarah asked sarcastically, not buying his reasoning.

Roland said, "No, them dead kids are the victims. Hawkins went creeping on them. They said no. He put a bullet in them to hide his tracks."

Clyde added to the conversation. "Wait a sec. The victims were all of legal age."

"You shut up," Roland barked.

"Roland, he's okay," Cathy said, rubbing Roland's arm.

Roland fumed. His nostrils flared like a bull about to charge Clyde.

"What's your problem, man?" Clyde asked.

"Your dog is my problem," Roland shouted. "The mutt

killed my chickens. I put him in a hole to give him the punishment he deserved, and you brought it back here."

"What?" Clyde was confused.

"You heard me. That dog is a hellhound. It killed my chickens. I'd kill it, but a quick death is too merciful."

"Focus, Roland," Sarah said.

"I hate dogs," he vented. "See these scars?" He pointed to little scarred holes on his neck. "One tried to bite my throat when I was nine. I got my vengeance, I tell you what, and boy, did it taste sweet. No mutt was safe around these parts."

Sarah asked, "Why do you think Hawkins killed those kids?"

"He'd been planning it for years," Roland said. "You can only keep people quiet for so long. Once they were out of their parents' care, they could tell the world."

"Their parents knew about it," Sarah said, hand on her hip.

"No, but it's easier to kill a young adult than a kid," Roland said.

"You learn that from experience?" Sarah asked.

"It's common sense, woman," Roland barked.

Cathy said, "We should get going."

"One last question," Clyde said. "Where were you the night of the shooting?"

"I tell you about the chief and now I'm a suspect? Nuh-uh. You want to hear more about my night, you talk to my lawyer," Roland replied.

"You don't have one," Sarah said.

"I ain't stupid, woman. There's a hell of a difference between a DUI and four homicides. Now I want all of you out, and don't you dare come back without a warrant," Roland threatened.

"Roland..." Cathy said softly, begging him to listen.

"Out! All of you!"

The three of them exited.

The door slammed behind them and locked.

Clyde saw the feathers, chicken poop, and dried blood in the coop. Pathfinder must've killed a dozen.

"Nice guy," Sarah said sarcastically. "That whole rumor about Hawkins was a lie."

"Keep an eye out for him," Clyde said. "We don't want anyone to slip through the cracks."

"Wait a minute," Cathy said. "You guys are already investigating Chief Hawkins? Is that why you want the investigation to stay under the radar?"

Sarah's face turned pale. "You best not tell anyone."

"I won't... I think it's rather exciting," Cathy said. "I'll make you a deal: I'll keep quiet, but I get to be a part of your investigation."

"Not happening," Sarah said.

"What? I'm trapped at home all day. Give me something fun to do," Cathy answered. "You need an ear to the ground. Someone who is part of the people."

"I have Clyde, so no thanks," Sarah said.

"The locals don't know Clyde. Why should they trust him? My family has been in Hartwell for over a century. The roots run deep," Cathy tried to convince them.

Sarah checked her watch. "I don't have time for this. Come on, Clyde."

"I'll take him," Cathy said. "You don't want to be late, after all."

Sarah turned to Clyde, waiting for his response.

Clyde said, "I'll go with Cathy. We can talk about the next steps."

Sarah said, "Don't escalate things."

"You don't have to worry about me," Clyde said.

"Fine. Whatever. Do what you want. But if this rumor gets back to me or anyone on the station, it won't be good for either of you." Sarah got in her car and drove away.

Cathy smirked. "She's hot-headed, isn't she?"

Clyde sat shotgun. Cathy reversed away from Roland's trailer.

"What makes you so interested in this case anyway?" Clyde asked.

"It's a part of this town," Cathy said. "Not a proud part, but an important one. I want to have a hand in fixing it. Like I said before, I knew the victims."

"Did you know my uncle? Andrew Barker."

"I know he killed himself," Cathy said. "I'm sorry for your loss by the way."

"I barely knew him," Clyde replied.

Cathy said, "So when I can start helping?"

"Cathy, I don't want to disappoint you, but Sarah is right. We can't escalate this. Not until we know what we're working with," Clyde said.

Cathy was offended. "If you really wanted to solve this case, you'd be getting all the help you could get."

"I'm sure you'll do wonderfully, but this is a sensitive matter," Clyde replied.

Cathy's eyes watered.

Clyde said, "I'm sorry. Thank you for getting us to Roland though. It wasn't what we needed, but it was still something."

Cathy said, "You know, I've lived alone a long time, and time after time, people come into my life, they use me, and they toss me out like trash."

Clyde pursed his lips. He didn't expect her to be set off so easily.

Cathy wiped a tear but held her angry expression.

Clyde kept quiet the rest of the ride. He had Cathy drop

him off at the woods where the murders happened. She was confused about why. He told her that he wanted to jog.

When her truck was out of sight, Clyde started his sprint. He pushed himself until he forgot about his troubles. His uncle's home welcomed him and was a fast reminder of all the little chores he needed to complete. He changed into his work clothes and entered the living room. Parts of the walls needed to be repainted, furniture needed repair, Pathfinder needed feeding, and large chunks of the moldy ceiling needed to be replaced. He took care of the dog first and let her run around outside.

Clyde's mind raced as he worked. What if Cathy was the killer? The ghosts pointed to her. She seemed to be jealous of the victims. Nevertheless, a sixteen-year-old girl killing a bunch of people seemed unlikely. What about her friend Glen? He was a mysterious figure that kept coming up in conversation. The young man vanished a few years after the killings. Was he running from something? If so, Clyde's attention was in the wrong place.

Roland was off his rocker and a drunk, but would he have killed the girls? What motive apart could he have? Despite him being one of Uncle Andrew's lead suspects, Roland didn't strike Clyde as the killer.

Curtis Lowry had the criminal history and expertise to enact the shooting, but no discernable motive. Maybe something triggered him. Did the murders occur during one of his blackouts?

Don Fegan had secrets and grand ambition, but what was his connection to the victims?

Last was Hawkins. Clyde knew so little about him that he couldn't make an assessment. Everything was conjecture and hearsay. He needed evidence.

Clyde fixed up the living room. He sawed out the

portions of the moldy ceiling and replaced it with white wood. Reaching a good stopping point on the inside repairs, he decided to gut the porch. He stood in the hole and sledgehammered the rest of it. It was cathartic to smash the wood. Feelings of power and control surged through him.

Pathfinder watched, her head tilted and her blue eyes full of wonder. Clyde carried the scrap wood to the backyard and tossed it into a pile. He added more junk to the mound, planning to burn it when it got big enough.

Sarah stopped by late in the evening. She brought a greasy bag of hamburgers and fries. She hiked up the cinderblock stairs to the front door.

"I can see you made… progress," Sarah remarked.

"It's going to get worse before it gets better." Clyde sat at the little kitchen table. The ceiling light above cast a nasty yellow hue over them.

Sarah took a big bite of the burger and talked as she chewed. "How was your ride with Cathy?"

"I believe we've come to a mutual understanding," Clyde replied. "She's not happy that she's not involved, but it's better this way."

"Did she tell you any more about Glen or Roland?"

"Nope," Clyde said, disappointment in his voice. "And asking around isn't going to get us what we need. I think we should adjust our methods."

Sarah eyed him. "You're talking about spying."

Clyde replied, "I hate the idea of it, but..."

"When did you become such a rebel?" Sarah asked.

Clyde shrugged. He suddenly remembered he was talking to a cop. "Just to clarify, I'm not saying I'm going to do anything illegal."

"Relax. In small towns like these, little laws get broken all the time and no one says anything," Sarah replied. "I guess its the idea that if we're all guilty we can't be tried."

"Speaking of which, how is Hawkins?"

"Word has gotten out about the newly-discovered remains. A few journalists are already taking an interest in the case," Sarah said. "Hawkins is flipping out. News like that can hurt Hartwell."

"Is it the town's interests he's trying to protect or his own?" Clyde asked.

"Beats me. The word is coming whether he likes it or not. It could go national. People love small-town true crime," Sarah said.

"I wonder how our suspects will react when their lives are back in the spotlight," Clyde replied.

"We'll have to watch and see."

They began planning ways to get hard evidence.

13

FRESH BLOOD

Clyde hiked through the woods. Andrew's binoculars knocked against his chest with every step. The morning sun cast its rays through the canopy of trees. He kept his compass open, remembering his hiking trips through the Appalachian. He stayed eastward for two miles and stopped. A mannequin's dirty arm rested on the floor of the calm woods. Five feet away, the mannequin stood. Tattered bungee cords secured her torso to a tree. Bullet holes peppered her chest. Buckshot caved in her featureless face.

Clyde was getting close.

Secured to high treetops and lingering behind bushes, a colony of decrepit mannequins lingered in the wild. Dozens of bullet holes testified to Curtis's frequency through usage of the homegrown shooting range. Beyond the tree line was a yard where his cabin stood.

Clyde lifted his binoculars to his face. Shirtless, Curtis stood beneath the shed's awning and splashed a bucket of water over the deer's bloodstains. He returned inside his house. Clyde sat on a felled tree and waited. Strange guilt pinged at his conscience. He had spent his career searching for ways to prove people's innocence. He now watched for faults.

The hair on his right arm stood.

He glanced over.

Elizabeth Mara sat beside him. Broken leaves clung to her blonde hair. Light dirt powdered the left upper portion of her forehead. She was silent.

"I've been waiting for you," Clyde admitted.

The dead girl turned to him. Her motion was jerky, mechanical even. Her lifeless pupils peered deep into Clyde. The rest of the world seemed to fade around her. Clyde's pulse quickened. Waves of chill bumps danced up and down his body. It was like she was an energy black hole. As toxic as it was, Clyde was drawn to her on a deep, existential level.

He lifted his hand and drew it near her face. *What are you doing?* Clyde freaked himself out. He hovered his fingers inches from her pale cheek. The strange, tingling feeling fueled his intrigue. He gently touched her skin. His fingers brushed through her as if she were air.

He withdrew his hand. He said, "Sometimes I wonder if you're just in my head."

Elizabeth grabbed his wrist. Her icy fingers dug into his skin. She forced his hand to her face. Clyde's breath quickened. Elizabeth brushed Clyde's knuckles against her cold cheek. He felt the soft texture of her flesh. He twitched, feeling how lifelike it was. She took his hand away from her face and held it tightly.

"Justice," she said, her endless gaze still unbroken.

"I'm trying," Clyde said. "Tell me who killed you."

Clyde heard something snap. He reared his head, watching one of the tree-bound mannequins turn her burlap sack-covered head to him. Its neck popped as it moved.

Clyde fought the fear welling inside him. He swallowed a large glob of spit. "I'm hoping you moved that."

The corner of Elizabeth's lip twisted into a partial grin.

Clyde studied the mannequin, trying to understand. It was the only mannequin shrouded by a bag. A thought came to mind. "The killer wore a mask."

Elizabeth let go of Clyde. Her handprint stayed on his skin.

Clyde rubbed his wrist. "Was he male or female?"

Elizabeth's face betrayed nothing.

Frustration strained Clyde's voice. "I'm grateful for your help, but I need more. What did you see that night?"

Elizabeth got on her hands and knees and used her fingertip to draw on the dirt. Clyde watched in awe and fascination. Her back was to Clyde. When she finished, Clyde saw a stick figure wearing a cloth mask. It held a rifle and two eye holes cut into the mask. Elizabeth slowly twisted her head back in a way that wasn't humanly possible. She tapped on the stick figure's chest.

"He is who you saw that night," Clyde thought outloud.

Elizabeth stood. Dirt stained her knees.

"What about Catherine?" Clyde asked.

Hundreds of yards away, the cabin door opened and stole Clyde's attention.

Elizabeth vanished. The drawing in the dirt was gone. The bagged-head mannequin faced forward again.

Clyde shuddered. He lifted the binoculars.

Wearing a fogged gas mask and army cargo pants rolled up at the ankle, topless and shoeless Curtis carried his automatic rifle through the backyard.

"What the..." Clyde mumbled.

Curtis stopped. He raised his weapon and aimed right at the woods.

"Oh f—"

Bam-bam-bam!

Birds scattered from the trees.

Bullets ripped into two mannequins forty feet away from Clyde. He dashed. A root snagged his ankle and he hit the forest floor.

Gunfire sounded.

He twisted back and raised the binoculars.

Curtis ran into the tree line, heading Clyde's way.

Clyde cursed and scrambled to his feet. He took a step and felt a pain shoot up his ankle. He grunted through his teeth. It was a minor sprain, but a sprain nonetheless.

Despite his age, Curtis Lowry moved quickly. He swiveled his waist back and forth and shot the mannequins with great precision.

Clyde ran, but the pain became unbearable. His run dissolved into a limping jog.

The gunfire grew louder.

Curtis was nearing him.

Clyde wouldn't be able to outrun him. A nearby tree beckoned Clyde. He jumped and grabbed on to the lowest branch. Using his upper body strength, he pulled himself onto the branch and straddled it. He needed to go higher. He grabbed the next branch and the next, scraping his torso against the bark as he climbed. He reached a thick branch. It bowed beneath his weight. He stopped his ascent and crouched. Keeping one hand on the tree trunk and the other on the branch, he waited.

Bam-bam-bam!

Curtis slowed his run one hundred and fifty feet away from Clyde. He kept the rifle stock snug against his inner shoulder. Scars marked his torso. The gas mask lens fogged over. There was a good chance he could only vaguely see his targets.

Clyde kept completely still, narrowly letting a breath escape his lips. He hugged the trunk. His height was a weakness.

Curtis stopped walking. He pulled up his mask, revealing his angry mug. He took a knee, seeing the disturbed dirt. The man scanned the area. "Hello?"

The sound of the wind replied.

"Come out!" Curtis shouted.

His voice echoed through the woods. Grumbling, he slid his mask back over his face. He continued to walk forward, passing under Clyde.

He fired a burst into a mannequin hoist in a tree opposite of Clyde's. The mannequin's head snapped off and plopped on the dirt.

Curtis vanished into the woods.

Clyde quickly climbed down. Upon reaching the last branch, his sprained ankle slipped and he toppled backward. He free fell for an instant. His spine hit the earth, kicking up a small cloud of powdery dirt. He inhaled. The sharp tree tops reached into the afternoon sun. The lack of gunfire alarmed him. He forced himself to rise. His back throbbed. Hobbling and slightly hunched, he hurried back to his car.

Twenty minutes later, he reached the edge of the road. His Cadillac was parked a little beyond the shoulder. Tall bushes concealed it. Clyde smiled in relief. Salvation was in sight.

He took two steps forward.

Curtis Lowry stepped out from behind a tree fifty feet to Clyde's left. Gas mask on, the black man's attention was locked on the car.

Clyde backed away and took cover behind a tree, unsure if the man saw him.

Curtis approached the car. He circled it, keeping his gun aimed. He took his hand off the rifle and tried the door handle. Locked.

Clyde wanted to step forward, but what would he tell the man? Did Curtis recognize his car? Possibly.

Curtis walked around to the back of the car and eyed the license plate.

Clyde cringed.

A twig snapped nearby.

Curtis turned that way. Clyde saw a squirrel scurrying up a tree. Curtis couldn't see it from his angle. He probably thought it was someone else. He followed after the noise.

Clyde slipped out from behind the tree. Hunched, he limped to the driver-side door, put the key in the lock, and got inside. Not seeing Curtis, Clyde started the car. Beads of sweat rolled down his cheek. He slowly backed out of the woods, trying to make as little noise as possible. He backed into the road, turned the car around, and gunned it.

Curtis stepped out of the woods behind him. He lowered his rifle, the fogged glass eyes of his mask looking Clyde's way.

Clyde cursed under his breath. He might've seen his face. Clyde would have to tread carefully.

Roland was an easier target to follow. The old hick watched Chief Hawkins on the morning news. He leaped from his seat and tossed his bowl of cereal at the screen. Milk and glass exploded on contact. The screen glitched, further infuriating the man. He grabbed whiskey from the cupboard before storming outside. Clyde stayed hidden behind the shed. Roland got in his truck. He took a swig from his whiskey and sped out of the driveway.

Clyde dashed for his own car parked off the side of the road. His sprain made the run a chore. The moment he was back in the Cadillac, he floored the accelerator. For five minutes, he sped and kept his eye out for Roland, eventually catching up with him down a two-lane road.

Trailing six car lengths behind him, Clyde drove the speed limit. He wished his car were less distinguished in design. He never thought he'd be doing private investigating. Roland turned his truck onto a dirt road. Clyde followed after his dust cloud. The road ended at a scrapyard. Rust rotted the chain-link fence surrounding the property. The afternoon sun beat down on the mountains of discarded metal. Parking his truck on the other side of the fence, Roland locked the gate and entered into the labyrinth of junk cars. He took a swig of his whiskey as he walked and let the bottle dangle at his side. The grip of the gun stuck out the back lip of his jeans. Sarah was right. Clyde should've brought his own gun.

He parked his Cadillac off-road and hiked to the fence. A chain and master lock prevented him from entering. Clyde put his hands on his hips and glanced at the twelve-foot fence. *Easy enough.* He grabbed hold of the rusty metal and ascended, then sat on the top and jumped down. He landed with a roll. Brushing off the dirt, he entered the maze. Twisted metal jutted out from the scraps. He crunched broken glass under his feet. The place was a death trap waiting to happen.

Gunshots sounded.

Clyde climbed a stack of old Fords. A headlight broke under his weight. He caught himself and stood still, hoping that the noise didn't alert anyone.

Bam!

The gunshot was far off.

Clyde reached the top of the cars. The roof dented beneath him. He crouched and moved from vehicle to vehicle. A car teetered on another. Clyde put his arms out to his side to keep his balance. The dangerous journey ended on top of a 1980s Oldsmobile. Its front end was crunch like a stomped soda can. Clyde lowered to his belly and army crawled to the edge. Eighty feet away, Roland sat on a lawn chair at the center of a clearing. A beach umbrella shaded him from the sun. Bottle in one hand and gun in the other, he took aim at a series of rusty cans and glass bottles standing on different cars.

Bam!

A bottle exploded into a hundred crystal shards.

Roland took another swig of whiskey.

He rested the loaded gun on his crotch and reached into the back pocket of his chair. He removed an old tin tobacco box, popped open the lid, and sifted through the contents.

Clyde watched from a side view. He lifted the binoculars around his neck and saw Roland sifting through Polaroid photographs. He stopped at one. Clyde couldn't get a good look at it.

Roland drank. He looked at the photos for a long time, lost in thought. After hours of intermediate napping, drinking, and thinking, Roland put the box back into his chair, closed it, and walked to a Volkswagen van. He opened the sliding door and put it inside. After sealing the van door, he slid a piece of rusty metal over the door and headed out of the maze of vehicles.

Clyde lifted himself up. The vehicle's sun-heated metal burned his forearms and torso. He climbed down carefully to avoid getting snagged on sharp metal. He went towards the Volkswagen van, removed the metal sheet, and opened the sliding door. The seat rotted away inside. The lawn chair rested propped against half a dozen lawn chairs. Clyde opened the back pocket and removed the tin box.

He leaned out of the van, making sure Roland had not returned. Seeing he was clear, he popped open the lid. He found a silver dollar, a bullet from the Civil War, a charm bracelet belonging to a female, a golden tooth, a few wedding rings, and a stack of photos. The first was of a dead dog. A sea of maggots packed the gaping wound in its stomach. The photo sickened Clyde. He flipped through half a dozen more, seeing more dead dogs.

Sick bastard, he thought bitterly. The last pictures were of Elizabeth, Tommy, Gena, and John – the victims. Their pictures were taken from a distance. Clyde studied their outfits. The photos were taken the day of the murder. Clyde felt chills. *Did Andrew know about this? Is that why he was following Roland?*

Clyde used his phone to snap pictures of the contents of the box. He put them back in the chair and exited the van. He shut the door and placed the sheet metal against the door. He took pictures of that too. Feeling a high from the investigation, he quickly escaped the scrapyard. Back at his Caddy, he called Sarah.

She answered, "What's up?"

"I have photographic evidence that Roland was stalking the kids the night of the murder," Clyde said swiftly.

"Slow down," Sarah said.

"It's at his scrapyard in a van. You need to get a warrant from the court and search it. I can point out where," Clyde said.

"I need something to bring to the court," Sarah said.

"I can send the photos anonymously," Clyde said.

Sarah said, "I'm on traffic today and can't do anything to help."

"What if I send them to the station directly?" Clyde asked.

"Don't do anything just yet," Sarah replied.

"Why? We got what we needed."

Sarah explained. "We bring Roland in, they'll convict him and Hawkins will shut the case for good. If he's not the guy, we'll never have another chance to catch the real one. Now, if you're certain it's Roland, you let me know and I'll see it to the end."

Clyde blew air out the side of his mouth. He had the connection to Catherine like the ghosts suggested, a violent reaction to news of the case, and proof of interest in the victims. He didn't have a motive, but proof outweighed that every time. If Clyde went against him in court, Clyde would probably win.

"Clyde?" Sarah asked. "Are you still there?"

"Yeah, I, uh, I think we should wait. It's a twenty-year-old case. What are a few more days? Do you still want the pictures?"

"Nah. If the courtroom checks my timestamps, it would confuse things. Print them out at your place to have a back-up, though," Sarah said.

"Good idea," Clyde replied. "I'll keep on his trail. Where does he usually buy drinks?"

"Alistair's Pub," Sarah replied.

"Cool. I'll stop by there when it opens."

"See you tonight, Clyde."

"You too."

Clyde ended the call. He drove home, walked the dog, took a shower, and changed. He examined the purple bruise on the side of his foot. It was a lot worse than he realized. He'd have to stay off it a few days. He hated not being able to run. It just felt wrong. He put his socks and dark jeans on before heading *Alistair's*.

The Irish pub had fine wood panels and sturdy stools. A few old farts chatted at the bar, but otherwise, the place was empty. The news played on the TV above the bar. It showed pictures of the victims' bones. The reporters would be talking about it all day. Everyone loved a good serial killer story. Clyde took a seat in the back corner that had a clear view of the front door. He nursed a pint and checked his voicemail.

New clients had called him and asked for his immediate help while old clients were angered by his negligent. Clyde made a few phone calls to sort out business. Tommy Demko and John Roth stood on the sidewalk, watching him through the window. Blood leaked from their wounds. They weren't pleased with his distraction.

"I'll call you back," Clyde hung up his phone. He gave his ID to the bartender as a promise of his swift return and headed out the door. He followed the dead boys into an alley. The nearer he got to them, the more chills he got.

Tommy and John turned a corner. Clyde followed and both were gone. Clyde paced around the back but failed to find anything of importance. He returned to the sidewalk just in time to see Roland park his truck. The front-wheel bounced up the curb. He rolled the car back, getting the wheel back on the road. He got out of the car and slammed the door. Cursing under his breath, he entered the bar.

Clyde peered around the corner. He watched through the window. Roland sat at the bar and shouted at the bartender. Clyde couldn't hear the conversation, but it was obvious that the bartender wasn't going to serve Roland in his drunken state. Roland hammered his fist on the table, demanding a drink. The bartender pointed him to the door. Roland drew back his fist to strike him.

One of the patrons grabbed his arm, trying to calm him.

Roland elbowed him in the face. The patron stumbled back into the stools and hit the floor. Blood gushed from his nose. Roland gave the middle finger to the bartender and stormed out. He got back into his truck and sped off. Clyde left his hiding place and returned to the bar.

A few of the patrons helped the injured one stand. He held napkins over his leaking nose.

"You okay?" Clyde asked.

The bartender got a pack of ice.

The man held it against his face. Tears welled in his eyes. "I just need another drink."

"I saw what happened," Clyde said. "You could sue him for assault and battery."

"Nah, Roland's just being Roland. The man has little enough as is."

"I'm a lawyer. I'll work for cheap," Clyde said.

The patron shook his head. "I told you. I'm not suing him."

Clyde gave him a business card. "If you change your mind, let me know."

He closed his tab, grabbed his ID, and left. He returned to Roland's house and spied on him. The mean drunk spent the rest of the day inside.

Clyde headed home after dark. All the scouting left him exhausted. He sat on the couch. The husky snuggled up next to him.

"I'll bring you along to the next one," Clyde promised.

He needed to talk to Don. The sooner Clyde could start crossing names off the list, the better. He shut his eyes to sleep.

Someone knocked on his door.

He got up and opened it. Sarah held up a six-pack of PBRs. "May I?"

Clyde stepped aside and allowed Sarah to enter. When she sat on the couch, Clyde brought over the printed pictures of Roland's tin box. Sarah looked through the printouts.

"Andrew didn't have any colored ink. Sorry."

"Is this a tooth?" Sarah asked, holding up one photo.

"A gold one, yeah," Clyde said.

"Creepy," Sarah replied.

"The news set him off today," Clyde said as Sarah examined the next photo.

"Oh, why the dogs?" There was dread in Sarah's voice.

"I don't know," Clyde replied. "Must be that vengeance he talked about for his childhood throat bite."

Sarah eyed the picture of the victims. "How do you know this was taken the day of the killings?"

"The clothes," Clyde replied as if it were the most obvious explanation.

Sarah stared at Clyde.

"What?" he asked.

"I was reviewing the case file today, and even I don't remember what clothes they were wearing," Sarah said.

"Good memory. It's a staple of every good lawyer," Clyde lied.

Sarah was suspicious. "Uh-huh."

An awkward silence filled their conversation.

She knows I'm lying. Clyde thought. *I can't tell her the truth. I can't tell anyone.*

"Can I see the evidence your uncle compiled?" Sarah asked.

"There is not a lot there." Clyde grabbed the folder off the lounge's desk and returned to the living room. He handed it to her and she flipped through the photos.

Sarah said, "He was following the suspects."

"Indeed," Clyde said. "It's hard to say what he found."

"There are no photos of the victims."

"No. The police must've kept that under wraps," Clyde said.

Sarah's eyebrows lowered in suspicion. "Then how do you know what their clothes look like? I sure never told you."

"The parents told me," Clyde lied.

"Each of them described the outfits?" Sarah asked, not believing a word Clyde said.

"Not all of the parents," Clyde replied. "But the ones that did have a pretty good recollection. It was the worst day of their life, after all."

"Why are you lying?" Sarah said.

Clyde's palms sweated but he stayed calm. "I'm not," he said, feigning absolute certainty.

Sarah didn't buy it. She said, "Whatever."

"I remember what my mom wore when she died," Clyde replied. "Take it from me, these things stick with you for a long time."

Clyde sat next to her and turned on the TV. Every local news network talked about the reopened investigation. It might go national. Sarah stayed for an hour more.

The next day, Clyde called Don, asking about his next fishing trip.

"Sorry, Clyde, I'm leaving town soon," Don said.

That was a red flag. "Oh, where are you going?"

"It's a business trip," Don said.

"New client?" Clyde asked.

"Potentially. The long and short of it is that I'm not sure when I'll be back," Don said. "Keep me in your prayers."

"Wow. What company?"

Don asked, "You're curious."

"It's part of my job," Clyde joked.

"Anyway, if you're still around when I get back, we'll grab a bite. Sound good?" Don deflected.

"Have you decided when you're leaving?"

"Early tomorrow morning."

"What if we got lunch today?"

"I don't know, Clyde. I'm really trying to get things in order."

"It'll only be an hour. I'll pay," Clyde suggested.

"Clyde, I—"

"You've helped me a lot in the short time we had. If I don't see you again, I want to make you know how much it meant to me," Clyde said.

Don sighed. "Fine. You'll have an hour."

"Thanks, Don. Where's a good place to eat around here?"

"Early-Birds. They're cheap," Don said, sounding peeved.

"Great," Clyde said. "I'll you at noon."

They said their goodbyes.

Early-Birds. Clyde checked the phone for his notes. It was the place where the waitress Hannah Granger worked—Don's suspected lady friend. *Interesting.*

Clyde spent the morning working on house repairs. His swollen ankle annoyed him to no end. The pain nagged at him as he put on his shoes. He thought about wearing his suit, but it was still dirty. He put on Andrew's light blue polo. It was a size smaller than what he usually wore, but it made him look strong. He kept on his tennis shoe.

He arrived at Early-Birds at 11:50 am. Don pulled up at the same time. He and his wife stepped out and greeted Clyde.

"This is my wife, Mary," Don said.

"We've met," Mary said.

"Oh," Don said, intrigued.

"I stopped by the other day," Clyde said.

Don remarked, "You got one taste of fly fishing and now you're hooked."

"Nice pun," Clyde replied.

Mary rubbed Don's arm. She smiled at Clyde. "Don't get him started. He once went on for hours."

Clyde grinned. He held the door open for the couple. Both of them were dressed in nice shirts and shorts, though nothing too fancy. They took a seat at a booth.

Hannah Granger waited on their table. She avoided looking at Clyde. Don avoided looking at her. They ordered their drinks.

"Well, that was something," Mary said.

"What's that, dear?" Don asked.

"Our waitress barely even looked Clyde's way," Mary said.

Don glanced up from his menu, eyeing Clyde. "Is that so?"

"I think you are looking too much into it," Clyde gaslighted.

The three of them engaged in small talk. Mary asked a lot about Clyde's job. He tried to keep his descriptions brief, hoping to get Don to open up about the murders, but Mary stole the conversation. All the while, the waitress barely waited at their table. Don seemed unfazed by her absence. He let his wife talk on and on, and Clyde was unable to get Don to discuss his business trip. By the end of the meal, Clyde learned nothing. He hated losing the time.

Don paid for the meal with his personal credit card despite Clyde's insistence. Before leaving, Clyde headed to the restroom. He held the sides of the sink and looked into the mirror. It was his last chance to get information out of Don. He needed to act fast. An idea came to mind. He exited the restroom. Walking by the table, he saw the receipt face down. Don and Mary were outside. Using a bit of sleight-of-hand, Clyde turned over the receipt. The meal cost around thirty bucks. The tip was two hundred.

Clyde joined Don and Mary by their car.

"It was a lot of fun talking to you," Mary said. "You'll have to come over sometime."

"Well, I know you're packing up for a big trip tomorrow. I could help," Clyde said.

"No need," Don said.

"Nonsense, Don," Mary said. She turned Clyde. "We'd be grateful for all your help."

"I don't pack all that much, Mary," Don said.

Mary didn't notice his hints and said, "You can follow us over, Clyde."

"Fantastic," Clyde shook Don's hand. "See you soon."

"Yeah," Don said, sounding annoyed. He got into his car.

Clyde waved them off and followed behind in his Cadillac. They arrived at Mary's nice home. She invited Clyde inside and pointed him to Don's room. Don organized his briefcase and left his open suitcase on the bed.

Clyde looked into his shirt closet. Nice shoes, tailored suits, and other accessories were neatly displayed. "You tell me what you want and I'll make sure it's neatly packed away."

"You don't have to," Don said, faking a smile. "I'll handle it."

"What would you like me to do?"

"Just..." Don stopped himself before raising his voice. "Here, why don't you, uh, fluff the pillows or something."

Clyde did as he asked.

Don focused on his briefcase, completely uninterested in a conversation with Clyde.

"Have you watched the news lately?" Clyde asked.

"What about it?"

"They found those kids' bones," Clyde said. "The police reopened the investigation."

"Good for them." Don sealed his briefcase and walked into his shirt closet.

"Twenty-year-old murders…" Clyde mused. "I wonder how the killer is coping with the news."

Don grabbed a few shirts and carried them to the suitcase. "Who is to say he isn't dead?"

"What makes you think that?" Clyde asked.

"There hasn't been any killing since," Don replied.

"Good point," Clyde replied. "Still… it's sick stuff."

"I'm sure you deal with plenty of vile people," Don said.

"Here and there," Clyde said. "Most just make a mistake. There was no mistake that night. Those kids were hunted."

Don opened his dresser drawer. His shoulders sank. "No socks. I'll be back."

He hurried out of the room.

Clyde silently walked to the door and watched Don go down the hallway. Clyde looked around the room. He wasn't sure what he was trying to find, but it could be the only time he got to see Don's stuff. He checked the drawer in the bedside table and the dresser. Nothing, of course. It was stupid to think he'd find something that would say *"Hey look, I'm a killer."* Clyde stepped into the closet. Old shoeboxes were stacked in the back. Clyde reached up and grabbed a few. Empty. He put them back. He checked behind the finely-pressed shirts. Nothing.

He returned to the bedroom.

Don returned, carrying a few pairs of freshly dyed socks.

"Where's your restroom?" Clyde asked.

"Down the hall. To the right."

Clyde exited. He traveled down the hall, passing by pictures of Don and Mary on the wall. On his way to the restroom, he opened various doors. He found a storage closet. He flipped the light switch, seeing stacks off old file boxes, family photo albums, toys, and other things from their childhood. Checking the hall a final time, Clyde slipped inside the closet and quietly shut the door behind him.

He took the top off a box, finding old books and accounting records. He put the top back on and noticed it was labeled by date. He glanced at the various boxes, going back decades. He removed two boxes before reaching a plastic tub. He moved it aside but spotted something inside that caught his eye. He opened the top and lifted out one of the headless GI Joes. There were dozens of headless action figures. He pulled a forty-four-year-old yearbook out of the bottom. Don would've been twelve at the time. Clyde flipped through the pages. "Xs" were drawn on different teachers' eyes. In the margins of certain pages, weapons and stick-figure battles were drawn. Clyde shut it. He slipped it halfway into the front of his pants and concealed the other half with his shirt. He shut the box top and put it and the others back in place.

He turned off the light and opened the door an inch. There was no one in the hallway from the angle the door opened. He waited a moment before exiting and shut the door behind him. He glanced down, seeing the outline of the book under his tight shirt. He used an arm to cover it the best he could as he leaned into Don's room.

The fifty-six-year-old fisherman hovered over his open suitcase.

"I'm going to head out," Clyde said. "Thank you for lunch."

"Drive safe," Don said, back still to Clyde.

Clyde hurried down the stairs.

Mary dusted the fireplace's mantel.

Clyde avoided her and made it to the front door.

"Oh, are you leaving?" Mary walked his way.

Clyde turned the doorknob. "Duty calls."

Mary smiled widely. She kept moving closer.

Clyde was out the door before she reached him. She stood in the threshold, confused and hurt.

Clyde got away as fast as he could. To avoid burning any bridges, Clyde sent Don a text, thanking him and asking him to say a proper goodbye to Mary.

He returned home and sat on the sofa. Pathfinder curled up at his feet. He opened the yearbook and went page by page. The violent drawings didn't phase him. Everyone was a kid once. It was the teachers' crossed-out eyes that set off alarms in his mind. He searched for them on the web. Only a few had Facebook. The rest were either retired, dead or didn't use the Internet. The lead was a bust. Clyde didn't have anything on Don other than his spontaneous business trip on the day after the murders and his strange connection with the waitress.

Curtis was also evidence-free. His firing range was creepy and the man suffered from blackouts, but there was nothing to say that he would kill four random people. Roland was still suspect number one.

Clyde leaned over and scratched the husky. "I don't know what to do, girl. Maybe I should just turn in Roland and be done with it."

He leaned back and shut his eyes. After clearing his mind, he continued repairing the living room. He went to bed early that night but didn't get much sleep. He sensed the dead watching him, though he couldn't see them. He asked them for their input, but they were silent.

The next morning, Curtis jogged. His ankle killed him, but he didn't back down. Morning fog lingered over the road. He turned back after a mile. Pathfinder trotted beside him. He did a hundred push-ups and sit-ups when he got home. His muscles burned, but he enjoyed the workout. Shirtless and wearing gym shorts, he took a seat on the couch and clicked on the TV. Pathfinder jumped on the cushion next to him and watched the screen intently.

The local news anchor spoke with a sobering tone. "…live at the scene. Jim, we're going to you."

The camera switched the woods. The reporter gestured to the police activity going on behind him. "Thanks, Karen. Behind me, Hartwell PD is cleaning up the body of a young woman. In fact, she was discovered at the same place in the woods where four locals were murdered two decades ago. Officials have not been forthcoming with the details but are certain it was a homicide. Chief of Police Robert Hawkins will be giving a formal address later this evening."

Clyde covered his mouth.

There had been another murder.

14

REAPER

News vans and police cars flooded the scene. Clyde slowed down the Cadillac, stuck behind a line of traffic. Volunteer police officers ushered cars away from the scene. No rubbernecking allowed. They placed long lines of police tape around the woods, connecting it from tree to tree like a thin spider web. Clyde set his jaw. If not for his sprain, he could've arrived at the scene an hour ago. He saw Sarah deep in the woods, putting down yellow markers. Clyde drove slowly. An officer shouted at him, forcing him to keep going. He made a U-turn.

He headed home and changed out of his exercise clothes, slipping on another polo and jeans. Being unable to access the crime scene, his new goal was to check on the suspects. Don was the closest. He sped to the house, knocked on his door, and saw Mary.

She wiped a tear from her eyes. It appears she'd been crying this morning.

"Is everything alright?" she asked.

"Sorry, I think I left my wallet upstairs yesterday," Clyde lied.

Mary allowed him inside.

"I'm sure you watched the news."

"It's horrible," Mary sniffled. "Hartwell is a nice town full of nice people. This type of thing shouldn't have happened."

"How has Don taken the news?" Clyde asked.

"He hasn't heard it." Mary wiped away a tear.

"Did he leave last night?" Clyde asked as he followed her up the steps.

"At 4 am," Mary said.

"You watched him go?" Clyde asked.

Mary eyed him suspiciously. Clyde needed to be careful how asked certain questions. Mary answered nonetheless, "He sleeps downstairs the nights before business trips. I never heard him leave."

It could've been at any time in the night. Clyde thought. "You must be exhausted. What time did you finally get to bed?"

"Eleven. Don went to bed earlier. He knew he'd be driving all day."

Clyde walked through the bedroom. He pretended to look around. When Mary had her gaze elsewhere, he drew out the pretend wallet from under the bed. "Found it."

He gave Mary a hug. "Thank you."

"You're welcome anytime," Mary answered.

Clyde rushed to Curtis' house next. Parking the car away from the cabin, he limped to the driveway. His tarp-covered motorcycle was still in the driveway. The lights in the house were out. He peered into the bedroom window. The blinds were closed. Clyde guessed he was asleep. He walked to the shed. He couldn't see inside. The door was locked. Clyde left and went to Roland's place next. The man's truck was gone.

Clyde headed back home. He drove by the woods on the way back. The press and fanfare were long gone. One cop remained. The police tape formed a shape connecting the trees. Clyde made it home. He got inside and paced for a moment, trying to think of his next step. He called Sarah. It went to voicemail. He sent a text, saying that they needed to talk. She didn't reply. He couldn't proceed until he knew the details of the murder.

The day inched by. He felt trapped in his home and waited for the victims to show themselves, but they were suspiciously silent. Clyde buried his face in his palms.

The sun fell away.

Clyde's phone dinged. He quickly grabbed it off the kitchen table and opened Sarah's text. "My place. 10 pm."

It was only 7 pm. Clyde drove to Main Street to grab dinner. Pathfinder rode shotgun. The town was suspiciously quiet. Few cars parked outside of restaurants. The traffic was nonexistent. The only place that had a lot of visitors was the pub. Nearly every parking spot was filled. The shockwave of the most recent murder had already reached the life of every local, and they didn't even know the victim's name.

Clyde purchased dinner and ate by the lake. The moon reflected on the calm waters. Clyde chewed, enjoying the fried chicken. He went home and waited. To keep his mind occupied, he worked on a few projects while the news anchors reported a feed of the same information. Hawkins was keeping the cards close to his chest.

Sarah texted him at 9:45 pm. "I'm home."

Clyde told her to brew coffee. He put on a jacket and raced over to her house. Sarah answered the door. She wore her police uniform, but her hair was down. Dark circles underlined her eyes and her jowls were tight.

The house was a mess. Books cluttered the shelf, unwashed plates sat on the coffee table, and discarded underwear littered the floor. Some articles belonged to

Sarah. Others belonged to a male companion. She hadn't cleaned up the place since the party.

"Your boyfriend lives here?" Clyde asked.

"I don't have one," Sarah headed to the kitchen. "Wine?"

"No," Clyde said.

She poured him a glass anyway and gave it to him while the coffee brewed.

Clyde sipped the wine as a polite gesture but wanted to stay sober. He had to keep his mind sharp. "How was it today?"

"Horrible," Sarah said plainly. "The victim was young like the rest, not a month over eighteen. Her parents showed up, and, uh… I talked to 'em."

"Wasn't easy," Clyde commented.

Sarah's tired face turned to the floor. "Never is."

"I'm sorry," Clyde said.

"It's the job." Sarah took a large gulp of her wine. "We spent the day working the case. Hawkins is on edge. One mistake, one leak, and we lose our jobs. He wants a conviction and quick."

"You think it's politically motivated or is he hiding something?" Clyde asked.

Sarah replied, "Political, most likely. His career could live or die based on this case."

"Can you tell me about what you found?"

"You still want to be involved in this?" Sarah asked.

"I was brought here for a reason," Clyde said.

Sarah took another swig. She grabbed a file off the kitchen table and returned to the living room. She sat on the floor, resting her back against the couch. Clyde sat next to her. The coffee maker rumbled in the other room.

Sarah opened the file and laid out the crime scene pictures one at a time. Clyde felt the presence of the dead behind him. He glanced back. John, Gena, Tommy, and Elizabeth stood behind him, staring at the photos of the latest woman to join their ranks. The newest addition wasn't among them yet. Clyde had to wonder when she would show. Feeling a chill, Clyde shuddered.

Sarah gave him a sidelong glance. "Yeah, it's screwed up."

The victim's black dress matched her jet-black hair. Half her face was in the dirt. Her left blue eye stared endlessly. Bloodied tufts of hair surrounded the gaping hole. It was of similar size to the holes in the last victims. *.223 rifle round. Same gun?* The victim's arms and legs were twisted in a strange way.

"The coroner said she was running when she got shot," Sarah said. "Died before she hit the ground."

"What's her name?"

"Alana Campbell. Eighteen. She was going to her fall semester in a month."

"Degree?" Clyde asked.

"Horticulture... why does it matter?"

"She's human," Clyde replied.

"Please don't remind me."

"I want to know her the same as the rest of my clients," Clyde said. "It's hard to fight a case if you don't care for the person you're representing."

Sarah lifted a picture of her wrists. "Check it out."

There were red circles on her skin. "She was bound?"

"Before she started running, yes," Sarah answered. "According to her parents, she vanished on her bike ride back from her friend's house last night."

"What time was that?"

"She left home at 7 pm and was going to get back before 1 am. Apparently, that is normal for her. The parents were asleep. They didn't even know she was missing until noon today."

"Dang."

"She's a night owl," Sarah said.

"Where does she work?"

"Part-time at Bean Barn, a local coffee house," Sarah said. "It's a hipster place."

"Did she work that day?"

"According to her parents, yes. The police plan to pay it a visit soon."

Clyde took a note on his phone.

"We need to map it out."

Sarah brought over her laptop. They pulled up a satellite image of the town, input Alana's address and the friend's house, and connected the two dots. The distance between the two houses was less than a mile. The place where she was kidnapped was twelve miles from the woods where she died. In the other direction, it was five miles from Bean Barn.

"The stalker could've followed her home from work on this path," Clyde moved the mouse cursor down a winding road, starting from a strip mall and ending in the neighborhood. "And stayed hidden while at the friend's house here. When she headed back home, he could've grabbed her at one of these four spots."

Clyde pulled up pictures of her fingernails. They were painted black and chipped. "She struggled against him."

Sarah finished her wine. "There's something you should know."

The screen reflected in Clyde's eyes. "I'm listening."

"The coroner discovered vaginal tearing…"

Clyde's stomach churned. "Did he leave any… evidence behind?"

"He was wearing protection," Sarah replied.

Clyde pinched the bridge of his nose. He rubbed his eyes with finger and thumb and shook his head. Bile climbed up the back of his throat. He pushed it down. The taste lingered. "The last victims were never…"

"The man is a monster," Sarah said.

They decided to take a break for a few minutes. The case wore on them like a rash. Sarah put a frozen pizza in the oven. Clyde poured his cup of coffee. The black and bitter taste bit his tongue. Anger brewed in him. He wanted to scream into a pillow. It doesn't matter who you were, no one deserved to die like that. Clyde promised himself to bring the killer down, no matter what it cost.

"I'm sorry," Clyde said.

"For what?" Sarah asked, leaning against the counter.

Guilt tightened Clyde's lungs. "I… I spent the whole day running around, but the one night that I should've been out…"

"You're not a cop," Sarah said. "I'm the one who failed. If we find out it was that bastard Roland all along, I'll shoot him myself."

"He wasn't home this morning," Clyde said.

"If he's skipping town, he won't get far," Sarah said.

They ate the cardboard-tasting pizza, but neither of them had an appetite. Getting numb to the gore and death, Clyde reviewed the crime scene photos. Alana's skin was pale like porcelain. She had a ring in her eyebrow and bangs cut straight across her forehead. Her lips were naked. Her eye shadow was smeared. Her sheer sleeves were intricately designed. She was barefoot. Thorns and twigs pierced her soles. Clyde couldn't imagine the grief her parents felt. He understood what it was like to watch his parents die, but to lose a child was a complete violation of the natural order. He imagined Alana as a child, long before the stain of this earth was put on her. He wasn't able to save her in this life, but he could help her through the next.

Clyde stood up.

"Where are you going?" Sarah asked.

"It's late. I should really be getting back," Clyde answered.

"Stay with me," Sarah begged. "Just for the night."

Clyde pursed his lips. He lowered back to the floor and put an arm around her shoulder. Sarah propped her head against the side of his torso.

Keeping the file open on the floor, Clyde stayed on the couch that night. Sarah kept her door cracked. A little night-light shined inside. Clyde kept his eyes open and his fingers locked behind his head. He didn't sleep that night. Before sunrise, he got up and exercised. Afterward, he cracked a few eggs and made breakfast for Sarah.

Wearing an oversized shirt and panties, Sarah joined him in the kitchen. Yawning, Clyde served a plate.

"That much sleep, huh?" Sarah asked. "Me too."

He poured her a glass of orange juice. Eating from his own plate, he sat across from her. "I want to get into the morgue."

Sarah stopped mid-chew. She finished her bite, giving him a strange look. "Why the hell would you want that?"

"I need to see her," Clyde replied.

Sarah lowered her fork. "I can't just let some random guy oversee the autopsy."

"Try to make it work," Clyde said.

Frustration built on Sarah's face. "*Try to*—Clyde. Come on. I already got you the case file."

"Do you trust me?" Clyde asked.

Sarah's lack of response alarmed him.

"Well?" he asked, trying not to sound offended.

Sarah put her hand on his. "I do, okay?"

"Get me into the morgue then," Clyde said. His lack of sleep made him curt.

"I-I can't see a reason why," Sarah said.

"You just have let me have this one," Clyde said.

"I could check the body for you," Sarah suggested.

"It has to be me," Clyde said. "How soon can you schedule an appointment?"

"I can try to get us in this morning. Any later than that and they'll start taking her apart," Sarah compromised.

"Thank you," Clyde said, looking into her beautiful face. "Truly."

She broke eye contact and drew away her hand. She crossed her arms. "Yeah, well, you own me. A lot."

"You do this, I'm yours. Whatever you need," Clyde replied.

"I'll take you up on that," Sarah said, promising. "You better be a man of your word."

"I do my best," Clyde replied. "I'm going to head home and get changed. We'll meet there."

"Whatever," Sarah said.

Clyde washed his plate before leaving. He waved her goodbye and slipped out the door, then drove home and changed into his suit. He brushed off the dirt and used body spray to hide the stench. After quickly shining his shoes, he took the dog out for a walk. After almost stepping in dog crap, he realized it would've been smarter to change the order of how he did things. His body cried out for sleep. His bruised ankle was dying to get out of his shoes. Leaving a large bowl of food for the dog, he drove off.

He arrived at the Hartwell PD Coroner's office. The single-story building was less than two thousand square feet and located next to *Kind Farewells,* a local funeral service. Clyde parked in the visitor's spot and waited a few minutes for Sarah to arrive. She parked next to him and flattened out her uniform. They walked side by side.

"You let me do the talking," Sarah said before opening the door.

Clyde gestured for her to enter.

An overweight, grey-haired man stepped out of his office. He wore doctor's scrubs. His skin was soft like a baby. A small smile grew up his plump lips. "Officer Sullivan. What a pleasure." His soft hand shook hers.

"You lost some weight, Mitchel," Sarah said, putting on a beaming smile.

"Glad you noticed. I've moved to the keto diet. It works miracles. Who is your friend?"

Keeping quiet, Clyde did a two-finger wave.

"He's not much of a talker," Mitchel remarked.

"He's actually a forensic analyst," Sarah lied. "I was hoping you could give the two of us a look at the body?"

"Is he from State?" Mitchel asked.

"Uh, yeah. He's our temporary analyst before our main one shows up," Sarah said.

"Do you know Doctor Peterson? Ed Peterson?" Mitchel asked as if talking to a deaf person.

"I'm still trying to learn everyone's name," Clyde said.

"He's a good friend of mine from State," Mitchel said. "We have an online chess game we've played for weeks. You wouldn't believe it by looking at him, but Peterson is a genius. You should get to know him. He'll help you."

"I will," Clyde said politely.

"Mitchel." Sarah focused on the man. "Can we?"

"Of course," Mitchel said.

Clyde felt a weight lift off his shoulders.

Mitchel walked to the desk. "Let me just see check your IDs, badges, and medical license."

Sarah turned to Clyde. "You brought it, right?"

Clyde smiled nervously.

Sarah frowned. "You left it."

"I thought I brought it," Clyde said.

"Unbelievable," Sarah said.

"No license, no entry," Mitchel said.

She rested her forearms on the desk and spoke quietly. "Mitch, the guy is green. Can you cut us some slack?"

"The rules are rules," Mitchel said.

"I know, but—"

"My hands are tied," Mitchel said.

Sarah hiked her thumb back. "I've been with this idiot for less than twenty-four hours. He's been complaining nonstop the whole time about needing to see the body. It's driving me nuts."

"Why is State so concerned? I turned in a thorough report yesterday. The only thing we're waiting on is the toxicology," Mitchel whispered.

"It's a high-profile case," Sarah explained.

"And they send that buffoon?"

Hands in his pockets, Clyde walked around, reading the different plaques on the board.

Sarah leaned close to Mitchel. "Throw me a bone here."

"You know how much I hate breaking the rules."

"Mitchel, I'd never want to put you in that position, but I need help. Please. For me,"

Mitchel sighed deeply. "If he breaks anything, it's on your head."

"We'll be in and out in before you know it," Sarah promised.

Mitchel unlocked the door to the examination room and shut it behind Sarah and Clyde. The room was cold and had a sterile smell. They each grabbed rubber gloves from the wall-mounted dispenser.

Mitchel walked over to the aluminum table. The shape of Alana's body was visible beneath the sheet. Clyde neared, the hair on his arms standing. Mitchel pulled back the sheet, revealing her pale face. There was a small scab on her purple lips. Her skin was the color of curdled milk.

Where are you? Clyde silently asked. He saw a naked old man in the back of the room. He was curled up in a fetal position. Blood pooled around his feet. There was a seven-year-old girl facing the corner. She was soaking wet. Water dripped from her mouth.

"How much do you want to see?" Mitchel asked.

"All of it," Sarah said.

Mitchel completely removed the cover.

Clyde stood by the dead girl. Her ghost didn't show up. Sarah watched Clyde, waiting for him to do something. Even Mitchel was confused. Clyde circled the body. *Come on. Do something already*.

He completely circled her and looked into the woman's face, remembering how staring into the victim's eyes affected him. He moved his hand near the woman's face.

"May I?" He asked.

"Uh, sure," Mitchel replied.

Clyde pried open Alana's eyelids, trying not to flinch. He stared into her dry, soulless blue eyes. Nothing.

"Show yourself," Clyde said under his breath.

He touched her forearm and shut his eyes. "Alana. I'm here to help you," he mumbled.

Mitchel and Sarah traded looks.

Clyde focused completely, hoping somehow that would summon the spirit. He realized how little he knew about his power. He felt dreadful hopelessness. Sarah had risked her job, only to have Clyde hang his head in shame. He sensed body's presence strongly. That had to mean something. Sweat dotted his forehead. He gave up. Opening his eyes, he started to draw his hand away. *What will be, will be,* he thought. Just as his last finger was about to lift away from the body, he blacked out.

Clyde opened his eyes. Flashes of a mysterious man flickered in his mind. He aimed a pistol at her from his car.

"Get in," the man threatened.

Clyde was suddenly in the passenger seat. The man aimed a pistol at him and drove with the other hand. He told her to open the glove box.

Clyde blinked and the memory changed. Clyde was in the man's bedroom. The lights were off. The man was silhouetted in the doorway.

The incoherent flashback ended. He was back in the backseat. He was lying down in the backseat of a car. His body ached. He felt pain in his wrists. He blinked. He fought his binds but realized that his hands weren't his own. They belonged to Alana. Her fingernails were chipped and broken. He looked down at himself. He wore Alana's body like a suit. He felt what she felt. The car drove down a dirt path. Clyde kept still. He couldn't move if he wanted to. He was just a spectator. Alana was fully in control.

The car stopped. The front door opened. Alana's heart raced. Her breathing quickened. The back door opened at Alana's feet. A little key was tossed at her. It landed on the floor beside the seat. Trembling, Alana grabbed it and unlocked the handcuffs.

"Are you… are you letting me go?" Alana asked. Clyde wanted to yell, but he could only observe.

Fear fought to paralyzed Alana. The cuffs fell.

She slowly sat up. The door was still open, but no one

stood there. Trees stood in the dark. She was in the middle of the forest. The trunk was open, and the man rummaged around inside.

It's a trap, she thought. Nevertheless, it was her only chance at freedom. She scooted across the backseat and quietly stood up. Her knees quaked.

Her captor lifted a rifle out of the truck. It was a hunting rifle with a scope and laser sight.

Alana saw his face. They locked eyes. The killer shut the trunk.

Alana screamed and ran for the woods.

Harsh earth stabbed into the bottom of her feet. She zigzagged, racing through the trees. A thin branch slapped her in the cheek. Her heart was about to explode. She wasn't ready to die. All of this had to be a bad dream. She screamed for help. A few bats took off into the sky.

The red dot followed her. She kept running, weaving her way through the trees. She stepped on a thorn bush and hopped on one foot. In the corner of her eye, she saw the red dot move from the bark of a nearby tree to out of sight. *It's on my back.* She dropped to her belly and crawled.

Footsteps crunched behind her.

"Somebody help!" she cried.

She dragged herself. Tears poured down her face. She just wanted to go home. She'd forgive what he did to her if it meant staying alive. All she wanted was to cry in her mother's arms. For her father to comfort her. She wasn't the brave, no-nonsense woman she claimed to be. She was just a little girl. Scared, alone, and wanting comfort.

The footsteps stopped.

He was behind her.

Alana's breath got caught in her throat.

He was going to hurt her again.

She'd let him if it meant getting out alive.

She looked back through her life. She remembered running outside in the rain with her brother, she remembered lying in bed while her mother read to her, and also the puppy her father bought her. All of that childish joy died during puberty. Her parents' acts of kindness felt like a means for control. Their restriction on her boyfriends was unjust punishment. She'd seen so much injustice on the news and in school, yet her parents smiled like nothing was wrong. She thirsted for independence even if it meant diving headlong into the darkness. She put on dark clothes, went after boy after boy, hoping she'd find her own Prince Charming. She flunked out of her classes. She didn't want to be part of the system. Faced with death, all of that was petty. It didn't matter what she ate or wore, or all the grandstanding from her parents and other authority figures. She wanted love. She wanted to be back to a time in her life where there was peace and joy. She wanted to rebuild connections she so fervently opposed.

The rifle clicked.

Alana quickly turned her head.

Bam!

15

FERRYMAN

Clyde gasped and jolted upward. Drenched in sweat, he sat on the morgue's cold floor. Sarah was kneeling next to him. Mitchel stood over him, looking terrified.

"Clyde?" Sarah asked. She shook him. "Are you okay?"

He got to his feet. His legs felt like jelly. Waves of heat and cold washed over him. He took a step and the world spun. Sarah wrapped her arm around his back and supported him. "Easy, big fella."

"I'm fine," Clyde said before doubling over and vomiting.

Mitchel headed for the door "I'll get an ambulance."

"No!" Clyde shouted.

"I'm going home… just… dizzy." Clyde pulled himself away from Sarah. He blinked and was back in the woods. He could feel the dirt under his fingernails and thorns in his feet. He closed his eyes. His migraine pounded his forehead. He touched the back of his head. No bullet wound. He glanced down at his fingers. He saw blood. He gasped, and the blood vanished.

"I got to go," he said hastily and ran for the door. His

swollen ankle slowed him down. He burst through the door, even forgetting to take off his gloves.

Mitchel said to Sarah, "You said he was green, but has he ever seen a dead body before?"

"Excuse me." Sarah shouldered past him.

"Hey, aren't you going to clean my floor?" Mitchel shouted.

Clyde raced outside and caught his breath. He thought about punk rock, and kittens. He rested his hands on his knees and steadied his breathing. He smelled Alana's perfume and tasted her vegan dinner. How did he know she was vegan? How did he know that Josh Carmichael was Alana's first crush in the sixth grade? It was like his mind and Alana's were overlapping. He listened to the birds and watched the trees sway in the wind. Nature was so beautiful. He was seeing it with a fresh pair of eyes.

"Hey."

Clyde jumped and swiftly twisted back to Sarah. "Holy crap. Don't sneak up on me like that."

"Are you okay?" Sarah asked.

"I was her, Sarah. I saw everything," Clyde said.

"You what?"

"Alana and I—" Clyde shut up. *You've said too much. She thinks you're crazy.* "Sorry, I'm a little discombobulated."

"Clearly," Sarah said, concerned. "You want to go to the hospital?"

"Anything but that," Clyde said, suddenly hating hospitals and needles. Especially needles.

"I'll drive you home then," Sarah said.

"That'll probably be best," Clyde replied.

He sat shotgun, leaving his car at the morgue.

Sarah glanced over at him a few times as she drove.

Clyde asked, "What happened in there?"

"You fell over and started shaking and then you just went still. I think you stopped breathing for thirty seconds," Sarah said.

"I was only down there for that long?" *It felt like much longer.*

"Has anything like that ever happened to you before?" Sarah asked.

"No," Clyde replied, too jarred to think of a lie.

"Was it the body that did it?"

"I don't know!" Clyde barked.

"Chill out."

"Sorry. I just really want to rest," Clyde said.

Sarah dropped him off at his home. She reversed and headed to work. The moment Clyde got inside, he grabbed a pen and searched for the nearest piece of paper. He grabbed a blank sheet out of the printer, rested the page on the table, and started drawing the killer's face.

He was slightly overweight. His skin tone was on the lighter side, but in the dark, Clyde couldn't tell. He was balding and had a round face. No mask. Dressed in black. Clyde didn't remember the eyes or mouth shape. Clyde lifted his pencil and studied his drawing. It looked like a fourth-grader drew it. Art was not a talent of his, but at least he had a starting point. Unless Curtis was wearing serious make-up, he was no longer a suspect. Roland was too skinny and had a ponytail. It wasn't him either. The man had a similar body shape to Don and the police chief. Clyde tried to remember more, but all he had was the quick glimpse he had of the man before Alana had screamed and ran away. He grabbed Andrew's photograph of the police chief. They were both middle-aged and balding. The chief had a squarer face and less weight, but the dark made it difficult to tell the difference. The killer could've been someone Clyde never expected.

He needed to see where Alana would lead him. He was still shocked by the magnitude of his powers. He could sense the dead, see them, and live out their deaths through their eyes. How and what triggered these were unknown. He lay down on the couch but was still too anxious to nap. He needed to follow Alana's trail and see if he could find her. Going to her parents' house was too controversial. He checked his notes. The coffee shop where she worked would still be open. Taking the drawing and shoving it in his back pocket, Clyde washed his face and stepped outside.

He searched for a local cab service, but Hartwell didn't have one, so he downloaded the Uber app and waited for forty minutes before someone got him. The driver talked the whole way. Clyde ignored what he said.

"Do you believe in ghosts?" Clyde interrupted him.

"Heaven, you mean?" the driver asked.

"No, like actual ghosts."

"I believe in heaven and hell. Maybe there is something in between," the driver said.

"How do you know it's real?" Clyde asked.

"By faith. There has to be more to life than just what we see. Look at how complex everything is. From a flower to a skin cell, something must've done that," the driver said.

"Hmm," Clyde said, looking out the window.

"Do you believe in the afterlife?" the driver asked.

"I was on the fence for a long time, but recently I've come to understand that there's a lot I don't know," Clyde said.

"Seek the Lord, my brother. He'll sort things out," the driver said, grinning.

"I hope so," Clyde said. He didn't just need an answer to the murder. He needed answers to everything.

"You know Jesus?" the driver asked. In America's Bible Belt, that wasn't a surprising question.

"Am I a Christian? No," Clyde replied. "I'd say I lean more towards agnostic if I had to put a label on it."

"Well, you know what I believe? I believe God has a plan for us all," the driver said.

"Fate," Clyde replied.

"Yeah, but we still have to make a choice. Do we follow our own way or His?"

They arrived at the coroner's office.

Clyde thanked him and left a few dollars as a tip. *What is His way? What is mine?* The powers kept growing. It couldn't be by chance. Was it only for this case? Would they vanish after the dead found rest? Part of him hoped it did. Life was simple before the revelation, but he knew mediocre was ruined for him. Once he tasted something real, he was addicted.

Clyde arrived at the coffee shop. Bean Barn had a washed-out wooden look to it by design. Edison-style light bulbs dangled from its ceiling. Soft acoustic music played over the speakers. College and high school students hung out inside. It was mostly females and a few of their beta male friends. They were the artistic kids on the liberal end of the political spectrum. Inside of the rural Georgia town, this café was the closest thing to modern city culture.

Dark circles under his eyes, light stubble on his cheeks and dressed in a suit that smelled of sanitation chemicals and bile, Clyde stood out from the artistic crowd. He spoke to the barista.

"I need to talk to your manager. It's a legal matter," Clyde said.

Horrified, she went outside. She returned with a woman moments later. The woman was in her forties. Her short hair was dyed hot pink. She wore a size eleven and had a bull ring in her nose. Her lips were purple. She smelled of cigarettes and had a rugged complexion of common among lifelong smokers.

"What do you need, huh?" she asked in her raspy voice.

"I'm a lawyer. I need to know everything about Alana."

"And why should I tell you that?"

"The police are building a case. You help me out, and I'll make sure they don't implicate you," Clyde said.

The manager, her name tag reading Stella, invited Clyde to sit in a booth at the back. She sat opposite of him.

"You look tired as hell," Stella said.

"Alana worked here the night of her death, right?" Clyde asked, wasting no time.

"Eight to five. Three days a week," Stella said. "She was a good worker. I'm sorry to hear what happened. Probably a crazy hick that killed her."

"Did she act strange that day?"

"Not particularly," Stella said, "I already told the police this stuff yesterday. I was careful with my words."

"Doesn't matter," Clyde said. "I need to hear everything."

Clyde pulled out his sketch. He unfolded it and showed it to her.

"Your kids draw that?" Stella asked. "No offense, hun, but art ain't his talent."

"Have you ever seen this man before?" Clyde asked.

"He looks familiar," Stella said, "But a lot of people come through here."

"Was there anyone looking like him the day Alana was attacked?" Clyde asked.

"Two or three," Stella replied.

"He could've been following her the whole day," Clyde mumbled to himself.

"You need some sleep, man," Stella said.

"How long have you lived around here?" Clyde asked.

"Fifteen years."

Clyde was disappointed. The woman was not helpful.

"You want to find some creepy, middle-aged white guys, go to the skate-in at night," Stella said. "All the creeps come out then."

"When is the best day for that?"

"Fridays and Saturdays. That's when a lot of the younger girls are out," Stella said. "Alana was a regular over there."

Clyde asked her a few more questions about Alana and her relationships. Stella pointed out a few of the patrons but asked that he didn't bombard them with too many questions. Alana's death was an open wound in all their hearts. Clyde talked to Alana's friends. As he looked them in the eyes, he felt strong emotions toward them that made him teary eyed. One young lady cried and he gave her a comforting hug, holding back the tears. The logical part of his mind told him to back away, but his feelings were strong. He didn't know much about these people, but Alana had a strong liking to all of them. One of her friends was terrified that a serial killer was going to target him next. He didn't have a good reason for his theory.

All in all, Clyde learned a lot about Alana's interests and had multiple strong emotional experiences he hadn't felt since his parents died. That said, the patrons had no new information, nothing that would help him find the killer. The skate-in was something to look into, though.

He spent the daytime hours riding around town, hoping to spot Alana's ghost. Police tape formed a web around the woods. The cop that had been watching was gone, along with any other evidence. Clyde crossed under the tape and limped across the dirty ground. It was like Alana was hiding from him, playing an elaborate game of *catch me if you can.*

Darkness rolled over the sky like a blanket. Fog fell over the trees, surrounding their towering trunks in mystery. Clyde stopped a foot away from the bloody stain. Dark blood painted the dirt. Fingernail-sized skull fragments dotted the surroundings. Little ants climbed over particles of brain matter.

Clyde felt the presence of the dead. He drew in a deep breath of cool country air. The rich oxygen was coolant to his lungs. Something moved behind a distant tree. A shadow? A person? Clyde investigated. His ankle throbbed. The shadow, now a hundred feet farther away, slipped behind another tree and vanished.

"Hel-Hello?" Clyde's voice carried through the eerie woods.

An owl hooted.

Clyde followed the shadow. It stayed a hundred feet ahead every time he saw it.

He jogged, gnashing his teeth as a reaction to his pain. He traveled down a small hill. A stream appeared in the distance. Staying parallel to the stream, the water took him to a narrow gorge. Two eroded rock-faced cliffs stood at forty-ish feet over Clyde's head. The water spilled through the three-foot gap between them. Stepping on mossy rocks, Clyde slipped through the small gap and followed it.

His phone light guided him, casting strange shadows across the rocky walls. A strip of the night sky appeared through the gap above Clyde's head. He traveled through the enclosed area for fifty feet. His back rubbed against the cold cliff face. The pointy rock scraped his clothes and skin. Water sloshed on his shoes, wetting his toes. The cliffs widened like a funnel and formed a circle around a forty-foot diameter spring. The dark blue waters betrayed the underground cavern below. Mossy grass dressed the outer ring of earth surrounding the water. Patches of grass interrupted slabs of mostly-buried wet rock. Shafts of moonlight spilled over the water. Stringy dirt dangled from the thick roots bursting from just below the cliff tops. A dense ring of trees bordered the upper edge so closely packed together that only a child could squeeze between their trunks.

Clyde circled the water, peering into the deep blue underground cavern. Its colors transformed from a crystal surface to dark indigo to pitch black. Clyde had never seen anything like this place. It was like his own hidden paradise found in the middle of the most unlikely place. A highway of caves and caverns must run for miles underneath these woods. The trees' roots were deep, but the labyrinth of caves was deeper.

Clyde stopped at the edge of the water. His light pierced through the surface, barely revealing the shadowy figure far below.

Clyde lowered to a knee. The wet grass soaked through his pant leg.

The figure shot up faster than Clyde could process. He pulled his head back just as the hand burst from the water and grabbed his throat. He dropped his cellphone on the grass a second before getting pulled under.

The cold water enveloped him as the figure pulled him down. He fought against her, hitting her pale skin. Her black hair extended above her head as they sank. Her bangs swished to the side. Tears of blood left her eyes like rising crimson ribbons.

Bubbles flowed from Clyde's mouth. One of his large palms pushed against the woman's face. She was immovable and undeterred.

"Alana!" Clyde shouted, but the noise was muffled by the water.

He repeated her name.

Alana locked eyes with him. Clyde felt her looking into his soul. She Marked him. She raised Clyde up and burst to the surface. He breached the water. His back slammed on the rocky ground. Alana lay on top of him. Her cold body felt like a slab of rotting meat. Clyde turned his head to the side and coughed out a lungful of water. Pain flashed in his throat as he gagged. Alana grabbed his mouth, squeezing it hard and forcing Clyde to look at her. Somehow, her hair was dry now. Scarlet tears trickled down her cheek and out of the right corner of her mouth. More blood leaked from the bullet hole at the back of her head.

Shaky breath escaped Clyde's lips.

Alana studied his eyes keenly.

Clyde kept perfectly still.

The moonlight against her skin made her glow. She released his mouth.

"Alana," Clyde said hesitantly. "I know… I saw what happened to you. I saw his face."

Clyde's teeth chattered. Water puddled around him. The icy body chilled him.

Clyde said, "I know it's not fair, but I can help you."

Alana lifted herself off of him. She crawled a few feet away and pulled her knees up to her chest. Hugging her shins, she gazed into the spring.

Clyde sat up. A cocktail of fear and adrenaline pumped through his veins. Trembling from the cold, he scooted next to the girl. His senses were going crazy, from chills to raised hair to the intense pull drawing him to her.

Alana spoke softly. "I saw him." Her voice was chilling. "Here. In this place?"

"He took you here?" Clyde asked.

"He followed me," Alana replied. "Long ago, he watched me play in these waters." She slowly raised a finger to the line of trees on top of the cliff. "That's where he stood."

She lowered her gaze back to the water.

It felt strange talking to the dead. Clyde was fascinated and terrified. Despite this being his Gifting, he couldn't escape the strangeness of the situation. Him and a dead woman alone in the woods. It was unreal, except that it wasn't. "Did he ever approach you?"

"He watched. Nothing else," replied Alana.

Clyde noticed the gaping hole on the back of her head. "Does it hurt?"

Alana shook her head.

"I talked to your friends. Carmon, Denise, your boss Stella. They all miss you," Clyde said.

Alana gave no response.

"I'm still learning how to do this," Clyde admitted. He rubbed his upper arms to stay warm.

Alana turned to him. "You must not stop. There are more like me. Thousands. We sense the end pulling us, but we're chained to this place."

"How can you break free?" Clyde asked.

"Only you can do that," Alana said. "You must work quickly or there will be more."

Clyde lowered his head. He felt the burden of responsibility on his shoulders. No one would thank him for this work. No one would even know what he was doing. It was a life condemned to secrecy and completely unrewardable. Spiritually, the call was all-encompassing.

"What do you think comes after?" Clyde asked, eyes on the dark water.

"Heaven. Hell," Alana replied plainly. "I don't know, but it feels like the right answer. This life has to be building to something, right?"

"Do you know where you're going?" Clyde asked.

No reply.

Clyde lifted his head.

He was alone.

"Alana?" He called out her name. The answer to his question was not for him to know. He was just a ferryman between this life and the next.

Clyde grabbed his phone. The water weighed his clothes down and sloshed in his shoes. Drenched and freezing, he limped his way out and returned to his car. He drove home and switched his clothes. Dressing casually, he took Pathfinder out for a quick walk, fed her, and drove to town.

He couldn't escape the call in his heart. *Justice,* Elizabeth whispered. He glanced in the back seat. Empty. Keeping both hands on the steering wheel, he drove just under the speed limit and then eyed the town. Flashing tube lights marked the skate-in. Its design was as tacky as the bowling alley. After parking, he entered. The man at the counter pointed him to a shoe dressing room where he could change into his roller skates. Clyde refused and told him that he was just waiting for a friend.

To keep from looking too suspicious, he ordered nachos at the snack bar and followed the carpeted path around the large skate floor. Men and women, young and a few old, raced in a circle. A DJ played the latest hip songs and directed which direction traffic flowed. Clyde found a small table in the back corner. A burnt-out light hung above the table. *Perfect.* He sat down, embracing the shadow. He ate slowly, enjoying his vantage point of the entire room. He ate slowly and kept his eyes open for any creepy, middle-aged men.

A few were skating, but none matched the killer's description. It was a slow night but still packed. In a town the size of Hartwell, the skate-in was a major attraction. Clyde stayed until closing. He did the same for the next two nights. Exhausted from lack of sleep, he drank a cup full of burnt-tasting coffee. He pinched the bridge of his nose and yawned. A few people had already started to give him strange looks. They'd seen him around, but he had not skated once. Late on the third night, the place was crowded. Most of the local middle schoolers and high schoolers gathered around the large room. Chatter and obnoxious pop music filled the place with noise.

In walked a familiar-looking man. He was balding, middle-aged, wearing a striped polo tucked into jean shorts. He wore aviator-style bifocals and held his roller skates in one hand.

Clyde lifted his head. He looked across skating floor at the man. His appearance nearly matched the killer. Did this mean the police chief and Don were innocent? Clyde was looking at the wrong place the whole time.

The stranger put on his skates and cruised out into the floor. After putting in his headband earphones, he joined the chaotic circle and trailed behind a group of fourteen-year-old girls. The sight sickened Clyde. He watched him race around for hours, staying behind the same group of young female friends. Clyde snapped pictures with his phone. The in-motion shots were mostly blurry. The stranger left the floor once to get a bottle of water. He sipped it and watched the skaters. He was on the opposite side of the room. Clyde snapped his picture. He couldn't send it to Sarah until he had reason to believe this man was worth investigating.

After finishing his bottle, the man skated until exactly twenty minutes before closing. Clyde walked to the shoe-changing room. Cubbies full of skates and shoes lined the walls. Headphones on, the stranger sat on the bench, hunched over as he untied his skates.

Clyde sat next to him. Heart racing, he tried to think of some way to break the ice. *Simple's better,* he told himself.

"Hey," Clyde said.

The man didn't hear. Synth music faintly escaped his headphones.

"Hey," Clyde replied, his sweaty palms resting on his own thighs.

The stranger glanced at him. Sweat droplets spotted his forehead. He pulled the headphones back. "What?" the man asked.

"I'm Clyde," he introduced himself, grinning kindly.

"I'm not a homosexual," the man replied in his weaselly voice and removed his shoe.

"I think you got the wrong idea," Clyde replied.

The man scoffed.

"You did good out there," Clyde said. "How long have you been skating?"

The man slipped on his walking shoes and left.

Clyde stayed seated, running his tongue behind his bottom lip. He got up and followed the man.

He spotted his sedan in the parking lot. It was a 2001 Mazda. Clyde didn't recognize it. He knew Alana had been in a similar car but it was so dark that night, Clyde didn't remember. He casually walked to his Cadillac. Dirt and dust painted the panel behind the tire. He slipped inside. The stranger left the parking lot. Clyde stalked him. He stayed a few paces behind. Still new to tailing people, Clyde relied on similar situations in buddy-cop movies to help him out. The stranger arrived at a small house in a populated neighborhood. His single-story house sat on an acre and a half of land.

Clyde drove past him. He parked at the turn of the road, where he could still see the stranger's house, but didn't draw attention. The stranger went inside. Clyde got out of his car. He walked the sidewalk. The light from the neighboring houses projected from their windows. Clyde kept his head forward and down. He reached the stranger's house. His window curtains were shut. Clyde circled the house, trying to find a way inside. Out of luck, Clyde returned to the car. He watched and waited. Hours passed. Clyde nodded off multiple times. He awoke in the middle of the night. The stranger's car was still in the lot.

Morning came.

Clyde opened his eyes.

The stranger, wearing a work polo and slacks, got into his car. Clyde rubbed the sleep from his face and turned the key. Exhausted, he followed the stranger through the outskirts of town. The stranger arrived at a small gas station named "Fuel Up." It had outdated pumps, cracks on the concrete parking lot, and decals plastered all over the windows, advertising cigarettes and Mountain Dew.

Clyde drove by, seeing the stranger unlock the door and go inside. He must've been the cashier. In a small station like that, Clyde would be surprised if there were more than two employees there. The stranger would be in there for a while. Clyde headed home, nodding off at the wheel. He blacked out a few times on the road but somehow ended up back at the house without crashing.

Pathfinder jumped on him the moment he opened the door. The dog wanted a walk. "Not now," Clyde replied.

He dragged his feet to his bedroom and crashed on the bed. He awoke some time later. A puddle of drool wetted the pillow by his lip. He pushed himself up from the bed. The sun shone through the window. He checked his phone. It was fifteen minutes after three. He walked the dog and spent a few hours on home repairs. It felt good to reset and do something that didn't require too much brainpower. Sarah hadn't called him lately. Alana's murder was still being blasted over the news, so she was probably booked.

In the latter part of the afternoon, Clyde drove by the stranger's gas station. He saw that the man's car was still there. He must've been working a long shift.

Similar to the times Clyde scouted other suspects, he parked nearby and watched the shop from a nearby field. After the stranger's twelve-hour shift ended, a second car showed up. A man took over for the night shift. Clyde hurried back to his car and followed the stranger down a country road.

Ten minutes through the winding roads, the stranger floored his accelerator and zoomed far ahead of Clyde.

16

APPREHENDED

Clyde groaned, unsure if he should follow.

He stomped on the gas pedal and raced after the stranger.

The road zigged and zagged. Clyde gained on him. He smelled burning rubber as his RPM needle climbed and wobbled. The stranger took a sharp turn at a T intersection. His tires slid as he drifted. Trying to straighten out, he overcorrected and passed into the other lane.

Clyde tackled the same corner at a slower speed, keeping better control of his vehicle.

The stranger's mistake cost him much of the distance between him and Clyde.

Clyde squeezed the steering wheel, his knuckles becoming white. His heart pounded intensely. He'd never been in a real car chase before. It was terrifying. *What are you doing?* he asked himself. The hairs on his right arm stood. He glanced over. Alana sat in the passenger seat. Memories of the woods and the pain returned to him. Thinking that the killer assaulted the young woman before killing her infuriated him. Lips pursed, his nostrils flared in rage.

The stranger turned onto a single-lane road. Ditches lined either side. Beyond were cattle fields and farms.

Ding.

Clyde's low gas light blinked on. He frowned and accelerated.

The stranger rolled down his window and shouted.

Clyde could barely hear him over the engine's roar.

They had forty feet of distance between the vehicles.

The stranger slammed on his brakes.

He skidded, coming to a harsh stop.

Cursing, Clyde stomped on his brakes as well.

Unable to stop fast enough, Clyde jerked the steering to the left. His car plowed into the ditch. The airbag exploded instantaneously. Time seemed to slow as the car bounced and rolled.

Clyde dangled upside down. The airbag deflated. His head pounded. His insides felt like they'd been shifted. There was a massive pain in his neck. Grimacing, he rubbed his forehead. "Idiot," he said to himself.

He heard a car door close. He glanced over, seeing the lower half of the stranger approaching him.

Heart racing, Clyde put his hand on the roof below him and unbuckled his seatbelt. He hit his head on the ceiling.

The stranger neared. Aching all over, Clyde climbed out of the driver side window and dragged his belly across the grass. He pushed against the dirt and stood to his feet. The world spun around him. He wobbled, nearly losing his balance. His back hit a wooden post surrounding a cattle field, keeping him upright. The stranger stood on the other side of the car.

The night shrouded most of his face. There were no road lights here.

"What the hell do you want?" the stranger shouted.

Clyde rubbed his hand through his hair. He felt a pain across his chest. The seatbelt had bruised him.

The stranger said, "You almost got me killed. Give me your insurance info."

Clyde breathed heavily.

"Hurry up," the stranger shouted.

"Where were you the night Alana died?" Clyde asked, wincing in pain.

The stranger balled his fists. "Screw you, man."

He turned around and started walking to his car.

"I know you did it!" Clyde shouted.

The stranger stopped walking. His back stayed to Clyde.

Still leaning against the post, Clyde said. "You watched her in that hidden spring, huh? It was tempting after the last victims. You went twenty years exercising self-control, but the news broadcast got you all riled up. You couldn't resist Alana anymore. Old passions died hard."

The stranger stood still for a moment. He boxed his shoulders and walked to his car.

Clyde replied, "You won't get away with it. I was an eyewitness to the whole thing."

The stranger reached into his car. He withdrew his hand, holding a pistol at his side. Keeping it by his side, he walked toward Clyde.

Clyde backed himself tighter against the fence.

The stranger walked around the flipped car. Clyde twisted back and quickly climbed over the fence. He felt pain across his neck and chest. He backed up a few steps. His right foot landing in a cow pie. The foul smell burst into the air.

The stranger walked down the ditch.

Clyde glanced around the field. It stretched for acres. There was nowhere to run. Nowhere to hide. He was unarmed and couldn't think of a worse scenario. The man neared. Clyde felt chills around him, but there weren't any ghosts. He was sensing danger.

The stranger raised his weapon. Even in the dark, Clyde looked into the eye of the barrel. His entire body was covered in goosebumps. The man stopped on his side of the fence.

"You did it, didn't you?" Clyde asked.

The stranger was as silent as death.

"You can hide my body," Clyde replied. "But you won't be able to get rid of the car. The police will come after you."

The stranger said, "Why do you think it was me? It could've been anyone."

"Alana told me," Clyde said.

The stranger glared at him, starting to sweat profusely. "Get on your knees."

"There's no scenario where you get out of this without the evidence pointing back to you," Clyde replied, standing his ground.

"You'd be surprised," said the stranger.

Clyde stood firm. He wasn't going to die a coward. He wasn't planning on dying at all. The dead would step in anytime. He just needed to trust. Fate was on his side. Fear crept into his mind.

"Down," the stranger commanded.

"Turn yourself in," Clyde said. He shifted his eyes. *Come on, Alana. Elizabeth, Mara, anyone, do something. Quickly.*

"You don't want to listen, fine. Get over here," the stranger said. "We'll talk like men."

Clyde carefully approached, knowing there was a chance he could take the weapon. "I'm a lawyer. We don't have to be enemies."

"You take me for an idiot?" the stranger replied.

"On the contrary, I think you're brilliant, which is why you haven't pulled that trigger," Clyde said.

He stopped a few feet away from the fence. Clyde said, "I have a contingency plan if you kill me. All the times you stalked Alana is clearly documented in her personal journal. If I don't make it home tonight, it's going public."

"I don't believe you," the stranger said, getting sweaty.

Clyde built upon his lie, "You think I'd chase after you without some sort of fallback?"

The stranger eyed him, uncertain whether Clyde was being genuine or not.

Clyde said, "I could've turned you in at any point. I chose not to."

"You want to talk? Is that it?" the stranger asked, "I have cuffs in the back seat. You put them on and we'll have a long chat."

Though separated by the fence, Clyde inched closer. "Deal, but you lower your weapon."

"You're a funny guy," the stranger said.

Clyde moved within arm's reach. The gun barrel was aimed at his chest. The dim moonlight showed a fraction of the stranger's face and was captured in the lens of his glasses.

The stranger said, "You come over the fence. Nice and easy."

Now's my chance.

Hesitation would kill Clyde.

He swiped at the gun.

His fingers slapped against the cold metal. He squeezed, shocked he was able to get it. He forced the barrel upward. The stranger used his other hand, trying to aim the gun back at Clyde, but he wasn't strong enough. His finger was stuck in the trigger guard, but he didn't shoot.

The stranger gritted his teeth. "Son of a –"

Clyde yanked the gun from his hands.

The pistol discharged, shooting into the sky.

The loud pop rang in Clyde's ears.

As Clyde twisted the pistol around, the stranger hastily climbed at the fence. Clyde took aim. The stranger tackled him, bringing them both to the ground. The pistol was knocked from Clyde's hands. He pushed the man off of him. The stranger rolled back and punched him in the jaw.

It hurt, but not as much as it could've. The man wasn't a fighter. Clyde slugged him back, busting the man's nose.

Howling in pain, he covered his face. Blood leaked from under his palm. Clyde crawled to the pistol. The pain from the car wreck sickened him. His palm pressed into dusty cow dung.

The stranger jumped on his back. Clyde tried to lift him off, but couldn't in his weakened state. The man grabbed Clyde's hair and slammed his face into the earth. He did it again and again. Clyde took mouthfuls of dirt. He groped blindly for the weapon, but only found dewy grass. He snatched a cold rock. Twisting his hand around so the rock was outward, he struck the stranger, knocking out a tooth.

The stranger shouted. Inspired by the small victory, Clyde pushed against the earth and got the man off of him. Still on the ground, Clyde twisted around and struck the rock against his cheekbone.

The stranger rolled to his side. Clyde scooted away. He pulled out his cellphone and dialed 911, lifting the phone to his ear.

The stranger lifted the pistol.

Clyde's heart stopped.

Leaving the phone behind, he jumped on the stranger. The stranger smacked the side of Clyde's head with the butt of the pistol.

Everything went black for a millisecond.

Clyde tasted copper. He opened his eyes and grabbed the pistol. The two men fought over the weapon, attempting to aim the barrel at the other one.

Clyde's consciousness was fading in and out. He was getting weaker. He blinked, seeing Alana behind the stranger. He blinked again and she had vanished. The stranger struck Clyde one more time, knocking him over.

Getting on top of Clyde, the stranger pressed the barrel against his forehead. The metal burrowed into his skin. He looked into the stranger's cold eyes.

"Go to hell," the stranger said.

Clyde opened his mouth to speak.

The stranger pulled the trigger.

Click.

Clyde drew in a deep breath. It took him a moment to realize that the gun had jammed.

The stranger's eyes widened.

Clyde socked his face, busting his already-busted nose and knocking him to the side. Clyde ripped the gun from his hand and removed the magazine.

Holding his hand over his nose, the stranger crawled away from Clyde.

Clyde stayed on his back, catching his breath.

The stranger reached the fence and slipped through the planks.

Wobbling, Clyde got to his feet. He collapsed before reaching the fence.

The stranger got to the other side. He grabbed the Cadillac's bumper and pulled himself up.

Clyde crawled over the fence, flopping to the other side. He gasped. The pain across his body was unbearable.

Slightly hunched and leaving behind droplets of blood,

the stranger crossed the road. He fished the keys out of his pocket and unlocked the car.

"Hey..." Clyde said, getting off the ground. "Hey!"

The stranger sat in his car and started the engine. He slammed the door and sped away.

A siren wailed.

Red and blue lights flashed in the distance.

Clyde reached the side of the road. A cop car pulled up to him. Clyde pointed down the road. "That way!"

The cop rolled down his window. "What?"

Clyde didn't recognize him. He pointed down the road. "He went that way."

A second cop car raced up to the scene. The first cop picked up his radio and told the other cop to keep going down the road.

Clyde touched his temple, feeling blood. He felt dizzy. He doubled over and vomited.

"Sir, I believe you have a concussion. Just wait, okay? Help is coming," the cop reassured him.

Clyde passed out.

He awoke to the soft beeping of an EKG machine. He was in a small hospital room at a local clinic. His head pounded. He was parched. Discombobulated, he spent a moment remembering where he was and how he got here. It was all a blur after the fight. His heart rate spiked, thinking that the stranger might've escaped. He glanced down at his wrists, seeing handcuffs that bound him to the bed.

The doctor and nurse entered. "Glad you are awake, Mr. Barker. How are you feeling?"

He lifted his wrists, making the chain go taut. "Why do I have these?"

"You assaulted a man, Mr. Barker. Do you remember?"

Clyde stopped himself from speaking. The stranger could

try to turn this around legally if it went to the court of law. Silence could keep Clyde from jail.

"You're not much of a talker," the doctor said. "Mr. Barker, you've had a concussion. There is blunt force trauma on the side of your head and also bruising across your chest from a seatbelt. I suggest you rest. The police will be arriving soon and they have questions for you."

Sarah arrived twenty minutes later. She had another cop with her. "Wait here," she told the other cop.

He stepped outside of the door.

Sarah approached Clyde's bedside. She glanced over his wounds, fighting to hide her horrified expression. "Clyde, what happened?"

Clyde scooted up, resting his back against the upper portion of the bed. "Is my car still salvageable?"

"Hell if I know," Sarah replied. She glanced over her shoulder, looking back at the slightly ajar door. She whispered. "You're in big trouble. You better start talking."

"I didn't do anything wrong."

"That's what the other guy says," Sarah replied.

Clyde whispered, "He killed Alana. He killed them all."

The revelation shook Alana. "What proof do you have?"

"Ask him, and he'll break. Trust me, Sarah."

"That's kind of hard right now," Sarah said. "If you have evidence, why didn't you show me?"

"You just have to talk to him," Clyde argued.

Sarah eyed Clyde. "You've always known a lot about this case. Too much, I'd say."

"You think I did this? You think I killed that girl?"

Sarah replied. "I don't know. But it's convenient that you find someone to blame but have nothing to show for it."

"He'll break, Sarah," Clyde said. "You just have to push him."

"Clyde, I'm interested in talking to you right now."

Clyde kept his mouth shut.

"What were you planning on doing with him when you found him?" Sarah asked.

Clyde stayed quiet.

Sarah put a hand on her hip. "Is that how you want to do this?"

Clyde refused to reply.

Sarah asked him question after question. He said nothing. Sarah eventually gave up on him and left. For five hours, Clyde waited.

A few cops entered his room. Clyde looked at them, waiting for them to speak.

One of the cops said, "You got the bastard."

"What?" Clyde asked.

The cop unlocked the first cuff. "He confessed."

Clyde replied, "To which one?"

"All of them," the cop replied. He removed the second cuff.

"See you around," the cop said, heading to the door. He turned back before leaving. "Next time you have a problem, call us. You won't end up in this place looking like you do now."

Clyde rested his head on the pillow. A smile grew across his face. He rested. He suddenly awoke in the middle of the night.

Alana lingered on the right side of the bed.

"Hi," Clyde said softly.

"It's over," Alana said. "You did it."

Clyde shrugged. "The police were the ones that arrested him. I still don't know the bastard's name."

Alana took Clyde's hand. "I'm going home now."

Clyde smiled weakly. "I'm glad for you."

Alana let go of him.

Clyde said, "Are the others going too?"

"Others?" Alana asked.

Clyde replied, "Hmm, they passed to the other side already."

Clyde felt strangely empty. He wished he'd gotten greater closure.

Alana headed for the hospital door. She opened it and stepped out, vanishing forever.

Clyde went back to sleep. He awoke the next morning, unsure if it were a dream. Two days later, he was able to go home. He took a cab and was dropped off at his house. It sucked that he lost his car, but the insurance would recompense him. Clyde hugged his husky. Sarah had been feeding her while he was hospitalized.

Being cooped up for so long, the dog ran a few laps around the lawn.

Standing where his porch once stood, Clyde watched her. He felt cruel for wanting to bring her back to his Atlanta apartment. It was confined and unclean. He wanted a place where she could run around. Nevertheless, he had to get back to work ASAP to pay off the remaining medical expenses. The trip was costly, but it felt right. He'd probably cut his losses on his house and sell to whoever wanted to rebuild it. He returned inside. Pathfinder followed him and rushed to the water bowl. Tail wagging, she drank up.

Clyde headed to Uncle Andrew's folder. He flipped through the pictures of the suspects and closed it. He removed the maps from the wall, folded them, and slipped them inside the file. Holding it under his armpit, he headed downstairs. His head pounded. He reached into his pocket and pulled out a bottle of pain pills. They rattled as he pulled one out and swallowed it down. He reached Andrew's safe.

He took a knee and twisted the dial. The hairs on his arms stood up. He paused, hearing a footstep behind him.

He turned around.

Partly concealed in shadow, he saw a figure wearing a red cloth mask and aiming a scoped rifle at him.

"Oh sh—"

Bam!

The bullet knocked Clyde into the safe. Intense pain thundered through his body. The papers from the file scattered. Resting against the safe's door, he glanced down at the bloody hole in his stomach. Every breath hurt. There was blood. Lots of blood. His blood.

The killer cocked the rifle.

Clyde's eyes widened.

17

DIGGING

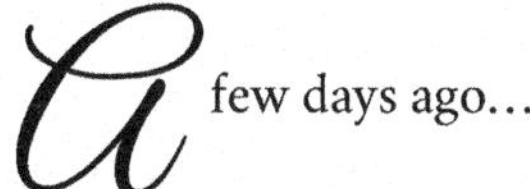

few days ago…

ARMS CROSSED, Officer Sarah Sullivan stood in the dark observation room, the live video feed of Interrogation Room 1 reflected in her bloodshot blue eyes. Her red hair was pulled back in a tight ponytail. The gender-neutral uniform masked the curves of her body. Her lips scrunched to the side of her mouth. On the grainy video feed, bruised and bloodied Terry Wells rested on his head on the tabletop. Handcuffs bound him to the table. His graying hair was balding with age. Dirt and droplets of blood stained his gas station work polo and khakis.

"This is the guy?" Officer Rivera asked. He stood next to Sarah.

The Hispanic cop had a buzz cut and a youthful face. Being in a cop in Hartwell meant you were more of a people-person than an arbiter of the law. Hosea Rivera was one of the nicest officers you'd ever meet. Somehow, he could even get smiles out of the person being ticketed.

"The press is calling the killer the Hartwell Huntsman," Sarah said.

"It blows my mind what names they come up with," Rivera replied.

Sarah leaned closer to the screen. Terry lifted his head. His eyes looked dead with depression and mumbled to himself.

"What are you thinking?" Rivera said. "You think your buddy in the hospital is right?"

Sarah glanced on the digital wall clock. It was almost 4 am. "He's marinated long enough."

Rivera cracked a smile. "Lead the way, Sully."

Sarah stepped out of the dark room into the lit hallway. Collecting herself, she grabbed the knob to the interrogation room. She took a deep breath and opened it.

Terry turned to her. "Hey, beautiful. I didn't realize they'd send you."

"I volunteered," Sarah replied, walking around the aluminum table.

"I'm a lucky man," Terry flirted. His eyes had dark circles. One had a ruptured blood vessel. A bandage patch was on the right side of his head. He had a swollen lip, and medical tape held a gauze pad to his nose.

The air in the room was freezing cold and bland. A wall-mounted camera watched Terry from the far back corner. Rivera joined Sarah's side. The two of them sat across from Terry. He nervously rubbed his hands together.

"You want to tell me why I'm here, sweetheart?" Terry asked. "I've been nothing but cooperative and you've kept me waiting."

Sarah said, "Sorry, Mr. Wells –"

"Terry. Please," He interrupted.

"Okay, Terry. I'm Officer Sullivan. This is my partner Officer Rivera."

"What are your first names?"

Rivera said, "Hosea. That's Sarah."

"Lovely name, Sarah," Terry said.

Sarah flashed a smile his way, silently reminding herself that this man might've raped and killed a woman days ago. *Innocent until proven guilty*. She said, "Hosea and I have been busy trying to clean up the car wreck. Small town. We all wear many hats."

"And you do a good job, but I have a feeling you didn't bring me in here to debate me fleeing the scene of the accident," Terry said.

"You and the driver had a lengthy conversation before you fled," Sarah commented.

"There wasn't much talking," Terry replied.

Hosea asked, "What did he do to you?"

"He followed me," Terry replied. "I didn't want that. I even tried to get ahead of him, but he kept coming after me. When he crashed, I approached him and then he attacked."

"But you attacked him and fled instead of calling the cops," Sarah said.

"Sweetheart, I was caught up in the heat of the moment," Terry replied.

"How well did that turn out for you?"

"We traded a few blows," Terry said, his ego shattering.

Rivera opened a folder and studied the crime report and a few photos. "A pistol was found at the crime scene. Does that belong to you?"

Terry replied, "No."

Sarah folded her hands together on the tabletop and leaned forward. The bottom of her breasts rested on the aluminum, drawing Terry's attention just as she expected. "Terry, we're in the process of the running the Colt's serial number. If you lie to me about it, it's going to make your life harder."

"I'm already hard," Terry said, a wry smile growing on his ugly face.

"Funny," Sarah said dryly.

"I hear girls like funny guys," Terry replied.

Rivera asked. "You like girls, Terry?"

"Who doesn't? Sarah, you might be old for my taste, but I could make an exception."

"I'm flattered," Sarah replied.

Terry grinned, revealing his missing bottom tooth.

"What about Alana Campbell?" Sarah asked.

Terry's smile fled. He tried to keep a neutral face. "Who is that?"

"Black hair. Goth-looking. She's been all over the news," Sarah said.

"Oh, *that* girl," Terry nodded. "What's she got to do with anything?"

"She was raped and killed," Sarah replied. "You wouldn't happen to know anything about that?"

Terry said confidently, "I was at home that night."

Clyde believed this was the killer, enough so that he almost lost his life going after him, but he didn't have any evidence back up his claim. Sarah pushed Terry. "Do you have an alibi to back that up?"

Terry replied, "Yeah, my flatmate, Dillan. He's always around."

Hosea jotted that down.

Sarah said, "You know Alana was going to college for Horticulture. I talked to her parents. She wanted to plant gardens in big cities. It was an effort to save the environment. She was a good girl. Had a big heart. It must've taken a real monster to kill her."

"I don't know why we're talking about this," Terry said. "She has nothing to do with the crash."

Sarah said, "We searched your car this evening."

Terry's confidence wavered.

Hosea showed him a picture of handcuffs and a few strands of long black hair. "We found these in the back seat."

"I'm a kinky guy," Terry replied.

"We have the hair at a lab right now being run for DNA. What are the odds it will match Alana's?" Sarah asked.

Terry's face turned red. He couldn't look Sarah in the eye.

"Terry," Sarah said sweetly.

He glanced up at her.

"Is there something you want to get off your chest?" She asked

"I..." Terry stopped himself.

Sarah and Hosea waited.

Hosea said, "It's okay. You can talk to us."

Terry shook his head. "This is ridiculous," he mumbled.

The three of them waited in a long, uncomfortable silence. Sarah wanted to grill him for the answers, but sometimes patience was key to a confession.

"I haven't been totally honest," Terry said.

Hearts pumping, Sarah and Hosea exchanged glances.

Terry nervously fidgeted with his hands. He sucked in his lips.

"What are you not telling us?" Sarah asked.

Terry sighed. "I've known Alana since she was a young girl. Thirteen, fourteen. Her father used to buy cigarettes from my gas station. He'd always get her KitKat bar. I saw her around the skating rink, too. We used to follow in the same lane. She was a talented girl. Smart, too."

Sarah listened, recalling painful memories of her own childhood.

"You liked her?" Hosea asked.

Terry shrugged. "Like. Love. They're all chemicals in your brain, right? Needless to say, she was something else. She was a little demon on the Roller Derby team. She never noticed, but I was there for all her games."

"So what made you want to assualt and kill her?" Sarah asked.

Terry looked down at his hands. "With the news coming out about the discovered skeletons, I thought it was time to… to get back in the saddle."

Sarah felt sick. She buried it behind her emotions, but she was always an expressive person.

Hosea asked, "You killed all those people?"

Head down, Terry nodded.

"I need you to say it," Sarah pushed.

Terry locked eyes with Sarah. "Yes. All of them. I killed all of them."

Hosea's eyes went wide. He glanced up at the camera and back to Sarah. "I'll get a notepad and paper. We'll take your confession. You good with that, Terry?"

Terry lowered his eyes and nodded.

Sarah could scarcely believe what she was seeing.

Hosea exited the door.

Sarah rested back into her chair. "Twenty years ago… what happened?"

"I was young," Terry paused for a moment. "I saw those kids. They, uh, they seemed so vulnerable. I had my hunting rifle at the time --"

"You still have it?"

"Not that exact gun, but I have a similar model," Terry said. "It's in the garage."

Sarah nodded. "We'll get some people out there to check it out."

Terry tapped his finger on the table.

"So, you just decided to shoot those kids because...?" Sarah asked.

"They were easy targets. It was a time before cellphones," Terry said.

Something about this felt wrong. Sarah couldn't explain it. "Did you even know their names?"

Terry said, "I don't... I don't remember."

"The killing was completely random?" Sarah said.

"Yeah. I guess I'm just a bad guy," Terry explained.

Hosea re-entered. He placed the pen and notepad in front of Hosea. Resting a palm on the table, he gestured to the paper. "Just write down the series of events leading up the killing."

Terry looked at him, confused. "I start with my name or..."

"That's fine. As long as you sign it afterward," Hosea said.

Terry nodded.

Sarah watched him write a three-page report of Alana's murder, detailing the way he stalked, held her at the road at gunpoint, got her to strip, assaulted her, forced her to redress, and drove her out to the woods.

Hosea filed it away and asked Terry to recall to the best of his ability the murders of Elizabeth Mara, Tommy Demko, John Roth, and Gena Cobbs. That report ended up being half of the page.

Terry was escorted out of the room afterward.

Sarah stayed seated, her mind racing.

Hosea returned a few moments later.

"Holy crap," he said, not one to swear.

"Is he being processed?" Sarah asked.

"Everything is ready to go," Hosea said. "I still can't believe it."

"Yeah, it has been a crazy night," Sarah said.

Hosea picked up on her uncertainty. He yawned. "I'm heading back home. C'mon. We'll let the guys on the morning shift handle the rest of it."

Sarah got up. Her knees popped. She stretched.

Hosea walked her out to her car. "Hawkins is going to be happy. We might just become Chief's new favorites."

Sarah flashed a false smile. She sat in her car. Hosea said, "I can get someone to drive you if you're feeling tired."

"I'm fine," Sarah said. "Have a good night, Hosea. Tell Sophie I said hi."

"You got it." Hosea patted the car roof twice before backing off.

Sarah drove home. She couldn't get it out of her head. The man who walked into the interrogation room wasn't the same man who left.

She went inside and took a long shower. Head bowed, she let the steaming hot water pound her neck. The water ran over her curves and the razor scars on her thighs. They were mementos of her troubled youth. She shut her eyes. *Slut,* the guys would say. *Whore,* the girls whispered behind her back.

She remembered one kid in junior year, a sweet guy named Drew Anthony. He was one of her few friends of the opposite sex she hadn't fooled around with. One day, his friends dared him to ask Sarah to spend the night with him. Sarah was at the lunch table, watching him trembling with his head down as he asked her in front of the whole school. His friends snickered. The other girls gawked. Sarah remembered Drew's expression vividly. His expression read *I don't want to do this, but I have to show off*. Terry Wells had that same look tonight.

Sarah stepped out of the water. The skin on her back was red from the hot water. Enduring the pain, she dried off and went to bed. She slept until noon. She awoke but stayed in bed, the covers half-concealing her body. She didn't want to move. She didn't want to get up. She closed her eyes. Two hours later, she got up. Wearing an XL t-shirt from one of her past lovers, she walked to the kitchen and cooked scrambled eggs for herself.

Finished, she took her paper plate and cup of orange juice and sat cross-legged on the couch. She clicked the remote. The TV turned on.

The news anchor discussed Chief of Police Robert Hawkins's press junket this morning. A clip played.

Hawkins stood in front of a few mics. A line of flagpoles stood behind him. He spoke with confidence. "We have a suspect detained. He has confessed to all five murders and will be going to court shortly. I want to take this time to thank everyone involved in the apprehension of the suspect, and I would also like to take a moment of silence to remember those we lost. They will be forever in our prayers."

Within twelve hours, Hawkins had already gone public. It didn't sit right with Sarah. She changed the channel and watched crappy reality TV. It was usually a night she'd go out on the town, but she was too lazy to get dressed. She ate a TV dinner at 8 pm and was in bed by 2 am.

She got up at six and hurled herself out of bed. After all these years, she still wasn't a morning person. She put on her uniform and belt and lastly put her hair into a tight ponytail. She only put a small amount of blush and eyeliner. No one took a dolled-up cop seriously, and Sarah preferred war paint over heavy make-up any day. As per her daily ritual, she drove to the local donut shop and got a discounted cup of Hartwell's finest coffee. It was a medium roast hazelnut with two sugars and three creams. Sarah added more sugar and drank it like a dessert.

When she arrived at the station, she stepped into the bullpen and was met with loud applause. The other four officers, two volunteers, and Hartwell's clerk stood from their desks, clapping their hands and cheering her on.

Sarah was confused and shocked. "Did I forget my birthday or something? What's going on?"

The plump clerk, Margery Patten, was on the verge of tears. "Oh, darling. Look at you. The town's hero."

"I don't understand."

"You got him," Margery said. The woman wore a polka-dotted shirt and thick glasses. Her hair was dyed brown, short and puffy. "After twenty years, you got him."

Chief Hawkins lingered by his office door, a little smile on his handsome, nearly symmetrical face. A centimeter of greying hair ran around the sides and back of his head. The ceiling light reflected off his bald crown.

"Alright, everybody," Hawkins said to the crowd. "We're in the news now. Let's keep up the good work. We'll make sure something like this never happens in Hartwell again."

The cops sat down.

Hawkins gestured for Sarah to follow him.

She stepped into his office.

It was nicely decorated. Pictures of his family decorated his wall. His father and grandfather were both chiefs of police before him. He had a large family, three brothers and two sisters. All of them were Hartwell locals, mostly all occupying significant roles in Hartwell's small government. There was a crude joke that the Hawkinses liked to keep it in the family. It stemmed from a rumor that Robert's older brother and sister had a romantic fling. It was a story that every local knew but no one ever talked about, especially to an outsider.

Hawkins took a seat at his desk. A half-smile lingered on his face. "Have a seat, Sully."

She lowered herself to the seat in front of him.

Hawkins sipped his coffee mug, reading "#1 Dad." "I was going to call you yesterday, but I wanted to let you rest. It was a long shift."

Sarah gave him a pursed-lip smile.

Hawkins lowered his mug to the desk. "You're quiet today."

"I'm just in my head."

"I can get you counseling. That case did a number on us all. That confession made my skin crawl. The sicko described in detail how he and Alana… Well, you read it."

"Chief, I don't… I don't think he killed those people," Sarah said.

"Okay? But he confessed," Hawkins reminded her.

"I understand, and I do believe the evidence points him to Alana's murder."

"What's the problem?" Hawkins asked, annoyed.

"I don't think he killed the others."

"Who did?" Hawkins asked hostilely.

"I don't know, but something about Terry doesn't sit right," Sarah said.

"Look, Sully," Hawkins locked his fingers together, keeping them on the desk. "I know it's hard to believe, but a confession is a confession. The guys is looking at multiple life sentences and possibly death row. Why would he lie?"

"Fame," Sarah replied. "This is the only big thing that ever happened in Hartwell. The trial will go national. He'll get a name that lasts forever. I looked into Terry's records. He's unmarried, has a crappy job, and is going nowhere. The man has nothing to lose."

"Which is why he killed those people," Hawkins said.

"But what if he didn't?" Sarah said. "What if the real killer is still out there? "

"Sully, you're a hero because of this case. The families have closure after decades of pain. Do you want to reopen those wounds when there is no evidence? You want to lose your legacy?"

"I feel it in my gut, Chief. We're missing something."

"If the justice system was based off anyone's gut, we'd all be in big trouble," Hawkins replied.

Sarah sulked.

"I have a nice raise for you, Sarah," Hawkins said. "But, it wouldn't be fair to give it to you if the case wasn't closed. I can give it to you now if you'd like, but only if you agree to drop these crazy theories the moment you step out of my office."

Sarah crossed her arms. She had wanted a raise for years. The money tempted her. A possible promotion tempted her even more.

"Well?" Hawkins asked, pulling out Sarah's employee file.

Sarah sighed, "Okay."

"We have a deal."

Sarah nodded.

"Fantastic," Hawkins crossed out the amount listed on her employment contract and added another four grand. "I'll call my accountant and get that finalized. It's just a starter, too. You keep up the good work and you'll get another boost before the end of the year."

He extended his hand to shake.

Sarah shook it.

She left the room, thinking that she should've been happy. Instead, she felt like she had just made a deal with the devil.

"Oh, Sully!"

She caught the door and looked back at him. "Yeah, Chief?"

"Take down the case board, will ya? Move it into evidence."

"You got it, Chief." Sarah let the door close behind her.

She entered into the briefing room. Multiple suspect photos were taped to a whiteboard. Sarah removed the DMV pictures of Roland Alcott, Curtis Lowry, and Clyde Barker. She tucked them away in a file and erased all the dates, locales, and other notes she and the rest of the department had slaved away at for days. When she finished, she felt empty. It was her first real serial killer case, and the joy of overcoming evil wasn't there.

She spent the rest of the day around the office, helping Rivera finish up police reports. He had a grin on his face from ear to ear. "Drinks are on me tonight."

"I'll pass."

"Whoa. That's weird," Rivera said.

"What?" Sarah said, seeing if she missed something on the form.

"You not drinking," Rivera clarified.

Sarah relaxed. "I want a little me-time. Ain't nothing weird about that."

"Whatever you want, but I bet you fifty bucks that drinks will be free for all of us if you show up to *Alistair's*. Just saying," Rivera nudged her.

"I'll think about it," Sarah said.

"When a woman says that, it's a *no,*" Rivera said.

"Tell your wife that."

"Oh, no no no. I'm not ending up on the couch again. Not after last time. She'd walk around all day, wearing practically nothing just to taunt me. I was blue-balling for weeks. A man can't live like that," Rivera said.

"Sounds like cruel and unusual punishment," Sarah said dryly.

"Exactly!"

Rivera clocked out of work before Sarah. She stayed after, with one other cop working the night shift. He went to take his evening deuce. That was usually a twenty to thirty-minute affair.

Seeing he was gone, Sarah got up from her desk. She jogged through the bullpen and approached Hawkins's office door. It was unlocked. One of the many safety hazards of a small, casual office. Sarah shut the door behind her. Keeping the light off, she turned on her phone flashlight. *Don't do this, he'll catch you,* Sarah thought as she scanned his desk and shelves.

She was looking for anything that might give him a reason for wanting to drop the case. She pulled open the desk drawers. She found knick-knacks and Post-Its. Her seven-minute search through the office yielded nothing. *Duh. It's because he's innocent.* She barely believed herself. Clyde was certain he was a suspect and all this time, she'd yet to find anything to point him to the killers.

She started to dial Clyde but stopped. He was in the hospital. It would be raising too many red flags if she visited him. Sarah slightly suspected him, but the other officers were after his blood. They had spent days searching through dirt in the past to bring him into the station but didn't find anything outside the death of his parents. Also, Terry could sue him for assault. Sarah didn't want to deal with that mess. She submitted her work and went home.

The next day was her day off. She had a granola bar for breakfast and worked through an hour-long CrossFit video in her living room when she got a text.

Winded, she paused the video and checked the phone. It was from her mother. *Dinner tonight?*

Sarah's shoulders slumped. She hated their outings. Nevertheless, she typed, *Yes.*

Her mother, Julia, named the place and time.

Sarah put her phone aside and exercised harder.

She spent the afternoon watching her favorite cheesy soap opera. Ben, an old ex, called her, wanting to chill. Though hesitant at first, Sarah headed over to his house and got an exercise of a different sort. She left a little happier and got home to get changed into something nice. She wore a violet blouse, leaving the two buttons undone as well as a black skirt.

As she straightened her hair, Julia sent her a different text. *I didn't get my hair done so no fancy place for me. I'll meet you at the diner in fifteen.*

Sarah groaned. "Well, I'm not changing," she thought aloud.

She arrived at the local diner. Julia was already in her booth. She was skinny and had voluminous red hair. In her fifties, she was still a bombshell, but a life of smoking gave her face a coarse complexion.

The sun-kissed waitress Hannah Granger served her a Diet Pepsi.

"There is too much ice. Get me another," Julia said to her.

Hannah humbly took back the glass and walked away. The moment she turned her back, the waitress frowned.

Sarah arrived at her mother's side and spoke in a low voice. "You've been here for two minutes and you're already pissing off the waitress."

Julia said, "And you're dressed like a slut. You trying to steal her tips?"

Sarah sat down across from her.

"Seriously, button-up or don't wear it at all," Julia rudely pointed at Sarah.

"Mom, I'm thirty-two. You can't talk to me like that," Sarah said.

"You want to be a slut, keep being a slut. I don't care," Julia said, clearly caring.

Sarah flipped through the menu. "Did you order anything yet?"

"Nope, the waitress is an airhead. I want another one, but I think she's the only one working," said Julia.

Hannah returned holding the Diet Pepsi. She smiled at Sarah. "And what can I get for you?"

"Water is fine," Sarah said.

Hannah walked off.

Julia asked, "Since when did you start drinking water? Trying to trim off that extra fat?"

Sarah would've laughed at the comment if her mother wasn't completely serious.

"How was work today?" Sarah asked, perusing the menu. Under the table, she squeezed her little belly, riddled with self-conscious thoughts.

"The girls are fighting," Julia said.

Sarah said, "That must be hard for you."

"It's what they do," Julia replied.

The waitress arrived and took their order. Sarah ordered a hamburger and got a judgmental look from her mother. She quickly switched to a salad. Julia got soup and a BLT.

"Two of the girls are becoming a real problem. They attacked each other," Julia said.

"Verbally or physically?"

"I'm not telling you that," Julia replied.

Then why bring up? Sarah thought cynically.

Julia asked, "Are you making any money now?"

"I just got a raise yesterday," Sarah said proudly.

"Send some of it my way. This lawsuit is raping my finances," Julia said.

Her words made her Sarah cringe. She asked, "Which lawsuit is that?"

"Against the club," Julia said as if it were the most obvious thing in the world. "It's always against the club. You know, I do everything I can to keep my girls and my patrons happy, and time after time, stupidity happens. I'm losing my mind. I should've become a cop like you. All I'll have to do is sit around in a car all day, making people's lives miserable."

It took a strong measure of self-control to keep Sarah from leaving. "Why did you want to come out here tonight?"

Julia got offended. "I'm not allowed to celebrate my daughter's achievement?"

"You know I got the killer?" Sarah asked, shocked and almost flattered.

"Everyone knows," Julia replied. She scoffed and shook her head. The waitress returned with their food.

After putting down her plate, Julia grabbed the woman's wrist.

Hannah looked terrified.

Julia asked, "You know this is my daughter, right? She's the one that saved the town."

"Oh, I heard. I didn't realize it was you," Hannah said.

Julia let go of her. "Well, kind of. The killer confessed all on his own. Sarah was in the room though. That's something, I guess."

Hannah smiled awkwardly. "You must be very proud of her."

"I wasn't expecting any less," Julia replied.

Sarah masked a smile.

Julia continued, "Excellence shouldn't be rewarded. It should be expected. Remember that."

She spoke as if talking to a child, but the waitress was around her same age.

"Enjoy your meal," Hannah said insincerely and left the table.

Julia started eating.

Sarah rested an elbow on the table as she forked the salad.

Julia stopped mid-chew and glared at her.

Sarah moved her elbow.

Julia went back to eating normally.

Sarah thought for a moment. After finishing her bite, she said, "I actually wanted to ask you something, but you have to promise to keep it between us."

Julia said, "You tell me what it is first and we'll see."

"I'm serious," Sarah replied.

"Fine, whatever. What are you going to say?" Julia replied. "Gawd, I wish I could smoke in this place."

Sarah had reservations about asking her. *What's the worst that could happen?* She asked, "Does Bob Hawkins ever visit your girls?"

"Not recently, unless the girls are going behind my back," Julia said.

"How soon is recently?" Sarah asked.

"Five, ten years," Julia replied. "He only did escorts. Less eyes on."

"Does he have a type?" Sarah asked.

"Young bunnies," Julia said, "But he likes to go as low as he can go. Legally, of course. You better not blackmail him or harass my girls about it."

Sarah nodded, abiding by her threat.

"Why do you care anyway?" Julia asked.

Sarah said, "I'm just exploring different possibilities."

Julia replied, "I like Bob. He treated me right. Still does. Don't screw that up."

"Don't worry about that," Sarah replied. "How can I get any worse than I am now?"

"By opening that can of worms," Julia said. "I should've never told you."

"Too late," Sarah mumbled.

Julia dabbed the side of her mouth with a napkin. "Well, if you're looking to extort him, I can find other dirt."

"Mom, no," Sarah said.

"What? Just because I don't agree with your methods doesn't mean I can't help."

"I'm done talking about this," Sarah said.

"If that's the case, I don't want you bringing it up again. Not to me or my girls," Julia said defensively.

The rest of the meal dragged on as Julia complained about her landlord, her lawsuits, and her girls. Sarah tuned most of it out. Julia left a small tip and the two of them left.

"I'm going home," Julia said. "Where are you going?"

"To sleep," Sarah replied.

"Good. Don't be chasing any boys. No one is going to want to marry damaged goods," Julia, the woman who had two failed marriages and countless boyfriends, replied.

"Okay, Mom," Sarah said dryly.

Julia got into her luxury Mercedes and sped away.

Sarah's back slumped slowly. *Damaged goods,* she heard her mother say. She returned to her car. Conversations like this used to make her cry, but now she got angry. She thought about going home, but she had a better idea.

She left Hartwell and arrived at the neighboring town, Royston. Its population numbered under three thousand. On the side of the hallway, conveniently located between a truck stop and a cheap motel, *Princesses Playhouse* stood. It had darkened windows, a packed parking lot, and a tall neon sign of a woman's leg lifted up and down like a Rockette.

"Nice place, Mom," Sarah mumbled. She shut off her car and looked at her hair. It wasn't every day a single woman went into a strip club. If anyone questioned her, she was a cop. That would keep the creeps from getting touchy-feely.

Sarah remembered coming here as a kid. Her mother performed on stage while Sarah stayed in the back. She was always in on the latest gossip. Sarah's father was obviously never in the picture. All Sarah knew is that he was a patron until Julia got knocked up. He hadn't come back since.

Sarah approached the bouncer outside. The young man had large muscle like Clyde and a cue-ball head. He didn't recognize Sarah. She never came by. Too many bad memories. The place had an oppressive atmosphere, too. The raw lust and desperation drained her soul. After getting a pat-down, she entered.

Dim lights shined over the room. A pink phallic-shaped catwalk jutted out at the back third of the room. Multiple round dance pedestals stood at half-circle booths. Neon signs decorated the wall, mostly beer ads and promiscuous words. Half-naked women grinded on middle-aged patrons and worked the pole. The bartender was a tatted guy wearing a black ball cap. He wiped down the bar top and chatted with the patrons. One of them slipped him a large tip. The bartender gestured to the serving girls. Money jutted from the band around her upper thigh. She approached the man and whispered in his ear. He nodded. She walked to the Employees Only hallway. The man left, presumably going to the motel.

Darn it, Mom. You said you didn't do that anymore, Sarah thought.

Sarah found a seat near the back of the room and

watched the showgirls and patrons. Curtis Lowry drank by himself, seated by the catwalk. The black man wore a camouflage jacket, a ball cap, jeans, and work boots. He was too preoccupied with the dancer to recognize Sarah.

One of the dancers approached Sarah. She wore a server's apron and panties. "Hey, gorgeous. Would you like a drink? Cocktails are half-price. My treat."

"You look sexy."

"Thanks, girl. Call me Fonda."

"Sully," Sarah introduced herself. "You work here long?"

"Since I was eighteen, sugar."

"Now what are you?"

"Nineteen," Fonda replied.

"I want to know something," Sarah gestured for her to come closer.

Fonda lent her an ear.

Sarah said, "Do they treat you right?"

"Only when I say to. Sometimes I like a little punishment," Fonda replied.

"You ever do anything a little *extra*?"

"Not me, sugar. Talk to Fantasia." Fonda pointed to the current dancer on stage.

"Thank you, doll. I'll just have a water bottle, please." Sarah didn't trust any glass from a strip club, no matter how many times they were washed.

A few patrons looked Sarah's way. One waved to her. Sarah didn't wave back.

Fonda returned with the bottle. "Are you sure I can't get you a real drink?"

"Maybe later," Sarah replied.

Fonda walked to the next patron.

Ten minutes after her dance set, Fantasia approached Sarah. The glitter on her hair and chest glistened in the light. She scooted next to Sarah, resting her hand on Sarah's thigh. "I heard you're interested in something personal."

Sarah cringed internally. Her mother should tell her girls to be more careful. A cop might get the wrong idea.

"I am," Sarah said. "I wouldn't mind having a little alone time with you."

"You saw the motel across the street, right?"

"I was hoping we could do something out back," Sarah replied.

"It'll cost you more," Fantasia replied.

"$85 work?" Sarah said.

"That'll be fine," Fantasia said. "We'll be quick."

Fantasia told Sarah to meet her behind the club. It smelled like dumpster trash. An unpackaged condom and cigarette butts littered the cracked ground. One of the dancers stood on the lit side of the back door, smoking a cig. A can of pepper spray was strapped to her thigh.

Wearing a jacket, Fantasia stepped out a moment later. The other girl went inside. Fantasia approached Sarah. "What are you looking for?"

Sarah replied, "You know your clients, right? Any of them look like this?" Sarah showed her a picture of Bob Hawkins on her phone. He wasn't in uniform.

"Never, precious," Fantasia replied.

"You sure?"

"We have a don't kiss-and-tell policy here," Fantasia said.

Sarah said, "You'd help me if you knew who you were talking to."

"Why is that?" Fantasia pressed her body against Sarah.

"I'm a cop," Sarah said.

Fantasia whispered in her ear. "I love roleplay, Officer."

"Badge 82483," Sarah replied.

Fantasia pulled away, suddenly realizing Sarah wasn't acting. "Oh no."

Sarah nodded. "And you're going to help me out."

Fantasia teared up. "Please. I have two little girls. I can't lose this job. I can't."

"And you won't if you do as I say," Sarah promised.

Fantasia hyperventilated. "I just got off parole. Please, don't do this."

Sarah showed him the picture. "Have you seen this man?"

"No. Never," Fantasia replied, wiping away a tear. More kept flowing.

"Have any of the others?"

"It's a middle-aged white dude. That's 90% of our clientele."

"Who has been here the longest?" Sarah asked.

"Julia, our manager."

"I'm not interested in her," Sarah replied curtly. "Who else?"

"Bunny. She's been around here for three decades," Fantasia answered.

"Bunny..." Sarah thought out loud. She hadn't been in the club since she was twelve. She might've seen her, but didn't remember her face. "Where can I find her?"

"She works at the truck stop."

"Anyone else with tenure?" Sarah asked.

"Julia rotates us out at the age of thirty," Fantasia replied. "You aren't going to turn me in, right?"

"If you keep quiet, you'll never see me again," Sarah replied. "I'll know if you tell Julia, so don't try it."

Sarah headed over to the truck stop. A few semi-trucks were parked beside the building. A bell rang as she stepped inside. Georgia merchandise was displayed in a mini souvenir shop. Sarah walked to the counter, seeing the middle-aged man. He had so much hair on his arms he looked like a gorilla. His face was ugly with a pig nose. He breathed with his mouth open. His upper lip was naturally curled upward.

He stared blankly at Sarah.

"Hey, big fella, I'm looking for Bunny," Sarah said.

The man cupped his hands around his mouth. "Hey, Bunny!"

"What?" A voice sounded from the back of the store.

"A customer needs you!"

"I'll go to her," Sarah said, following the sound of Bunny's voice. She arrived at the back of the merchandise section.

Bunny, a skinny sixty-year-old woman with wiry hair and a saggy, dolled-up face, hung shirts on a rack. "What do you want?"

"I need to talk to you about your job across the street," Sarah said.

"And who the hell are you?"

"Sully," Sarah replied.

"I don't owe you any explanation about my life or my choices, Sully," Bunny replied rudely.

Sarah showed her the pictures of Hawkins in civilian attire. "Have you seen that man?"

"That's Chief of Police Hawkins from Hartwell. His face has been all over the news lately," Bunny said.

"Have you ever seen him at the club?"

Bunny chuckled. "You're not getting any information out of me. I'm not a snitch."

"Julia has already told me he was there five or ten years ago. I'm only asking you to confirm a story."

Bunny put another shirt on the rack. "You're looking to stir up trouble, more like."

Sarah said, "I know that club does more than dancing.

With the insight I have, I can bring that whole place down. Those girls would lose their kids to protective custody and probably get arrested themselves. The ones that wouldn't will probably end up as full-time tricks. You want that on your conscience?"

Bunny glared Sarah. "You're a sick woman. Those girls got nothing against you and you'd ruin their lives. For what? Gossip?"

"Maybe," Sarah replied. "You talk, and it won't have to be that way."

"What if I don't know anything?" Bunny asked.

"I find that hard to believe," Sarah said. "I know you're one of the longtime girls. I'm sure you've seen plenty of things."

"If any dirt comes out of Hawkins, he'll shut us down," Bunny said. "We lose either way."

"I'm not interested in exposing the information. I just want the facts."

"Blackmail," Bunny said, hand on her hip.

"Truth," Sarah corrected.

"Well, you want me to help you, you better make it worth my while."

Sarah shook her head. She fished out sixty bucks from her wallet. The women reached for it. Sarah drew back her hand. "Not until after you talk."

"So you can ditch me? I wasn't born yesterday," Bunny said.

Sarah gave her twenty. "Here's a show of good faith."

Bunny pocketed quickly. "That ain't much."

"I can destroy you, "Sarah kindly reminded her.

Bunny was suddenly content with the twenty dollars. "Hawkins showed up seven, eight years ago for a friend's bachelor party. He got hands-on with one of the girls."

"Did they move past second base?" Sarah asked.

"No."

"You worked there twenty to thirty years ago. Did he frequent the club back then?"

Bunny glanced down at the money and then back to Sarah.

She gave her another twenty.

Bunny pocketed it. "Hawkins used to come around a lot. Maybe once a month. He always paid for side services."

"Did he have any particular tastes?"

"Not really," Bunny said.

Roland's rumor about Hawkins being a kiddie-lover was false. Sarah expected as much.

"You want to know about his involvement with the killings," Bunny said, a twinkle in her eyes.

Sarah's heart skipped a beat. "You know something?"

"What are you? A cop or an investigator?"

"I can't tell you that," Sarah replied.

"Smart," Bunny replied. "I like to yap."

Sarah gave Bunny her last forty dollars. "That's it."

"There's an ATM down the road," Bunny said.

Sarah glared at her. "Tell me about Hawkins."

"About twenty-four years ago, I started working at the club and got into a few side services, if you know what I mean. At the time, Hawkins was trying to curry favor with the locals as a wholesome man, but he had nocturnal activities. The story circulated that while he was in bed with a barely legal, and I mean *barely* legal, dancer, a teenage girl saw him. I don't know how she got into that position, but she told her parents. They knew Hawkins. They offered to keep his little secret... for a price. Hawkins paid up. The rumor went away. A few years later, the teenage girl who saw him was one of the murder victims."

Sarah said, "And you think Hawkins wanted to shut her up for good?"

Bunny shrugged. "Maybe. He had motive."

"And the stripper that slept with him?"

"She died in a car wreck a few weeks before," Bunny said. "Someone cut her brake lines."

18

BOGEY

Sarah drove down the dark country road, listened to the hum of the tires. She kept one hand on the steering wheel and other on the door's armrest. The wind brushed against her face. *Would Hawkins really kill someone to hide a scandal? Were the other three deaths purely collateral?* She had questions, but nothing convinced her that he was the killer.

Driving away from the strip club, she fell into a memory. She was eight at the time. Her mother told her to hide in the motel room bathroom while she took care of a client. Sarah was at the age where she started to understand what her mother really did for a living. Being around promiscuity her whole life, she saw it as normal. She waited for the man to leave and kept quiet. When her mother opened the bathroom door, she gave Sarah a hug and said, "*Good girl.*"

The next night, the man returned. This time he saw Sarah as she hid in the bathroom. She closed the door before he could get a good look at her.

"*Cute girl,*" he commented, his voice muffled by the door.

"*You got the cash, right?*" Julia asked.

"Always."

A week later, Sarah was playing with her Barbie and Ken on the hotel floor. The afternoon sun streamed through the window. Mom was out somewhere. She tended to be gone most days and didn't want to take Sarah to daycare. She claimed that the other mothers were too judgmental.

There was a knock on the door.

Sarah got up. She stood on her tiptoes and looked through a peephole. It was blacked out.

Someone knocked again.

Sarah stayed quiet.

Knock. Knock. Knock. *"Room service."*

Sarah twisted the doorknob and opened it a crack.

The man was back. He was average-looking in every way and had a soft, non-threatening smile. *"Hi,"* he said, leaning down to her level. *"Is your mom home?"*

"You're not with room service," Sarah said, keeping the door cracked.

"You got me," the man said. *"I left something of mine here last week. It was my watch. May I get it?"*

"Wait here," Sarah closed the door.

She walked around the room, checking under the bed and bedside tables for the watch. Unable to find it, she opened the door again for the stranger. *"It's not here."*

"May I look?" the man asked.

"No one is allowed inside," Sarah replied.

The man shouldered into the door, bursting it open.

Sarah staggered back. *"Get out."*

"Relax. Just relax." The man closed the door behind him.

Sarah pulled the car over. She quickly opened the door and vomited into the ditch. She wiped her mouth with her sleeve. The taste of bile lingered. She spat. Being so close to the strip club brought back all that old junk from her past.

Instead of heading home, she made a split-second decision to visit a bar. She drank, danced, and screwed until she felt nothing. At 5 am, she drove home, almost crashing her vehicle twice. Still dressed, she fell into her bed and spent most of the day there. She'd be back to work tomorrow.

She got up at 2 pm. Her head pounded. She took a cold shower. Everything from the night before was a blur. *Good,* Sarah thought. She knew she was trapped in a self-destructive cycle, but didn't have any hope of breaking it. She sat in her bathtub, letting the cold water wash over her.

The man that had ruined her was still serving time. He had six years left. Julia never discussed the attack with Sarah after the fact. She was just happy that Sarah didn't get pregnant. Sarah lowered her head to her knees and pulled them close. Trembling from the cold, she wept. *Don't cry,* she told herself. *You're not a little girl. Don't cry.* Her body didn't listen.

She got out of the tub a few minutes later. After drying off, she got dressed in her civilian clothes. She drove by the police department. Hawkins's car wasn't there. She kept going, eventually passing by his house at the lake. He wasn't there either. Sarah thought about the pictures Clyde's uncle had taken. Reminded of a clue, she drove to the country club. She couldn't access the golf course the normal way and arrived at a hiking trail two miles away. Putting on the running shoes she kept in her civilian car's back seat, she took a jog through the woods. Winded, she arrived at the outskirts of the golf course. A ten-foot-tall fence surrounded the course. A few golf carts drove on the grass, avoiding the green.

Sarah followed the fence. At the second to last hole, she spotted Hawkins. He golfed with a few snowy-haired men. Sarah had seen them at police fundraising events and various business openings. She imagined that these were the folk that ran Hartwell. Sarah spied for a while, snapping a few photos of the men. She stayed until they finished before heading back.

Sarah sped up to the country club. It appeared Hawkins had already left. She followed the most logical path back to his house and saw his car there. There was nothing else she could do tonight.

She drove to the lake and sat on the grassy knoll. The water calmed her. A few families swam. Sarah shut her eyes and took a nap. A few hours later, she jolted awake. Grass was in hair. She spit out a little bug. "Gross."

Sick of wasting the day, she headed home and searched through local newspapers, finding pictures and names of Hawkins's golf buddies. She searched their names on the police database. Their records were spotless. As she suspected, they owned a lot of the local businesses. The chance that any of these men would rat on Hawkins was slim to none. Hawkins was a dying lead. Terry might've been the killer the whole time. Maybe Sarah just read him wrong.

That night, Sarah returned to the station and asked to see the evidence log for the Hartwell Huntsman. Alone in the evidence storage room, she sorted through the photos and evidence from the murders twenty years ago. She spent hours studying every shell casing, testimonial, and police report surrounding the case.

She sealed the box and put it back on the "Case Solved" shelf. Head down, she left the station. She'd be back on the beat tomorrow. After her shift, she'd check on Clyde.

19

TWIST OF FATE

Clyde gasped, as if he was breaching the surface of water just before drowning. The metal safe chilled his back. Panicked, he patted down his chest and stomach. No blood. No wound. Not even a hole in his shirt.

"Impossible," He mumbled.

Eyes wide, he scanned the basement. The masked man was gone. Clyde stood up, the contents of the file scattered around his feet. He twisted back to the safe, expecting to his body. Nothing. He pinched himself. He was fully awake and fully alive.

"What the hell?" He rubbed his hand up his scalp and kept it there. The pain of the gunshot, the sound of the bullet, it was all so real. He remembered tasting copper and feeling the blood roll over his fingertips. They were unstained. It was like his murder never happened.

The doorbell rang.

Clyde ignored it, still on high alert.

The doorbell rang again.

Leaving the file on the floor, he hiked up the steps. His

feet dragged. His mind raced. He needed an explanation, but nothing fit.

He opened the door before checking who it was.

Wearing her uniform, Sarah stood on the cinder-block step before him. A wry smile painted her face. "You really need to get your porch fixed."

Pathfinder heard Sarah's voice and bolted to her. Still disorientated, Clyde stepped aside, allowing Sarah to pet the husky.

"Who is a good girl? You are. You are!" Sarah rubbed her white and black fur. Clyde stared at the night sky. Sarah clearly saw him. He couldn't be a spirit.

"Are you going to invite me in?" Sarah asked.

"Oh, yeah. Sorry," Clyde moved aside.

Sarah entered. "You really cleaned up the inside of this place."

Clyde didn't reply. He buried his hands in his pockets.

"How are you holding up?" Sarah asked.

"Uh, fine," Clyde said.

"You don't sound like it," Sarah replied. "I heard you took a pretty good hit to the head."

"Multiple," Clyde replied.

"Concussions can be rough," Sarah replied. "They got you on any painkillers?"

"A few," Clyde replied. "What, uh, what are you doing here?"

"I'm glad to see you, too," Sarah said sarcastically.

Clyde replied, "I apologize. I'm just a little scatterbrained."

"Tell me about it," Sarah replied, sitting the couch. "Nothing has felt right since Terry's confession."

"Terry?" Clyde asked.

"The guy who almost killed you," Sarah replied.

"Oh," Clyde said.

"I know he killed Alana, but the rest of them doesn't seem likely. The guy had no logical motive," Sarah said. "His confession only hit the broad strokes. I get there is a twenty-year delay, but you don't forget something like that. You were following him that day? What made you think he was the killer?"

"Well—"

Clyde was interrupted as Elizabeth, Gena, John, and Tommy stepped out of the dark hallway and kitchen. They glared at Clyde. Their angry gazes silently cried out for justice.

Sarah blinked at Clyde. She turned to where he was staring, not seeing anything. "What?"

Clyde lost his voice.

Out from the darkened hallway stepped a fifth person. He wore a red mask and all camo. He held the rifle in both hands but wasn't aiming at anything. Through his tattered holes cut in the face of his mask, his dead, dry eyes watched Clyde.

Clyde trembled. He took a step back. "No, you..."

Sarah was alarmed. "Clyde. You're freaking me out."

The man in the mask shouldered through the rest of the dead and approached Clyde. He stood a foot away from him. Chill bumps rose all over Clyde's body. The killer was unmoving and unblinking.

Sarah eyed Clyde. "You need to talk to me, man."

Clyde slowly turned to her, the terror visible in his eyes. "There was a fifth victim."

"Yes, Alana," Sarah said. "You want to have a seat?"

Clyde said, "Not Alana. A fifth victim from the camp side massacre."

Sarah drew her eyebrows together in confusion. "All the bodies were recovered."

"You have to trust me, Sarah."

"Trust you?" Sarah stood up. "You need to start talking, Clyde. First the skeletons, then finding Terry, and now this new victim crap? Where are you getting your information? What are you not telling me? Don't just stand there. Speak up."

"I see them!" Clyde blurted out. He immediately wished he could take back his words.

Sarah didn't have any words at first. She then asked with extreme suspicion. "Who?"

"Forget it," Clyde said, breaking eye contact.

The five dead stood all around the room. The masked man was right there, still a foot away.

"No. You're not chickening out of this," Sarah said, nearing Clyde. "And don't blame it on your head injury either. You were acting weird even before your morgue episode."

Clyde said, "I see them." He glanced at each teen. "Gena, Tommy, John, Elizabeth. The fifth one."

Sarah looked at him like he was crazy.

Clyde tried to explain. "Ever since I got here, I sensed something was different, and one night they just showed up. That's how I knew what they were wearing when they died and where the skeletons were located. They helped me. In exchange, I help them."

"How much medication are you on?" Sarah asked.

"You wanted the truth. That's the truth," Clyde said.

"Spirits? You're talking to spirits?" Sarah asked.

Clyde nodded.

"This is unbelievable," Sarah mumbled. She wanted to leave.

"I'm not lying, Sarah," Clyde said. "They're right here."

"How come I can't see them?" Sarah asked.

"I don't—I don't have the answer to that," Clyde said. "Elizabeth, show her that you're here."

The ghost didn't move.

"Please," Clyde begged.

Elizabeth walked up to the lamp beside the couch, picked it up, and tossed it against the wall. Clyde flinched as it smacked the drywall. Sarah was unfazed and more confused.

"Didn't you see?" Clyde asked.

"See what?"

Clyde walked to the broken lamp. He took a knee and picked it up. Turning back, he presented it to her.

Sarah looked in horror. "You're joking with me."

"You see it now, right?"

"There is nothing in your hands, Clyde," Sarah said.

Clyde glanced down. His hands were empty. The lamp was back up in its original position, completely undamaged.

Sarah approached him. "You want to go to the hospital?"

"No, no! I'm not—" Clyde eyed the ghosts around him. He spoke calmly. "I'm not crazy. It was a... a bad joke. It's not very funny now, come to think about it."

"It's not funny at all," Sarah said bluntly.

Clyde stood up. "It's getting dark out."

Sarah scoffed. "You want me to leave?"

Clyde didn't reply. He could barely look at her. *I'm not crazy. I know I'm not.* Doubt seeped into him.

Sarah said, "Let's get some help, Clyde."

"No, I'm fine," Clyde mumbled.

She approached him, putting a hand on his arm. "Clyde."

He recoiled at her touch. He locked eyes with her. "You've got to believe me, Sarah."

Sarah scrutinized him. She sensed he was telling the truth. Or at least what he thought was true.

Clyde pinched the bridge of his nose. "We can go around

and around all day. Nothing is going to change what I saw. What I see."

"So you admit to being crazy?" Sarah asked.

Clyde shrugged.

Sarah took a deep breath. "I'm going to get a drink."

She walked to the kitchen.

Clyde sat on the edge of the recliner. He bowed his head and shut his eyes. After a few seconds, Sarah returned.

Clyde opened his eyes and the dead had vanished. *Strange.*

Sarah handed him a glass of scotch.

Clyde nursed it. He wasn't a heavy drinker.

Sarah sat on the couch nearby. She took a sip of her glass. "So... like, this fifth victim. What does he look like?"

"Average guy," Clyde replied. "He wears a red mask. It's made of stitched cloth and has holes cut out where the eyes are. Strangely enough, he has the same model rifle that killed the others."

"You're saying that he's the killer?" Sarah asked, trying to follow.

"I thought so at first, but Alana passed on when Terry was arrested. The rest of the dead haven't. I don't know the rules of sending them beyond this world, but they're after justice. I believe that can only happen if the killer is apprehended."

"They want you to find the real killer and prove it was him, even after he died," Sarah filled in the blanks, trying her best not to judge her friend as crazy.

"Maybe, or the killer had an accomplice," Clyde theorized.

"I never thought of that," Sarah said.

They sat in silence for a long moment.

Sarah finished her glass. "Well, I stopped by here tonight to tell you that I'm done with the case."

"Is that still true?" Clyde asked.

"I don't know," Sarah said. "I certainly don't believe in ghosts."

"What do you believe?"

"I never put much thought into that," Sarah replied. "Some big questions we aren't supposed to know."

"I don't know about that," Clyde replied. "The truth is out there. We have to dig for it."

Sarah set his glass aside and leaned back in the couch. "I guess we better get our shovels."

Clyde was shocked she was still with him.

Sarah herself was unsure why she took him up on his offer. Ghosts, God, the supernatural, she hardly believed in any of it. Yet, Clyde knew things he should've never known. Out of every explanation, it was the only one that made sense. She kept her opinion to herself. She didn't trust him anymore. This could be a sort of con. If not for his age, she'd suspect him to be the killer. His Uncle Andrew wasn't out of the equation yet. That could be his inside source.

Sarah went home that night. Clyde waved her goodbye and locked the door. He thought about his next course of action. Sarah could get a list of local death records and see who else died around the time of the killings. Strangely enough, the rest of the victims looked like how they did on the day they were murdered, meaning that this man was killed wearing a mask. Clyde didn't see any bullet holes on the front half of his body. He'd need to check behind him.

Clyde lay in his bed, fingers locked behind his head. Solving the murder was one thing. Figuring out the paranormal phenomenon was another. He'd go to local churches tomorrow. Maybe they'd have answers. It wasn't much of a lead, but it was a start.

The next morning, Clyde used the local town map and website to contact and schedule a meeting with the various pastors around town. Sarah had work during the day, but she was happy to run the death records. There were a handful of other males that died that same year as the rest of the victims. She planned on visiting their loved ones on her own time.

Clyde got an Uber and arrived at the first two churches. He tried to get information on the supernatural, but they didn't have much to offer him. The last was a small church in a tin building. It looked like a storage garage, but longer and wider. The chairs inside were mismatched and likely donated. Christmas lights were strung down the wall's sanctuary. The platform had an electric guitar, keyboard, and large drum set along with a set of RGB lights above. In the middle of the afternoon, they were all turned off at the moment. Clyde found a man kneeling before the cross at the platform.

"Pastor Murry?" Clyde asked, stopping a few yards away.

The man stood and turned around. He was in his forties and short. The hair on the sides of his head was faded and pulled into a short manbun on top. He wore a maroon button-down shirt, skinny jeans, and boat shoes. He greeted Clyde with a smile and handshake.

"You can call me Murr," the pastor said.

Clyde glanced around the room. "Before today, I haven't been to a church in ages."

"Bad experiences?" Murr asked.

"Just busy," Clyde said.

"I get you," Murr said. "I work full-time at a pest control company to keep this place afloat."

He sat at the edge of the platform and gestured for Clyde to sit.

"Interesting place. Do you not have many people come through?" Clyde asked, sitting down next to him.

"We have a fair amount. Most of them are college kids. They're good, though. If there is one thing I know, it's that you don't need a lot of people to make an impact. You just need the right ones," Murr said. "Anyway, tell me a little about yourself, Clyde."

"I'm a lawyer from Atlanta," Clyde said.

"Nice."

"Single. Thirty years old. I drove over here to clean up my uncle's house. He recently passed, and the house needs to be put back on the market."

"I'm sorry for your loss," Murr replied.

"Don't be. I barely knew the guy," said Clyde.

"What got you interested in coming here?"

Clyde took a breath. "You believe in God, right?"

"I'd be in big trouble if I didn't," Murr said, chuckling.

"So what about the supernatural?" Clyde asked.

Murr gestured to the room. "It's all around us. I believe God is always doing something. We just have to have eyes to see."

I have them, Clyde thought to himself. "What about ghosts?"

Murr replied, "I don't believe in them."

"But you believe in the supernatural?"

"Of course, I believe in angels, demons, and the Holy Spirit. Jesus himself dwells inside of us who invited him. That's purely supernatural--"

"But not the spirits of the dead?" Clyde asked.

"Maybe there is purgatory. Some Catholic sects seem to believe so. Have you had experiences?" Murr asked.

"Yeah," Clyde admitted ashamedly.

"What are they like?"

"I see the dead. They talk to me sometimes," Clyde replied, realizing how crazy he sounded.

Still, Murr's look was without judgment.

Clyde continued, "Those teenagers that were killed all those years ago. They came to me and wanted my help." Clyde proceeded to tell him about finding the skeletons, stopping Terry, and the crazy experience at the morgue.

The pastor listened to his every word, not once interrupting.

Clyde felt good to unload. It went a lot smoother than with Sarah.

When he finished, Murr remarked, "That is quite the story."

Clyde was sitting, his legs parted, elbows resting on his thighs and his hands locked together. He stared at the concrete floor. "I'm not sure what to do."

"I'm not sure either," Murr admitted.

"Aren't you the expert?" Clyde asked.

"I'm a man like everyone else," Murr answered. "I don't know anything. I wish I did, but every day I discover something about God or the universe."

Murr sensed Clyde's disappointment. He said, "When I was younger, I had a similar experience to yours, but with night terrors. They were intense. I felt like I was pinned to my bed and had something invisible squeezing my throat. I was horrified and defenseless. One day, I got so desperate I just started saying Jesus over and over. And bam! They stopped. A few months later, I wake up late at night and see these dark figures standing around my bed. They're like shadows with little red eyes. They stared at me. One reached out to touch me. The Jesus thing worked again. With your situation, I don't know the answer. I'd like to say you're encountering demons. If so, Jesus is the answer to that too."

"They aren't malevolent," Clyde retorted.

"Have they tried to hurt you?"

Clyde was hesitant to answer. "Yeah, but the injuries weren't long-lasting."

"What exactly do they want you to do?" Murr asked.

"Find their killer."

"And then what?" Murr asked.

"Capture him, I guess."

Murr stroked his chin. "Hmmm."

"Are you sure there is nothing you can do, like show me a book or pray?" Clyde asked.

"I could do both," Murr said, "But it may not be the answer you are looking for."

"Well, I should probably get going then," Clyde stood.

"Hey, don't go running off just yet," said Murr.

Clyde listened.

"I want to help you through this," Murr said.

"Okay?" Clyde asked hesitantly.

"You mentioned your uncle passing away. Who was he?" Murr asked.

"Andrew Barker. He took his own life a few weeks ago," Clyde said.

"Andrew…" Murr said, thinking. His eyes widened. "Wait. *That* Andrew?"

"I don't know another one," Clyde replied.

"I heard rumors about him," Murr said. "He was also looking into those teenagers' deaths."

I know. Clyde thought.

Murr replied, "He never came to the church personally, but one of the members had a prayer request for him. He said that he was starting to lose his mind, namely talking to people who weren't there."

"So this ability I have might be genetic?" Clyde asked.

"That, or a psychological deficiency," Murr concluded.

"*Tomato,* Tomahto," Clyde replied. "Who was the person that wanted prayer for him?"

"Donald Fegan," Murr replied. "His nephew is a regular here."

Don knew that Andrew was seeing ghosts? Why didn't he tell me? Then again, that's not something that tends to get brought up in normal conversation.

Murr noticed his concerned look. "Clyde."

"Yeah..."

"I want to you to know that I'm here to help if there is anything I can do for you," Murr said. "I lost Andrew, though I never knew who he was. I won't make the same mistake."

"Thanks, Pastor." Clyde checked his watch. "I should get going."

"Can I call you sometime?" Murr asked.

Clyde gave him his cellphone and allowed Murr to type in his name and number. He texted Murr his information.

"If these spirits tell you to do something you're not comfortable with, let me know," Murr replied.

"Will do," Clyde said, "And thank you."

"Before you go, let's pray."

Clyde sat down beside him. He bowed his head. Murr lifted his hands and closed his eyes. "Father God..."

After they finished, Clyde left. He hadn't seen anyone pray like Murr before. It was passionate, raw, and felt really long. He wasn't the spiritual guide Clyde had hoped for, but he was a good guy.

In the church parking lot, Clyde called Don as he waited for his Uber. It rang a few times before the man answered.

"Clyde, how are you?" Don asked.

"Could be better," Clyde said. "How's the trip?"

"Business is business. I heard about the murder. Sick

stuff. I'm glad to see the killer was apprehended. A little bird at the police station told me you helped out."

"It was chance, really," Clyde lied.

Don replied, "I'm sorry about your car, but I'm glad you're okay."

"Me too," Clyde said. "When are you coming back into town?"

"In a while. It always takes time with these certain deals," Don replied. "I have a feeling you didn't just call to check in?"

"I was hoping we could talk about Andrew," Clyde said. "I heard from a source that he wasn't all there in the end. That he started having visions. Can you confirm that?"

"Yeah, he, uh, said he talked to dead people," Don said awkwardly.

"You never told me."

"I didn't want to tarnish the man's legacy," Don replied. "The truth eventually comes out though."

"What did these ghosts say to him?" Clyde asked.

"I dunno. I never cared to ask. I thought by not playing along with his insanity, it would go away…" Don went silent.

"Is there anything else you can share about his time leading up to his death?" Clyde asked.

Don replied, "He had this theory that the killer was still around. By the way he looked at me, I say he suspected me." He chuckled.

"Why would he do that?" Clyde asked.

"No one is spotless, Clyde. I'm no exception," Don said. "Murders that old could link back to anyone. That's what happens when there is not enough conclusive evidence."

"Still, he must've thought you had some sort of motive to make accusations like that," Clyde said, hoping to get answers.

"The man wasn't right in the head," Don said. "We can't trust anything he said or thought."

"You don't even have a theory?" Clyde asked.

"I don't," Don said firmly. "And that's a season of my life I don't plan on revisiting."

Unable to get any more information out of Don, Clyde changed the subject. "Did Andrew ever go to anyone to get answers for his *Spiritual Awakening?*"

Don thought about it. "I believe he mentioned visiting a shaman of sorts. Hartwell used to be the center of the world for the Cherokee Indians. All their roads led here. The man runs a spiritual shop on the outskirts of town. Look up Natural Herbs and Remedies. You'll find it."

Clyde made that his next destination. He swung back to the house to get Pathfinder. The dog needed some fresh air.

The Uber took Clyde fifteen miles outside of Hartwell and to a small shop on the lakefront. Tall trees and colorful honeysuckle bushes created a wall on either side of the road ending at the dockside building. With all the charm of the New Orleans bayou bait shop, it had an A-frame roof and washed-out wooden walls. Bushels of herbs dangled from the covered porch.

Her tongue dangling out of her open smile, Pathfinder walked alongside Clyde. She curiously turned her head back and forth and sniffed the grass by the entrance. Beyond the hut, a lake was visible. The water around this part was mucky and shallow, only good for canoes and kayaks. The docks from other homes jutted out into the water. Most were in disrepair. This wasn't what you'd see advertised on a Hartwell Lake brochure.

Clyde reached the front door. He fell a small pull on his back. He turned around, seeing a goat on the trail behind him. A crown of dry vines topped its head and dark blood oozed out of its slashed throat.

Out from the woods stepped five more goats, wearing similar crowns and having cut throats. Pathfinder didn't notice them. Clyde had never seen an animal like this before. His mind raced. Why was he seeing these goats and not other dead animals? Were they killed in ritual sacrifice? Was that why they were still around? It looked like something the occult would do, not the friendly Cherokee. Sickened by the sight, Clyde twisted around and entered the shop.

The pungent scent of herbs and spices assaulted Clyde's sense as he stepped on the inner welcome mat. Glass jars full of roots and vegetables lined a self against the wall. Seed packets dangled on a rack. Little plants grew on flowerpots. There was a wooden bucket full of different rocks and crystals. A line of beads streamed over the doorway behind the desk. Voice chatted in the room beyond.

A moment later, an old woman stepped out. Short and plump like a tomato, she had silvery-white hair, a red wrinkled face, and chapped lips. She wore a half dozen necklaces, some decorated with beads and other crystals. Her tiny eyes seemed like they were shut as she gazed up at Clyde.

"Hey," Clyde said awkwardly.

A tall Native American stepped out behind the woman. His silver hair flowed down his broad shoulders. His face was square and hard like a brick. The man looked as if he never smiled a day in his life. The odd couple stared at Clyde as if he interrupted something very important.

"I need to talk to you," Clyde said, bouncing his gaze between them. "Which of you owns the shop?"

The woman said, "What is this about?"

"A sale, most like," the man said to the woman, though he kept his dark, beady eyes on Clyde.

"Not this one," the woman wagged her finger at Clyde. "He wants something else."

Clyde cleared his throat. "My uncle stopped by here some time ago. He was looking for a shaman."

"Why?" the man asked sternly.

"Answers," Clyde answered. "He could see—"

"The dead," the man finished.

His response shook Clyde. "You know him?"

The man shook his head. "No, but I see *it* in you. You have the Gift."

20

SOUL TRAIN

Clyde brought the wooden bowl to his lips and sipped the herbal tea. The taste of grass and leaves swirled around his tongue. He sat crossed-legged on the hardwood floor. Storage shelves of strange relics and Cherokee antiques lined two walls of the shop's back room. A table supporting different mortars and pestles pressed against the third wall. The fourth had the "door" of string beads. The round woman sat to Clyde's left. Her beefy legs were crossed. She sipped her own bowl as she eyed Clyde. Much like the spirits of the dead, her expression was unreadable and she rarely blinked.

The beads parted, making a soft rattle, as the Native American man returned from locking the front door. He sat on the floor facing Clyde. Frogs croaked outside.

"I'm Clyde, by the way," Clyde said.

"Sequoyah," the man replied in his natural baritone voice.

"Waya," the woman introduced herself.

"Very good tea," Clyde said politely as he set it aside.

Clyde waited for Sequoyah to speak, seeing what else he knew.

Sequoyah said stoically, "If you have questions, ask."

Clyde had a lot. He started with the basics. "What is this Gift?"

"A curse," Sequoyah replied.

Clyde didn't like the sound of that. "Then why call it the Gift?"

"It is a gift to the dead, but a bane to the living," Sequoyah said. "When did it start?"

"When I moved into my uncle's house."

"Not before as a child?" Sequoyah asked.

Clyde fidgeted. "I don't remember much of my childhood prior to my parents' deaths… Do you know how to stop it?"

Waya cackled.

The joke was lost on Clyde.

Sequoyah said, "Once the Gift has blossomed, it can't be stopped."

"Have you tried?" Clyde asked.

"Yes," Sequoyah said, but his harsh tone was a hint that he didn't want to explain more.

Clyde said, "Great. You still haven't told me exactly what it is."

Sequoyah replied, "A few individuals get the ability to help the wayward dead cross to the other side. The nature of the Gift is to sense the dead, to see them and experience their final hours."

"To what end?"

"Bringing justice to those who wronged them."

"Makes sense," Clyde said as Sequoyah confirmed his theory.

The Native American man held up three fingers. "The Gift has three tiers." He lowered his ring finger. "The Sense: that strange chill you feel when They are near or danger is approaching." He lowered his middle finger. "The Vision:

seeing and interacting with the dead." He lowered his pointer finger. "The Reality: living out the victim's death. This is the most dangerous power and should be used sparingly."

Sense, Vision, Reality. Clyde committed them to memory. "Do you have the Gift too?"

"No," Sequoyah said.

Clyde gestured to Waya. "What about her?"

"Neither does she," Sequoyah said.

"Then how do you know about it?" Clyde asked.

"Legend, stories, and dreams," Sequoyah said.

Clyde was hoping for a real mentoring, but talking to this man was like having a professor who spent all his years in academia with no hands-on experience. "Do you know the origin of this Gift?"

Waya said, "From times of old, people have exhibited similar traits."

"Like who?"

"Their names are forgotten. Only the dead remember," Waya replied.

"It's a rather unrewarding calling then," Clyde replied.

Sequoyah nodded soberly. "It is your fate nonetheless. I can see in your eyes you've already decided to embrace it."

"What other choice do I have?"

Waya replied, "Your uncle chose otherwise."

"You spoke to Andrew?" Clyde asked.

"He stopped in once," Waya said.

Clyde turned to Sequoyah. "What did he say?"

"I was not in town," Sequoyah said. "Hartwell is not my home. Andrew spoke to Waya."

Waya said, "We discussed the nature of his Gifting. He could not accept it. A few weeks later, he joined the dead."

Clyde lowered his eyes. He wondered if he would share a similar fate.

"Be discouraged," Sequoyah said.

Clyde replied, "Uh, what? Don't you mean encouraged?"

Sequoyah replied soberly. "The moment you accept the full reality of your calling, you will be able to embrace it. It will be joyless most of the time, but you will change the tide of history. Lives will be saved by what you do, but no one will remember you or sing your praise. You'll suffer harm and be isolated from those you love. At the end of it all, you will most likely die alone."

Clyde rubbed his brow. "Don't be a salesman."

"I will speak truthfully. If you chose to follow your uncle's path, I will not fault you," Sequoyah said.

Clyde thought about leaving. Calling to mind the faces of Elizabeth, Gena, Tommy, and John, he stayed put and awaited more wisdom. "Who else has this Gift?"

"I know of another," Sequoyah said.

"Can I call them?"

"No, you will be a distraction to her," Sequoyah said.

"Thanks," Clyde said sarcastically. "I do want to meet this person."

"Ten thousand," Waya said.

"What?" Clyde exclaimed.

"Ten thousand dollars and we'll let you speak to her," Waya said.

Clyde laughed.

The odd couple was dead serious.

"Hell no," Clyde said.

"Then we can't help you," Waya said.

Sequoyah said, "If you're serious about this calling, you will find the money."

"And if you were serious about helping the world, you'd work for free," Clyde said.

Sequoyah glared at him.

Clyde shook his head. "Ten grand. Unbelievable."

"You will be back," Sequoyah said.

"Unlikely," Clyde said spitefully. He pushed aside the beads and exited. In a huff of rage, he jogged down the steps. He untied Pathfinder's collar from the porch post and called his Uber.

"Ten thousand," he grumbled. "Are they nuts?"

He went home and spent the rest of the afternoon walking around Andrew's property. Pathfinder rushed ahead of him, chasing after a bird.

Clyde searched the house, trying to find anything of Andrew's that hinted at his Gifting. He looked for a journal but found nothing. A few of his uncle's books were religious texts. Seated at his uncle's desk, Clyde leafed through the pages of the Holy Bible, Indian Sanskrit, and a dozen other manuscripts. Certain passages regarding spirituality and removal of different spirits were highlighted. Nothing led Clyde to believe that Andrew found the exact answers he was looking for. Disappointed by his search, Clyde checked Andrew's closet. He found old photographs of his uncle and a beautiful woman. In the same stack of photos, he found a pamphlet for a woman's funeral. There were a number of newspaper clippings pointing to a hit and run. The woman was tall and slender. She had a small smile, almost mischievous-like. By the looks of it, she was the love of Andrew's life. In a different life, their romance could've gone somewhere.

Clyde was reminded of his past love. He had a girlfriend a few years ago, but she got too close. She blamed him for not opening up to her. He tried to go beyond surface-level platitudes and conversations, but he struggled to make sense of his parents' deaths. No amount of therapy helped him. He shut that door to his life, not even allowing himself to look back. Now, he thought about Sarah. She had a beautiful smile and great personality, though perhaps was a little fast-paced for Clyde. Nevertheless, intimacy seemed very surface-level with her. Maybe Clyde was old school, but he only needed one woman to complete him. If she was the right one, the rest didn't matter. With the Gift, he wondered if he'd ever be able to find anyone.

Clyde put away his uncle's things and headed into the basement. He opened the safe and eyed his parents' file. Andrew might've left hints to clues inside. Clyde stopped himself from reaching for it. One case was too much for him now. He closed the vault and focused on the Hartwell Huntsman.

He sat on the couch. National news discussed Terry's trial. He entered a plea deal, confessing to all five murders. *Liar,* Clyde thought bitterly.

He checked the time. It was past 9 pm. Sarah should be off work. He debated calling her. He reviewed his suspect list. He couldn't rule any out, but there was one person that he still needed to research: the man in the red mask.

Clyde searched the web for any disappearances that occurred the same year of the massacre. The computer screen reflected in his bloodshot eyes. He took a few more pain pills. He felt the Sense. Looking over his shoulder, he saw the man in the red mask a few yards away. He held the rifle in his gloved hands. Clyde swiveled the chair around to face him. His heart rate quickened. The man's rifle still terrified him, even if it couldn't take his life. Clyde stood up slowly.

The man was completely still. His eyes stared through the hole in his mask. Clyde neared him, trembling just being at such close proximity to the man.

"Let me..." Clyde extended his arm to the man's face. His

fingers phased through him. Clyde withdrew his hand. "I need to see your face."

The man stayed silent.

Clyde tried to reach through again but got the same result. Clyde circled around the man, finding a small bullet hole in the back of his head. Clyde's stomach churned. The hole wasn't much larger than the width of his pinky. *9mm,* Clyde concluded.

The masked man stared at him, unblinking.

"What do you want?" Clyde asked.

The man did not react to him.

"Anything I can give you, I will. Just ask," Clyde said. He tried to grab the mask again.

Resting the rifle on his shoulder, the man suddenly grabbed Clyde's hand. He squeezed his fingers. Clyde's bones cracked. He cried out and dropped to a knee. The man squeezed harder. The agony shot down through his wrist. Clyde struggled to pull away, but the man's hold was unbreakable.

"Let go!" Clyde cried.

Using his free hand, the man tilted the rifle down at Clyde. He pressed the barrel against Clyde's chest.

"Please," Clyde begged.

Cold metal pressed against Clyde's skin.

Sweat dotted Clyde's forehead. "You want me to help you or not!?"

The spirit tossed the rifle aside. It clacked on the hardwood floor. Hand now free, the man grabbed the crown of his mask and removed it from his face, revealing the young man beneath. He couldn't have been older than twenty-five. Acne dotted the sides of his forehead. He had a hooked nose and long face. He looked almost like H.P. Lovecraft. He released Clyde's hand. Clyde fell back. His broken hand trembled. The pain was unbearable.

Clyde shut his eyes. After ten seconds, he reopened them. The pain was gone. His fingers were back to normal. He took a deep breath. Staying on the floor, he pulled out his cellphone and called Sarah.

"Clyde, I've been meaning to call you," Sarah said. "Hawkins promoted me today. He was so happy with the case, he thought that a raise wasn't enough."

"Congrats," Clyde said, though his mind was elsewhere. "I saw the fifth victim's face."

"How?"

"Doesn't matter. I need your help to identify him," Clyde said.

"I'm still at the office. Let me take a look."

"I searched everything for the year of the massacre, but I'm thinking he died afterward," Clyde said.

"Describe him."

Clyde did so to the best of his ability. Sarah searched through a number of deceased persons and photographed ones that matched the man's physical attributes. She sent them ot Clyde.. Staying on the line, Clyde swiped through them.

"None of these guys," Clyde said.

"Give me a sec," Sarah replied.

"Where are you going?"

"To get a coffee," Sarah replied.

They spent the next forty minutes going through hundreds of deceased locals in and around Hartwell in the few years after the massacre. Nothing Sarah sent Clyde matched the man's face. "What if he wasn't confirmed died? What if he just went missing?"

Sarah followed his hunch. An hour later and she got a match. Clyde reviewed Sarah's text. It showed the missing person's info along with a picture of his unsmiling face. Twenty-four years old, unmarried, and last seen in Hartwell three years after the massacre, Glen Iving went missing after a two-day vacation. His friend Catherine Barnes reported his absence.

"Well, that's interesting," Clyde said.

"Wasn't Glen Cathy's alibi?" Sarah asked.

"That's what she said. I say we pay Cathy another visit," Clyde replied.

"Agreed," Sarah said. "Call her and ask what time we can visit."

"You got it."

They ended the call. Clyde studied Glen's face. If he was the killer and already dead, how did he tie into this whole mess? The next night, Sarah and Clyde went to Cathy's home.

Cathy greeted Clyde and Sarah at the door.

She invited them to dine outside in her impressive garden. Plants grew tall and vibrant. Flowers of all types swayed in the wind. They sat around a stone table with elegantly engraved flowers curved into the rim. She poured them glasses of white wine.

Sarah got straight to business. "We wanted to talk to you about Glen Iving."

"He and I were good friends as I said before. He'd visit often. The age gap between us never bothered me," Cathy explained.

"And you were with him on the night of the killings?" Clyde asked.

"I was."

"Was there anyone else with you?"

"Just us," Cathy replied. "We were spending time in this

very garden. It wasn't as lively back then. And before you get too scandalized, Glen and I were not romantically involved. He might have wished we were at times, but that was not a step I was interested in taking."

"So you two spent the whole night here?" Sarah asked suspiciously.

"Not the whole night. Glen left at some point."

"Do you remember the time?" Sarah asked.

"It was twenty years ago, Officer. I was sixteen," Cathy said.

Clyde said, "You never told us that you were the one to report Glen's absence."

"Oh, that." Cathy sipped her wine. "His family cared little for him. They wanted him out of their lives and his absence was a blessing to them. I knew something was wrong though. If he left town, he would've told me. I filed the police report. They looked for a few days but gave up quickly. A real pity if you ask me."

"Did you know anyone who'd want to harm Glen?" Clyde asked.

Cathy replied, "There were a lot of people. He'd been caught stalking a few young women before and would steal metal from people to sell as scrap. The man wasn't well-liked."

Sarah said, "You don't seem too beat up by his disappearance."

"My time for mourning ended seventeen years ago," Cathy said. She lifted her glasses. "To lost loved ones. May we never forget them."

They toasted.

Cathy said, "Now, let's talk about something less cynical. You start, Clyde. What are your big plans now that your time at Hartwell is coming to a close?"

Clyde sipped his glass. He hated changing conversations. "I don't know yet. Going back to my attorney's office is the most likely scenario, but it's hard to say."

Sarah got annoyed. "I still have questions about Glen."

"What else do you want to know?" Cathy asked, faking a smile.

"You said that he stalked some young women. When did that happen?" Sarah asked.

"I hardly remember. Post-graduation maybe."

"Do you know who he went after?"

"No, but the boyfriends never filed a police report. They beat up Glen. He lost two teeth," Cathy said.

"Can you give me any more details?"

"I'm afraid I can't," Cathy said.

"Did he ever try to hurt you?"

"Never," Cathy said. "I was his princess. He'd do whatever I say." She brought her glass to her lips and sipped.

Sarah eyed her. "Like killing some people you don't like."

Cathy chuckled, nearly spilling her wine. "You think I'm behind this?"

"Are you?" Sarah asked.

Cathy replied, "No. Hell no. Terry whats-his-name admitted to the murders. You were the one who apprehended him."

Sarah was quiet.

"Unless you are lying," Cathy said. "Maybe I should talk to the Chief of Police and see if he wants to reopen the case."

Sarah boiled.

Clyde spoke up. "No need for that."

Cathy re-crossed her legs and relaxed her posture. "If I didn't know any better, I'd say you two came over here to interrogate me. That's not very polite."

Clyde response, "We're just talking about Glen because

Sarah wants to make a concerted effort to find him. With one cold case already closed, we thought it would be nice to investigate another."

"That's very kind of her," Cathy replied. "I don't understand what this has to do with the murders."

Sarah replied, "Maybe nothing at all. Or perhaps the Huntsman killed Glen too."

"My, that's horrible," Cathy shuttered. "I guess you'll have to ask Terry."

Clyde said, "Was Glen acting normal before he vanished?"

Cathy replied, "Now that I think about it, he wanted to get away from Hartwell. He was tired of his reputation. Could he have killed himself?"

"Someone would've discovered the body," Clyde said.

"Hartwell has a big lake," Cathy said.

Sarah asked, "Did Glen like to dress up?"

"What do you mean?" Cathy asked.

"Did he ever wear a costume or mask for any reason?" Sarah asked.

"That's an odd thing to ask," Cathy remarked.

"Did he wear a mask at all?" Clyde asked.

"I don't think so. I never saw him in one." She looked at the two like they were crazy. "All this talk is freaking me out. Can we discuss something normal?"

They spent the next half hour talking about useless things. On the ride back home, Sarah said, "She's holding something back."

"I know," Clyde replied. "But we don't have any evidence to pin anything on her."

Sarah said, "She mentioned Hartwell Lake. Any chance you could look for the body?"

"I might be able to get Glen to help me."

"Man, this whole ghost thing is something else," Sarah replied.

"Imagine how I feel," Clyde said.

They rented a boat at 5 am the next morning. Morning fog rested over the lake. The renter gave Sarah a discount for her services to the town. Sarah only had two hours before work, so they had to move quickly. Clyde sat up front. He held an extendable pole. Sarah steered. She hadn't driven a boat in a few years and was rusty. After ten minutes out in the water, she got the hang of it.

Hartwell Lake had an area of eighty-seven miles. They wouldn't be able to cover it all. The dingy fishing boat cut through the water, leaving behind a nice wake. The morning sun still hadn't risen. There was no one on the waters. They followed the area of the lake. Clyde kept a watchful eye and also let the Sense guide him. He focused intently, feeling a slight pull to the center of the lake. He pointed Sarah that way. He was surprised that she trusted him. If she had told him that she had the Gift, he probably wouldn't believe it.

The Sense grew stronger as they got to the center of the lake. Eventually, they reached a point where Clyde was completely covered in chill bumps. He raised his fist, gesturing for Sarah to stop. She put the boat in idle. Clyde shined a flashlight over the water. He saw a woman two feet below the surface. She wore a white dress that moved under the water. She was probably in her forties.

"There is a dead woman down there," Clyde said.

Sarah replied, "Okay…"

"Middle-aged. Strangulation marks around her throat," Clyde said.

"But no Glen."

The dead women opened her eyes, locking onto Clyde. He felt her Marking his soul with her gaze. He couldn't break eye contact. It felt like claws were tearing through his soul. The woman was tormented. "Get a few officers out here. Her remains are down there."

"But Glen."

"He can wait," Clyde barked. "This woman needs our help."

He sensed her pain and hurt. The woman had been betrayed, left here like trash. Sarah asked Clyde. "What should I tell the officers?"

"Anonymous tip," Clyde said.

"They'll want to check the phone records," Sarah said.

"Tell them you've got a hunch then," Clyde said.

"I don't like lying, Clyde," Sarah said.

"How else are you going to convince them to canvas the lake?" Clyde asked.

Sarah grumbled. She pulled out her walkie. "Hey, it's Sully. I got something you might be interested in."

"Go ahead, over," Hawkins replied, yawning.

"I received a letter this morning. An anonymous sender told us about a woman's remains at the bottom of the Hartwell."

"Bring in the letter when your shift starts. We'll talk about our next steps from there."

"Sound likes a plan. See you soon. Over and out." Sarah put away the walkie-talkie. "You better put together a letter real quick."

They cruised through the lake for thirty minutes. The Sense kept pulling Clyde back to the same woman. She needed to get cleared out of here before anything else happened.

They returned to the boat rental place. Sarah dropped Clyde off at his house. He used gloves to load fresh paper into his printer, typed a letter, printed it, and sealed it in a Ziploc bag. He gave it to Sarah. "Tell me how it goes."

"You'll hear soon enough," She replied.

Clyde stayed at home. He took a morning jog. It was more like a power walk. His ankle didn't hurt as bad, but the rest of his body was still recovering. He wondered who this new woman was. He didn't want to bother with another case, but if this Gift was his calling, he didn't want to neglect her either.

Three hours later, Sarah set him a text. *Divers in the lake. Don't make me out to be an idiot plz.*

No promises, Clyde messaged back.

By mid-afternoon, Sarah called Clyde. "We got it."

Clyde stopped fixing his bedroom dresser and said, "The woman?"

"Two skeletons. One male. One female. And they were discovered within twenty feet of each other. Bricks anchored them "

"Who is the guy?" Clyde asked.

"We're going to find out," Sarah said. "It may take Forensics a few days. Hawkins is pissed. He really didn't want there to be more murders in Hartwell."

"Too bad," Clyde replied. "We'll clean this town one body at a time if we have to."

They met at the local bar after Sarah's shift. The place was packed.

Sarah explained that male's skull was found with a 9mm bullet hole in the back of his head.

"That's Glen," Clyde said.

"You sure?"

"I saw the bullet hole myself," Clyde replied.

"Well, I'll be," Sarah said. "Who is the other girl?"

Clyde shrugged. "I haven't seen her since the lake. Maybe she'll stop by and I can get some answers."

"This is crazy," Sarah said.

"Yeah, another body this soon," Clyde replied.

"That, but also you."

"Thanks," Clyde said dryly.

"I didn't mean it that way," Sarah said, "All this supernatural stuff has my head spinning. No offense, but why you?"

"Fate, maybe," Clyde said. "I learned that my uncle had it too."

Sarah's eyes widened.

Clyde continued, "He couldn't handle it. That's why he took his own life."

Sarah cursed.

Clyde watched the football game replaying on TV. "It really puts things in perspective."

"I'd say," Sarah replied. "I never thought much of the afterlife. I believe... believed that this life was all we had, and we had to make it work. Now..." She rested her crossed forearms on the table. "I was ready to turn you over to the loony bin, you know."

"When?"

"This morning. I thought that the boating thing was such an extreme move, so I played along. There were only two possible outcomes: you were crazy, or you were right. History sided with you again," Sarah replied.

Clyde smiled. "My whole life, nothing I did fulfilled me. I think this Gift might be what I was looking for."

"What are you going to do with it?" Sarah asked.

"I'm not sure," Clyde replied. "I won't make any money off it, that's for sure. I guess I'll try to use it part-time while I figure out my career."

"That's going to be rough," Sarah said. "This *Gift* has almost gotten you killed multiple times."

"I'm aware," Clyde said. "But I guess going down using the Gift seems much more honorable than running from it."

Sarah said, "As cool as this power is, I don't envy you, Clyde."

"Maybe you have something, too," Clyde said.

"Like a power?"

"Yeah," Clyde replied.

"How would I know?" Sarah asked.

"I can't say, but if the supernatural is real, then who is to say what I have is the only type there is?" Clyde replied.

"You're moving into fringe territory now," Sarah said.

"Possibly, or we're onto something big," Clyde said.

The two shared a plate of beer-battered onion rings and sipped their drinks.

"How goes work?" Sarah asked, looking to change topic.

"Frankly, not good," Clyde said. "I've been consumed with everything else. My clients haven't been calling me. I'm afraid they might've dropped me."

"You could get a job as a Hartwell cop," Sarah said.

Clyde laughed. Seeing Sarah's straight face, he stopped. "You're serious."

"You'd have to go through the police academy, but I could set you up with a recommendation," Sarah said. "Within six months, you can be on the force. Hawkins would have to approve."

"I guess I never thought it was an option," Clyde said. "How much will the salary be?"

"Not much, but you'll be able to use your Gift," Sarah said.

Clyde thought on it. "That's a big commitment."

"We'll be partners in crime. Or law, in this case. I think it would be fun," Sarah teased. "You'll get to use handcuffs."

Clyde flashed a nervous smile. "From lawyer to paranormal cop."

Sarah raised her glass. "To a change in fortunes."

"Indeed," Clyde replied.

Three days later, the male skeletons was officially confirmed to be Glen Iving. The female was still unidentified. Clyde proceeded to rebuild the house's front porch. The new supplies ut a hurting on his bank account. Pastor Murry stopped by after Clyde called him and helped with the repairs. They talked about life. Murr said he tried every other kind of fulfillment before faith. He went into great depth about a major cocaine binge that nearly got him and his friends killed in a ski resort. Now, he was addicted to God. Clyde silently wondered if the Gift would become an addiction to him.

Sarah updated Clyde on the case. Since Glen's body was confirmed, a few people called in tips. Most of them told Sarah about Glen's reclusive personality, sociopathic tendency, and his violent temper. One old classmate of his said that only Cathy could calm him down. There was still no evidence to connect Cathy to the murders. Clyde wasn't entirely convinced either.

He decided it was time to start crossing suspects off his list. He wanted to find out the truth about Don first. Unable to get any information about the man personally, he sought after the only one who would know something. Hannah Granger, the diner waitress.

On a rainy night, Clyde and Sarah pulled up to the diner after work. They chose a table in the back and specifically asked for Hannah to serve them. Rain pattered on the window. An elderly couple were the only other guests. Wearing her yellow waitress outfit and waist apron, blonde-haired and shy Hannah approached their table.

Sarah placed her badge on the table and asked Hannah to sit. The woman nervously lowered herself into the booth.

"Let's talk about Don for a minute," Sarah said.

Clyde said, "Don't worry, Hannah. All we want is your side of the story."

"What story?" Hannah asked.

"Don wasn't in town during the Hartwell Massacre," Clyde explained. "Some sources say he was close to you."

"I don't know what you're talking about," Hannah lied horribly.

"You don't want to lie to me," Sarah taunted.

"Help us help you," Clyde said.

Hannah twiddled her thumbs. Her shoulders were tense. She refused to make eye contact. After a long pause, she started speaking. "Don and I… please, don't make me talk."

"Will he hurt you if you do?" Sarah asked.

Hannah looked at her like she was crazy. "Never."

"Then speak up," Sarah said. "I don't want to have to keep asking."

Hannah opened her mouth and shut it just as quickly. She shook her head. "I'm sorry. I can't." She started to rise.

Clyde said, "If you get up, we'll have no choice but believe Don was involved in those killings."

Hannah's eyes watered. She frantically looked around the store. She bit into her lower lip, keeping it from trembling.

Clyde gave her a sympathetic smile. "You can trust us, Hannah. We'll keep you safe."

"I'm not worried about me," Hannah blurted out. She covered her mouth, having said too much.

Sarah said, "Help us, Hannah. Unless you want us to bring both Don and you down to the station."

Hannah's face turned pale. She looked like she'd pass out.

Clyde waited patiently.

Hannah crossed her arms, making herself small. "Don's innocent."

"Why?" Sarah said. "And you better not bring up the whole *Terry confessed* BS."

Hannah wiped a tear. "I know Don's innocent because he was with me the night of the killings."

"Doing what?" Clyde asked.

Hannah blushed.

"So it wasn't a business trip after all," Sarah concluded.

Hannah whispered. "You can't tell anyone. It would destroy Don and everything he's built here."

Clyde asked. "Where were you two, you know..."

Hannah's face turned cherry red. "Ricktor's Cabins."

Clyde turned to Sarah for reference.

She said, "There's a chain of rental cabins forty miles south of here. Nice place."

"Do you have any way to back this story up?" Clyde asked Hannah.

Hannah replied shamefully. "You can ask Don. He's there now." She pulled out her phone and flipped through her texts. There was a picture of a bottle of champagne sitting in an ice bucket near a large bed.

Sarah said, "That's Ricktor's alright. I recognize the bedsheets."

The time stamp was from two days ago.

Clyde felt bad for Don's wife, Mary. She was a sweet lady and deserved better. Clyde and Sarah exchanged looks.

Sarah said, "Alright, Hannah. That's all."

Hannah got up quickly and rushed to the bathroom, starting to cry on her way there.

"Hey, at least he's not our killer," Sarah said, hoping it would cheer Clyde up.

It was good news, but Clyde hated to see his new friend

caught up in an affair. He left a twenty-dollar tip for Hannah and had their food to go.

Clyde ate at Sarah's house. He spoke aloud. "I say we get Curtis next."

Sarah replied, "His blackouts make him unreliable."

Clyde replied, "We should see him either way. Things with the murders are starting to blow over. Maybe something triggered him."

"Whatever you say," Sarah replied.

They arrived at Curtis's cabin on Sarah's day off. Dressed in civilian clothes, she walked next to Clyde. They knocked on the door.

Glass shattered on the other side, followed by a string of profanity.

Sarah knocked again. "Everything okay, Curtis?"

The front door yanked open and Curtis stood on the other side. Wearing a muscle shirt and boxers, cold sweat drenched the black man. His eyes were wide and crazy. "What the hell do you want?"

Sarah stared him down, unfazed by his uncouth behavior. "Relax, sweetheart. We just want to talk."

"You picked a bad time," Curtis replied.

Clyde stepped forward. "We wanted to check on you, Curtis."

"I'm fine," the man barked.

Sarah asked, "Is that why you're drunk at nine in the morning?"

"You don't know me, woman. You don't know what I've been through," Curtis replied.

Sarah flashed a smile. "I'd like to. May I come in?"

Curtis bounced his gaze from between Clyde and Sarah. "I have a better idea."

He turned back and walked to the other side of the living

room. Clyde and Sarah peered through the open threshold. Glass from a broken beer bottles littered the floor. There was a fist-sized hole in the wall.

Curtis grabbed a small key set from a nail in the wall and proceeded to unlock his gun cabinet.

Sarah slipped her hand onto her concealed pistol. "Uh, Curtis?"

Without replying, he opened the cabinet door. The glass door captured the man's angry mug. He drew out an AK-47. Keeping its barrel to the roof and his finger off the trigger, he twisted around. "You ever shoot one of these?"

"I can't say I have," Sarah replied.

"You?" he asked Clyde.

Clyde shook his head. "Never."

"Come on then." Curtis picked up a metal ammo bucket. Carrying the rifle and the bullets, he headed through the back door.

Sarah entered first. Clyde trailed close behind. They stepped out into the back lawn. Mannequins stood in the woods beyond the long yard. Curtis placed the ammo box on the ground and popped it open with the same hand. He stood in proper firing position and aimed down the sight. "Don't be shy," he said.

Clyde and Sarah approached him, standing to his right.

Bam! Bam! Bam!

Curtis fired into the woods, hitting one of his targets. He handed the gun to Clyde. "You try."

Clyde waited for Sarah's approval before taking the gun. He rested the stock against his inner shoulder, aimed, and fired. The recoil punched him. He missed all three shots.

Curtis laughed. "You thought I was the drunk one."

Clyde replied, "I'm not really a gun guy."

"How about you, woman?" Curtis asked.

Sarah took the rifle from Clyde. She fired at three targets in quick succession, only hitting two.

Curtis was impressed.

She lowered the rifle. "You want to tell us why you're all pissed off this morning?"

Curtis gestured for the rifle. "Hand it over."

Sarah hesitated.

"It's my gun," Curtis said coldly.

Sarah surrendered the weapon.

Curtis walked through the lawn, taking shots at the various mannequins in his line of sight. He hit them one after another.

Curtis picked up the heavy box of ammo.

Clyde shrugged at Sarah and followed after the crazy old man.

They walked a little further. Curtis put the ammo box down and removed his ammo magazine from his gun. He kept his eyes scanning the woods as if waiting for an attacker. He handed the magazine back to Clyde. "Load her up."

Clyde popped open the ammo box's top and fed the bullets into the magazine. Sarah pointed out the correct way to load the bullets.

His attention still on the woods, Curtis said. "You were spying on me."

Clyde stopped loading the ammo.

"You know I saw you, right?" Curtis asked.

Sarah asked, "When did this happen?"

"I should've slashed your tires," Curtis said. "I should teach you not to intrude on another man's land."

Clyde froze.

Not looking at him, the old man gestured for the ammo magazine.

Clyde held it. "We need to talk."

"Has it occurred to you I'm not interested in what you have to say?" Curtis said.

"You ever know anyone named Glen Iving?" Clyde asked.

"Who?" Curtis replied.

"It would've been decades ago. He was a white guy, long face—"

"You're asking me, the guy with the blackouts, if he remembers some white boy from that year?"

Sarah said, "His remains were recently discovered in Lake Hartwell."

"I don't know anything about that," Curtis said, lowering his rifle. He glared at Clyde, pissed that he hadn't given him the magazine.

Sarah said, "You seem to be having a pretty emotional response to the discovery."

Curtis gestured for the magazine.

Clyde didn't give it.

Curtis looked like he wanted to punch his face in.

Sarah put her hand on her hip.

Curtis straightened his posture, towering over Sarah and Clyde. "You want to know why I'm pissed? Fifty years ago to this exact day, my wife died."

Clyde lowered his gaze.

"If I want to drink and shoot, that's my business," Curtis said. "Now give me my magazine."

Clyde handed it to him. He put it into his AK-47 and proceeded into the woods. Clyde and Sarah lagged behind a few paces, watching him shoot his gallery of mannequins.

Clyde walked close to Sarah and spoke quietly. "Maybe we should try another day."

"We're here. Let's make the most of it," Sarah replied.

Curtis emptied his magazine by shooting targets. Resting

the gun on his shoulder, he turned back to Clyde and Sarah. "You mentioned that Glen guy. How did he die?"

"9mm to the back of the head," Clyde said.

"I don't own a 9mm," Curtis replied.

"Did you at one point?"

"Never," Curtis replied. "Too weak."

"Did you hear any rumors about Glen?" Clyde asked.

"This is the first time I've ever heard his name," Curtis said.

"But you were curious about what killed him?" Sarah asked.

"If someone blames you for something you didn't do, you'd like to know what they were talking about," Curtis replied. "Now do you got some evidence or you just blaming me for my past?"

Clyde and Sarah were silent for a moment. Sarah said, "We're not blaming you for anything. We just want to find out what happened to Glen."

"I wouldn't know, and I don't really care. You know, ever since my wife died, I've never been free. People accuse me constantly. They shoot their dagger eyes at me. They never asked me my side of the story. I say screw them, and screw you. I did my time. I worked hard. If you'd think for one moment that I'd kill another person after what I have to live through every day, you'd be mistaken. There is no greater pain than knowing that a loved one is dead because of you," Curtis said. "So go ahead, blame away. Lock me up. Or try, but I've served my time and if you come around here again, I will exercise my Second Amendment rights."

"Well," Sarah said, processing all that she heard.

Clyde could tell Curtis was telling the truth. He might have a disturbing way of blowing off steam, but unless Clyde was missing something major, he wasn't their guy.

"I'm sorry," Clyde said.

"Leave the bullets and get out of here. I'm sick of both of you," Curtis replied.

Sarah and Clyde did as he said and left. They made sure not to turn their back fully to him. They didn't have anything against him, nor did they have anything to convict him.

Clyde got a call on their drive back. It was Don. He said, "We need to talk."

21

THE HAND-OFF

Clyde sat on the park bench, his arm stretched over the top railing and wind in his hair. A few kids played on the jungle gym twenty yards away while their parents had a quiet argument under the covered picnic table area.

Sarah was in the parking lot, keeping a lookout. The sun was high in the sky, but distant dark clouds threatened the beautiful day. Clyde's stomach rumbled. His joints ached. Injuries didn't suit him. He missed running. He wanted to feel whole already. He was normally a very able-bodied person. Without the perks of his muscles and running ability, he was just your every day struggling lawyer… investigator.

Don rolled into the parking lot in the luxury sedan. He stayed parked but didn't shut off his car. His tinted windows prevented Clyde from seeing inside. Clyde waited. He anxiously tapped his foot. He had a feeling he knew why Don wanted to meet him so quickly but had to be prepared for anything. It was Clyde's idea to meet in a public place.

Don stepped out of his car. He wore a dress shirt, suit pants, and shiny black shoes. He had unbuttoned the button on his wrists and rolled up each sleeve. He approached Clyde, appearing to be unarmed.

Clyde stood to greet him.

Without as much as a glance Clyde's way, Don sat on the bench beside him. He stared into the distance. His jaw shifted behind his light stubble. The man was pissed and struggling to hold back his anger.

"Don, how are you?" Clyde asked.

"Shut up," Don said quietly. "And listen very carefully. If I hear so much as a peep out of you about Hannah to anyone, I will make your life a living hell. You understand?"

Clyde said, "It's not what you think."

"Do you understand?" Don said fiercely.

"Yeah," Clyde said, offended that their friendship had to go down this path.

"And don't you ever go back to her diner again," Don said.

Clyde was shocked by his words. He had never seen this side of Don before. The kind fisherman wasn't taking any chances.

Before Clyde could ask him any questions, Don got into his car and sped away. Clyde was left dumbfounded.

He approached Sarah's car.

She rolled down the window. "I see that went well."

"Very," Clyde said dryly.

He sat in the passenger seat. "He was pissed about the Hannah thing."

"I gathered as much," Sarah replied.

"I don't think the people in this town like me very much," Clyde said.

"Ah, you just haven't met the right people," Sarah said.

Clyde replied, "In some ways, I feel like we're trying to prove someone is guilty instead of innocent. It feels wrong."

Pursed lips, Sarah nodded.

Clyde said, "But, I think I know a way to move this case along quicker."

"I'm all ears," Sarah said.

"Let me touch Glen's bones."

"Okay, that sounds provocative," Sarah replied.

"When I touched Alana, I was able to see how she died. If I see how Glen died, I might just get a good look at our killer," Clyde said.

"I can't get you into the morgue after what happened last time," Sarah replied. "It just won't work."

"You can try to smuggle out the bones."

"How would I pull that off?" Sarah asked. "They're in a lab in Atlanta, having further testing being done. Even if I had the clearance, it would be impossible to get them."

Clyde stroked his chin. "We need to keep a close eye on Cathy. She was the one that suggested the lake."

"I've already talked to her," Sarah said.

"Wait, what?" Clyde exclaimed. "When did this happen?"

"The day after we discovered the bones, she came into the station. She told me all about Glen and how he was distant in the days leading up to his disappearance. She even had flight records saying that she was out of state during that time. The woman is notorious for keeping track of everything. I looked through them myself. She's clean," Sarah said.

Clyde gritted his teeth.

"It's a good thing," Sarah said. "We just have to fall back on the last two suspects."

"Roland and Hawkins."

"Yep. Little fish, big fish," Sarah said. "Between you and me, Hawkins is trying to pin Glen's murder on Terry."

"You think he'll take the rap for it?" Clyde asked.

"He's already sold out to his lie. What's one more body?"

Clyde hammered his fist on armrest. "Man, it's like we're so close, but we just need that final *umph*."

"I can help you out with that," Sarah teased.

"Not what I meant," Clyde replied. "I can go after the dead woman."

"You think she'll talk?" Sarah asked, almost scared to know the answers.

"She wouldn't have appeared to me otherwise, right?" Clyde asked.

Sarah shuddered. "Freaky."

"But pretty cool," Clyde smiled to himself.

"Say she tells you who killed her, how will we prove it?" Sarah asked.

"One step at a time," Clyde replied.

Sarah dropped him off at the lake before going her own way. "As much as I want to ghost hunt, it freaks me out too much. Don't get killed."

"Sound advice. Right back at you," Clyde replied.

"See ya, Clyde," Sarah drove off.

Clyde walked around the edge of the lake, unsure how to summon the ghosts. He set his mind on her, remembering the face he saw below the water and the way her dress squiggled like a jellyfish. His thoughts slowly drifted to Alana. The young goth girl held a special place in his heart. Part of him missed her. His interests were still swayed by hers even after she went to the great beyond. He'd learned to tune them out, but when he was alone, he felt a profound sense of isolation. Despite her friends, Alana was lonely. She died too young. Her killer may be behind bars, but that didn't change the damage he inflicted. *At least you can rest,* Clyde said to the spirit. He wondered if he could talk to her in the beyond. Probably not.

Clyde walked for an hour. He traveled through the trees

and spotted a woman in the distance. Water dripped from her white dress and puddled in the mud around her feet. She lingered at the edge of the five-foot cliff. One of her shoulder straps was torn and resting on her bicep like a ribbon. Her seaweed-like hair tumbled over most of her face and shoulders. Purple bruises painted her neck. She had a little belly, probably weighing around 150 pounds. Her dress was fancy enough for date night at a classy restaurant.

Clyde stopped behind her.

She kept looking out to the lake.

"Hey, I'm Clyde." It sounded stupid to say, but how else did you approach a ghost? Clyde felt he was talking to a girl for the first time. He didn't know how to proceed. He put on his lawyer face. He was after facts. Who, what, when, why? If the woman could answer that, he would be cruising.

She slowly turned her head, looking over her shoulder. She opened her mouth, and dirty water poured from lips.

"I was hoping we can talk," Clyde said.

The waterfall of water persisted. "Help. Me."

"Tell me who did this to you."

"Roland. Roland Alcott," the woman confessed.

And so the plot thickens. Clyde was shocked by how easy that was. "Why?"

"He didn't want it." She put her hand on her belly.

Clyde's countenance shrank. He always had a soft spot for children. "I'm sorry."

"Stop him," the woman said. "Please."

"How?"

"He has photos of me," the woman said.

"Where?" Clyde asked.

"Under his bed," the woman replied.

"I'll find them. I promise you that," Clyde said. "When you passed, was Glen with you?"

The woman stared blankly.

"Do you know Glen Iving?" Clyde asked.

The woman shook her head.

"What's your name?" Clyde asked softly, reminding himself that she was a lady despite looking like a monster from the depths.

"Lydia McCormick."

"I'll help you through this, Lydia. Stay close, okay? We're in this together now."

A small smile crept up Lydia's face.

Clyde smiled back. She was a lot sweeter than the other victims. "I have to make a call."

He dialed Sarah. The instant she picked up, Clyde said, "The Jane Doe is Lydia McCormick."

"Running her name now," Sarah said.

"Roland killed her," Clyde said, keeping his eye on Lydia.

"Oh boy," Sarah replied, getting excited.

"Lydia claims Roland has photographic evidence in his house," Clyde said. "You think you'd be able to a get warrant?"

"It's a tough call," Sarah said. "I want to confirm Lydia's testimony first."

"Fair enough," Clyde replied. "What would you like me to do in the meantime?"

"Get dates, times, and anything you can from this lady. Whatever we can do to tie this to Glen, the better."

"That's the thing. She doesn't even know Glen," Clyde said.

"They share the same grave," Sarah said.

Clyde replied, "I'm trying to figure this all out, too."

Sarah said, "I'll go back and look at the photos of Roland's secret box."

Clyde wished he could've forgotten about Roland's box of

mementos, but they were branded into his memory. Roland had a silver dollar, a bullet from the Civil War, a charm bracelet belonging to a female, a golden tooth, a few wedding rings, and a stack of dead dog photos. It was a sick fetish Clyde couldn't even imagine.

The phone call ended and Clyde directed his attention back to Lydia.

"I have a few more questions," Clyde said.

Lydia was an open book. She was an unmarried woman who died at the age of 42. She met Roland at Alistair's Pub seven years ago. She was in a low place in her life, and Roland, despite his many issues, was a kindred spirit. He too was lonely and living just for the sake of it.

Lydia said, "He was a strange man. Unpredictable and wild. I liked that about him. He'd race down the street just to see me or take me to some hidden nook on the outside of town where we'd picnic. He'd sing and dance, cook and live off the land. He captured the spirit of the south. I liked that, and he liked me. If a guy even looked my way, he'd cuss them out or bust their jaw. Some girls would think that was immature, but Roland was a protector. My protector."

"And then what happened?"

Lydia put her hand on her belly. "The baby scared him. He said he would never be a father. I tried to tell him otherwise, but that only made him angrier."

"And he attacked you?"

"He'd been drinking," Lydia said. "I told him that he'd have both of us or neither."

"I see he made his choice," Clyde said. "Where did it happen?"

"His bedroom," Lydia replied.

Clyde asked, "Is there anyone I should tell this to?"

"My sister. Jasmine."

"McCormick?"

"Dorshaw."

Clyde jotted the name down on his phone notes. "I'll reach out."

When he looked away from his screen, Lydia had vanished. Clyde called a cab. He headed home for the night. Sarah got him Jasmine's home address. She lived two towns over. Clyde got a rental car. It was a cheap Toyota minivan. The less flashy, the better. He was still waiting for his insurance company to pay him for his Cadillac, but they were stalling. A client called him on the way over.

"If you can't be here to represent me, I'll find someone else," the man exclaimed.

"I'm recovering from a car accident," Clyde replied.

"And I'm about to go to court without a lawyer," the man replied. "Screw it, Barker. I'm out."

"Kent—"

The man hung up.

The world was moving all around him, and he was in Hartwell, chasing ghosts. He expected ramifications for pursuing this case, but the cost increased by the day. He hardly slept, his body wasn't healing quick enough, rent for his apartment and office were due soon, and he was short on the money. He told himself Fate put him here. If he was truly living out his destiny, life issues would work themselves out... hopefully.

He arrived at Jasmine's suburban house. It was pretty, white, and clean. Children biked down the road. There was a basketball hoop and a minivan on nearly every driveway. Clyde pulled to a stop at the curb. *I'll blend right in.* He wished Pathfinder was at his side. He felt horrible leaving at her at home for so long. The dog needed to run free.

Clyde pulled down the overhead mirror and examined

his bruised face. The swelling had gone down, but there was still a lot of purple. Terry did a number on him. Clyde wasn't a religious man, but after the gun had jammed at the moment Terry pulled the trigger, Clyde was certainly a believer. A true supernatural experience was the death of rational science. No amount of Darwinian theory was going to change him now.

He combed his hair with his fingers. Clyde noticed a few grey hairs and plucked them out. *I'm too young to be going grey,* he thought as he stepped out of his car. It must've been the Alana in him that caused him to feel a sudden disdain for the suburban life. Setting his feelings aside, he rang the doorbell. He thought about what to say to the Jasmine but settled for the truth, or as close as he could get to it without saying ghosts.

A man answered the door. He wore a sweater vest, slacks, and slip-on shoes. Rimless glasses rested on his nose. He had a receding hairline and was probably in his fifties. One look at Clyde's face and the man was stunned.

"Does Jasmine live here?" Clyde asked.

The man adjusted his glass. "Why are you asking?" he said, faking a smile. The man was nervous. Clyde towered over him by seven inches.

"I'm a lawyer, and I thought I should talk to her about her sister's passing."

"Someone found Lydia?" the man asked.

"Remains were recently discovered in Lake Hartwell. There's a pretty good chance they belong to Lydia. I wanted to talk to Jasmine about her sister's passing."

"We never thought she was dead. We only thought she went missing," the man replied, stunned by the revelation.

"Is Jasmine home?"

"She's playing with the kids. I'll get her." The man shut the door.

Clyde stood outside, his hands in the back of his pocket. A few people watched him from the windows. He was going to be the neighborhood's latest gossip.

Jasmine and the man returned to the door. Jasmine had a ponytail and skinny frame. She wore a t-shirt and tennis shorts. She had her sister's luminous eyes. Though her husband was hesitant, Jasmine invited Clyde inside. They sat around the table. Outside, two little boys and one little girl played badminton. They were all between the ages of 8-12, the oldest being the girl.

Jasmine said to Clyde, "Why haven't the police reached out?"

"They want to run a few more tests," Clyde replied. "I have an inside source that claims it was Lydia. As an attorney, I want to make sure you're covered legally."

"We don't have money for that right now," the husband lied.

Clyde replied, "A little time is all I'm asking. Frankly, I'm trying to wrap my mind around another disappearance. Lydia's remains happened to be found in the same place as the man's body whose murder I'm trying to solve."

Jasmine replied. "That sounds like detective work."

"I'm a little unorthodox in my methods," Clyde replied. "Truth always matters more than a win in the court."

"You must be a bad lawyer," the man said, partly joking.

Clyde shrugged. "Probably, but someone has to do it."

Jasmine squeezed her husband's hand. "I can't believe this is happening, Peter."

"She's been gone for a long time, dear. It might not be as big of a shock as we'd like to believe," Peter replied, though the news was just as troublesome to him.

"Did either of you know Glen Iving?" Clyde asked.

The couple gave him a dumbfounded look. Seeing that was the best he'd get from them, he focused on Lydia. "Were either of you aware that she was seeing Roland Alcott during the time of her disappearance?"

"That man," Jasmine said distastefully as she wiped her eye. "He was a horrible fit for my sister."

"In what way?" Clyde asked.

"Every way," Jasmine said plainly.

"Did he ever abuse her?" Clyde asked.

"Maybe. All I know is that he stole her time," Jasmine said.

Peter spoke up. "Lydia rarely stopped by as it is. When Roland got into the picture, she cut all contact."

"How long did they date before that happened?" Clyde asked.

Jasmine said, "Right after they first started dating. That was, gosh, I'd say eight years ago. She went missing a year after."

"Were you aware they were dating at the time of her vanishing?" Clyde asked.

"I was, and the police even spoke to Roland about her disappearance. He was cleared though. No substantial evidence or body." Jasmine said.

Peter added. "His lawyer was an all-star."

"Who?" Clyde asked.

"I don't remember," Peter replied. "But he's a big shot."

Clyde stood up. "Well, thank you both for your time."

Jasmine said, "You're leaving so soon. What about Roland?"

"We'll figure something out," Clyde said. "If the cops come by, you just tell them everything you told me, okay?"

"We will," Peter replied.

Clyde gave them a small wave. "Enjoy your afternoon."

He met Sarah for lunch at a small pizza joint. She wolfed down a slice. "So what are you thinking?"

"We bring down Roland." Clyde said.

"How?" Sarah asked.

"He was a suspect in Lydia's vanishing. " Clyde took a bite. The cheese burned his tongue. Grease soaked his paper plate. "We might be able to bring him back in. Has Forensics confirmed it was Lydia?"

"I'm still waiting," Sarah said. "They were able to get Glen Iving confirmed quickly, but something is going on at the lab that is slowing it down."

"You think someone is tampering with it?" Clyde asked.

"No, the system has always been slow. The fact that we learned about Glen's ID so quick was a miracle," Sarah said.

Clyde lowered his piping hot cheese slice. He used a napkin to dab grease off the corner of his mouth. "We should recount what we've learned so far. It's a little trick I do to commit the case to memory."

"Okay, you want me to start?" Sarah asked.

"Be my guest," Clyde said.

Sarah said, "Elizabeth Mara, Tommy Demko, John Roth, and Gena Cobbs were murdered twenty years ago by a *single* gunman, though that might not be the case. At the time, the police suspected Curtis Lowry and Roland Alcott, but there was never enough evidence to convict either of them. Flash forward until a few weeks ago, you find the bones of two missing bodies—John and Gena. That sparked copycat killer Terry Wells to kill Alana Campbell. Suspicious of this, you were able to stop Terry, and I got the confession out of him. Now he stands charged on all five counts of murder."

"And potentially the murder of Glen Iving, if he chooses to confess to it as well."

"Hawkins is pushing for it," Sarah said distastefully.

Clyde stayed focused on the recap. "Judging from what I've seen, Glen Iving was one of the killers. Three years after the murders, he *vanished*, but was actually shot in the back of the head by a possible alibi. If the murders were solely his doing, the ghosts would've passed on."

Sarah asked, "Do you have to complete a ritual or something?"

Clyde shook his head. "Alana vanished the moment Terry was arrested. All we got to do is apprehend the killer, and the rest will leave too."

"And Roland is our number one suspect," Sarah finished for him.

"Yeah, Lydia McCormick's skeletal remains were discovered next to Glen's," Clyde said. "Roland killed Lydia. It's safe to say he killed Glen. If that's the case, he must've assisted in or known that Glen instigated the massacre. Stranger still, Roland was able to afford an all-star lawyer to represent himself."

"The man struggles with his monthly mortgage payment," Sarah said.

"Someone might've footed the bill. Someone who wanted to keep Roland safe," Clyde said.

"That's a bold theory," Sarah said.

"I'm just assessing the facts," Clyde replied.

"Who would want to protect Roland?" Sarah asked.

"You should ask him," Clyde replied. "Bring him into the station and see if he can open up. Meanwhile, I'll find the lawyer."

"Sounds like a plan," Sarah said.

They finished their meal. Clyde kept his mind focused on the case. He drove his rented minivan back to the house. Pathfinder was glad to see him. He took his phone and laptop outside and researched local lawyers. He called them one at a time, asking if Roland Alcott hired them. They all questioned why he needed such information. Clyde told him that Roland might be involved in some nasty stuff and the police might start digging. As a fellow attorney, he wanted to give the person in charge a heads up, and also ask for permission to take Roland on as a client. Eventually, Clyde got a hit.

Attorney-at-law Patrick Payas admitted to representing Roland. "The man was a mess. He'd show up drunk to most hearings and would rarely listen to my advice. Every time we shared a room together, he always wanted to add in his two cents or badmouth the cop interrogating him. If you want to represent him, by all means. I'd be happy if I never saw the man again."

"I noticed your rates are pretty steep," Clyde replied.

"You want people to see you as a professional, charge a professional rate. Let that be a little lesson," Pat said.

"I find it hard to believe Roland paid you out of pocket," Clyde said.

"He did. Cash, too."

"Do you know where he got it?" Clyde asked.

"I'm a lawyer, not a cop."

"He didn't have a benefactor?"

Pat replied, "Maybe. I was paid to defend the guy. I'm not going to dig up skeletons in his closet."

The phone call ended soon after. Roland was making money. Clyde didn't know how. He decided to follow him. He put on Andrew's old baseball cap, made sure Pathfinder was fed, and drove out to Roland's house. He wasn't home. Clyde was tempted to search for Lydia's photos, but he didn't want to tamper with evidence. He drove to the scrapyard next. Roland's truck was parked inside the fence.

Clyde stayed parked outside. An hour later, Roland left,

locking the door behind him. Clyde trailed behind Roland. He followed him outside of town and to a no-tell motel. It was located next to a seedy strip club called *Princesses Playhouse.* Clyde used his phone to snap pictures of the motel's sign. Roland hiked the stairs to the second floor and passed through a corridor between rooms. Clyde got out and jogged after him. He winced, feeling the bruises on his chest and the swelling on his ankle. He walked through the corridor and peeked around the corner. All the doors were closed. Clyde sighed. He kept watching. The case had tried his patience. 90% of what he did was watch people.

The hairs on the back of his neck stood. He twisted back.

Lydia stood behind him. Water dripped from her dress and hair. She smelled like the lake. Her hand rested on her belly.

Seeing her infuriated Clyde. Roland was a bad guy. The worst person Clyde had ever met. Since the death of his parents, he'd been good at keeping his emotions under lock and key, but the lack of sleep was causing him to crack. Part of him wanted to confront Roland now. It would be effortless to knock on the motel room door and… he didn't have a plan past that point.

"Is there anything you want to show me?" he asked Lydia.

"Excuse me?" a woman said.

She had been walking by and noticed Clyde talking to himself.

"Sorry," Clyde said. "Wrong person."

The woman walked along.

Great, now you look like a crazy person.

Clyde waited for five long minutes. He moved closer to the motel rooms, but they all had their window blinds drawn. He returned to his hiding spot. A minute later, a man in work polo and slacks approached him.

"Sir," the man said as he neared.

Clyde didn't reply.

The man stopped in front of him. He crossed his arms. The man had short, spiked hair. He was a few years older than Clyde. He stopped in a power pose, his legs slightly parted and his arms crossed. He was shorter than Clyde but could probably pack a punch. Not as hard as Clyde though. The man said, "You have to leave."

"Sorry?" Clyde asked innocently.

"I've been watching you on the camera." The man gestured to the mounted video camera in the upper corner of the wall. "You can't stay."

"I was meeting with a friend."

"Meet somewhere else."

"What's the big deal?" Clyde replied. "It's not even dark yet."

"You got something planned for after dark?" the man interrogated.

"No, I'm just saying—"

"Take a hike," the man said. "Don't make me call the cops."

Annoyed, Clyde conceded to the man's request. The man glared at him as he left. Clyde returned to his minivan. The man walked to the balcony railing and watched Clyde enter the vehicle.

"You got to be kidding me," Clyde mumbled. He turned the key in the ignition and drove to the strip club. He parked in the lot and turned off the ignition. He kept an eye on the motel, feeling like an idiot for not bringing his binoculars. Thirty minutes later, Roland left the motel and got into the truck. Clyde was torn between following him or investigating the person in the motel room.

Roland drove off. Clyde stayed put. He decided it would be better to see Roland's secret friend. It was probably a prostitute. Clyde had to be sure. He waited. No one came out of the motel for hours. Clyde drank gas station coffee and ate gummy worms to stay awake. Finally, someone he recognized walked through the motel parking lot.

"No way," Clyde said, seeing Chief of Police Bob Hawkins get into a white sedan. He wore a t-shirt, shorts, running shoes, and a ball cap. He drove away. Clyde tailed him, keeping a safe distance behind. He dialed Sarah.

"You wouldn't believe who Roland was meeting with," Clyde said.

"Hit me," Sarah replied.

"Hawkins."

Sarah cursed. "Why?"

"I don't know, but they left hours apart. The hotel manager didn't want anyone watching," Clyde said. "I got thrown out."

"Are you following them now?"

"I'm on Hawkins. Roland left first," Clyde replied.

"Keep on him," Sarah said.

"I am," Clyde replied. "Anything on the forensics front?"

"I've been stuck at the office doing paperwork all day. They reached out. They hope to have the results soon. I'll get a warrant for Roland immediately after the skeleton is confirmed… You're one hundred percent positive it's Lydia?"

"I saw her today," Clyde replied.

"Alright. There is something you should know about Hawkins."

"What's that?"

"There's a rumor circulating that he was with a prostitute over twenty years ago and one of the murder victims saw him."

"So what?" Clyde replied.

"It was when he was trying to build his brand as the

wholesome family man. Maybe he hired Roland to eliminate the witnesses," Sarah theorized.

"That's a bold response to a little problem," Clyde replied, driving with one hand.

"Reputation is important to Hawkins. He comes from a long line of police chiefs. The moral standard is high. He can't be having rumors like that going around or he'd lose his post," Sarah said.

"It still seems farfetched," Clyde replied.

"The stripper he screwed ended up dying in a car accident. Her brakes had been tampered with," Sarah said.

"Why are you just telling me now?" Clyde asked.

"Because I thought it was crazy too until you saw that Hawkins was meeting with Roland. Glen Iving and the two of them could've conspired in the murders. Of course, I don't have any proof, but it's a theory that just came to my head."

Clyde said, "I don't want him to get suspicious I'm following him. Talk to the victim's parents again. See if they can confirm the story. In the meantime, I'll keep tailing."

The call ended.

Clyde followed Hawkins down a series of back roads before reaching the street Clyde liked to run down. Hawkins pulled to the side of the road at the forest where murders happened.

Clyde drove by him to avoid suspicion. He followed another road and made a circle, eventually arriving back at the woods. Hawkins's car was gone.

Clyde pulled over to where he had been parked. Using the flashlight on his phone, he shined the light over the dirt. He saw vague footprints and followed them. About fifty feet back, the path ended and Clyde noticed a rock resting on a pile of leafy branches. He removed the rock and branches, uncovering a suitcase. There was a number combination lock on the suitcase. Not touching the brief case, he put the rock back.

Clyde glanced around. He walked over to a nearby tree. He silenced his phone, turned on the camera, and positioned it in the elbow of a tree and low branch. It would record for a few hours before dying. Clyde would come back in the morning to check. He drove home and lay in bed, unable to rest that night. The case was going in a direction he didn't expect. It was a rabbit hole he'd have to dive into to learn the truth.

The whole trip to Hartwell felt like a pursuit of truth. The truth about the afterlife. The truth about the massacre. The truth about himself. Clyde had natural patience and curiosity, but he never expected to be doing this. Not in a million years. His confidence rose in the midst of it all. Before all this, he thought he'd never be able to confront his own parents' murders. Now, there might just be a chance. His father was a lawyer. He wondered if he was insulting his memory by letting his practice slowly die. Thinking back, he enjoyed the idea of his job more than the work. Mankind was interesting that way. Sometimes they pursued things that they hated for a name or recognition. Everyone was searching for their identity. In some it was faith, in others it was their achievements. Some found it in family, and others in pleasure. Clyde believed in fate and destiny. Lying in bed alone, he imagined himself leading the dead home. He saw himself walking through graveyards and communing with the wayward spirit.

When he awoke the next morning, he felt like a train wreck. His body was sore. His head throbbed. He had little motive to rise from the bed. He stayed on his belly, half of his face pressed into the pillow. The night before, he was ready to embrace destiny. Now, he just wanted to sleep. His flesh was weak.

The Sense tugged at him like an invisible hand pulling at the corner of his shirt. He glanced over, seeing all six spirits eyeing him. They were getting restless. Clyde ignored them for a moment. They took a step closer. Clyde didn't like where this was going. He sat up and rubbed the sleep from his eyes.

He walked to the bathroom and took a shower. The sun was still down outside of the window. In an attempt to wake up, he stayed under the shower a longer time than usual. Despite the Gift, he was still human. The last weeks had already caught up to him. Now it was just worse. He got dressed and fed the dog. He thought about jogging to the woods, but opted for driving. He turned up the AC to full blast. The chill woke him up.

Morning fog hovered across the roads and snaked through the woods. Instead of parking at the entrance to the woods, he pulled the minivan off-road. The cabby bounced as he crossed rough terrain. Successfully hidden in the woods, he exited the van and walked in the direction of Hawkins's concealed briefcase.

He stepped over a felled tree and navigated around thistles. Eventually, he arrived at where the briefcase was located. The branches and rocks covering it had not been disturbed. Clyde stepped out from hiding and retrieved his cellphone. It was dead of course. He checked on the briefcase to be extra sure. It was still there.

Maybe it wasn't a drop point. Perhaps Hawkins was just storing it here. If that was the case, Clyde was tempted to take it. He was sure he would find a way to break the lock.

A motorcycle rumbled. It shut off. Someone had parked nearby.

Clyde dashed behind a tree. He lowered himself to the dirt floor and kept watch.

A man in a leather jacket and wearing a shaded bike helmet approached. He glanced around. Clyde stayed out of sight and kept still. The biker moved aside the rock and the branches. He retrieved the briefcase and started back the way he came. Clyde followed after him, trying his best to move silently. The biker put the briefcase into a mesh basket on the side of his Ninja street bike. Clyde committed the license plate to memory.

The biker sped away. There was a lot more going on in Hartwell than met the eye. Clyde just wanted to prove that Roland was the murderer. He returned to his minivan. After getting home, he charged his phone. He felt lazy today. Pathfinder joined him on the couch and rested her head on his lap. "I know, girl. I want us to go to more places too. It's just hard with all this sneaking around."

The husky glanced around. There was sorrow and boredom in her blue eyes. Thirty minutes later, Clyde's phone had a good charge. He quickly fast-forwarded through last night's video, found no new information and deleted it. He called Sarah. It went to voicemail.

"Heya," Clyde said, "Call me ASAP. Bye."

Clyde waited a few minutes. He thought about texting, but if Hawkins caught wind of Sarah's private investigation, he didn't want to have a paper trail. The phone calls were risky, but at least their conversations weren't recorded. He'd tell Hawkins that they were dating if things went different. It wouldn't be farfetched for him to believe it.

As much as he wasn't in the mood to, Clyde decided to do more work on the porch. After two hours, Sarah returned his call. Clyde wiped the sweat off his brow and answered.

"Hey asap, what's up?" Sarah said.

"What?"

"You said for me to call you asap."

"Funny," Clyde replied. "I need you to run a plate for me."

"Hit me," Sarah replied.

Clyde recited what he saw.

Sarah said, "It belongs to Sebastian Green. Twenty-four years old. He lives on Carter Lane. That's a trailer park in the less favorable part of town. Most of our dispatch calls lead us there. It's meth-heads galore. What pointed there?"

Clyde told her about the exchange between Roland and Hawkins.

Sarah cursed. "This is going deep."

"I'm interested in the murders. The rest is up to you," Clyde replied.

"Oh no no no. We're in this together. The whole way," said Sarah.

Clyde sighed. "Sarah, please. The dead don't care about drug deals."

"But mothers do when their children overdose," Sarah replied. "It's about time Hartwell got cleaned up."

Clyde said, "Whatever you want to do, great. Have you heard any word from the lab?"

"Still waiting."

Clyde gnashed his teeth. He was tempted to sneak into Roland's house and find Lydia's pictures himself. That would be enough evidence to bring Roland in. The hard part would be doing it in a way that didn't seem like Clyde steal it.

Clyde said, "I'll follow up on this Sebastian guy."

"Be careful," Sarah said. "That neighborhood doesn't take kindly to strangers." Despite her warning, Sarah gave Clyde Sebastian's address.

Clyde drove to the trailer park. It was built on a descending hill and the road that ended at a dead-end. Sebastian's house was near the back. Loud metal music blasted from inside the house. The bass shook Clyde's windows. He slowly cruised by. If he parked, it would raise too much suspicion from the locals. The trailer's windows were blacked out. Strong-smelling smoke wafted from the open back windows.

Clyde pulled out his phone and dialed 911. "Yes, I'd like to report a noise complaint."

He left the trailer park community and parked on the shoulder of the single-lane road outside. Not longer after, a cop car drove by and turned into the trailer park. Ten minutes later, two more cop cars came screaming down the road and turned into the trailer park.

Sarah called Clyde. The first thing she said when he answered was, "What the hell did you do?"

"Kicked the hornet's nest," Clyde replied.

"You think! We'll talk later. I have to go." Sarah hung up.

Clyde felt a rush. He had a theory, and it turned out to be correct. Sebastian was the drug dealer. Hawkins was the buyer. Roland was the middleman.

An ambulance raced down the road and into the trailer park.

All of this from a noise complaint. Clyde felt proud of himself. It was an easy victory and could bust open an investigation into Hawkins, Roland, and whoever else was involved.

Clyde went home. He called Pastor Murr and asked him to help repair the porch. The pastor obliged. They small-talked as they set the wood boards and nailed it in place. Clyde hoped to have it done by the late afternoon. It wouldn't be very flashy, but it would be functional. They enjoyed a quick meal afterward before Murr had to leave.

He asked Clyde about his visions.

"I'm learning to live with it," Clyde replied. "I'm looking into another murder."

Murr replied, "You want me to help you through it?"

"No," Clyde said. "But I'll show you this stuff is real after the convictions are in place."

Murr went home. Clyde waited for Sarah's call. The next day, Clyde contacted a few of his clients and gave them legal advice. Sarah reached out to him at lunch. They met at a mom-and-pop restaurant on Main Street. There were a few older couples inside, but no one else. Sarah was in uniform as she ate a fat hamburger. Clyde ordered a country-fried steak doused with white gravy.

Sarah said, "Good work yesterday."

Clyde asked, "Has Sebastian talked?"

"Not yet," Sarah replied. "He's not a snitch."

"What did they find in the trailer?"

"A meth lab," Sarah replied. "He was counting money while a chef was cooking up another batch. Judging by the excess residue on Bunsen burners and other things, they had been cooking for months there. None of the locals were brave enough to call it in, nor were they willing to give us any more information."

Clyde said, "If we can trace the money back to Hawkins, we can connect the two. That will lead back to Roland."

"Only if Sebastian talks," Sarah said. "The bills were clean. Hawkins is not stupid."

Clyde replied, "Is there any way to get Sebastian to open up?"

"It's going to be hard," Sarah said. "Hawkins has already taken a front row seat in the investigation. He wants to be in on every detail. He'll cover his tracks. I'm sure he's already in damage-control mode now."

Clyde agreed to watch Roland while Sarah stayed focused

on Sebastian. Instead of going to Roland's house, Clyde checked on the local bars. He remembered seeing him at one previously and hoped to spot him again. He got lucky. Roland was there, seated at a barstool and watching the soccer game on TV. He wore a stained shirt, straight-legged jeans, and muddy cowboy boots. His ponytail ran down the front of his left shoulder. A few stringy hairs curled out of his receding hairline. Clyde sat a few seats down from him and ordered a pale ale.

Roland recognized Clyde. "Your face looks ugly."

Clyde touched his bruised nose. "Yep."

"You still got that darn dog?"

Clyde replied, "Sure do."

Roland frowned. He sipped his beer.

Clyde took a sip of his drink as well.

"Sit over here," Roland gestured to the seat next to him. Clyde obliged.

Roland asked, "Are you and that cop still investigating?"

"Not really. Terry Wells admitted to the murders," Clyde replied.

"It's screwed up that you and that cop came blaming me."

"We weren't though," Clyde replied.

Roland said, "You two came to my house asking questions. I'm not a stupid man. I know when I'm being grilled."

Clyde replied, "Whatever you say, pal."

"Why did you care so much about those killings anyway?" Roland asked, attitude in his voice.

"My uncle killed himself looking into that case," Clyde replied. "I thought by solving it, I'd give him rest."

"RIP." Roland took a gulp.

Clyde watched the soccer game for a moment. Eyes on the TV, he asked, "You hear about those skeletons they found in the lake?"

Roland shook his head.

Clyde replied, "It's pretty crazy. Two sets of bones—one male and one female--dropped near the same spot, supposedly years apart."

"Who told you that?" Roland asked.

"It was on the news," Clyde said innocently.

"*Hmph,*" Roland replied.

"It's pretty crazy, huh?" Clyde asked.

"What?"

"All this stuff about Hartwell coming out all at once," Clyde replied. "It's like God decided it's time to execute justice."

Roland replied, "God ain't have nothing to do with it."

Clyde sipped his ale and put down his glass. "Have you ever been in love?"

"What kind of dumb question is that?" Roland asked.

Clyde shrugged. "Just wondering."

Roland stared at his glass. "There was this girl once."

"Pretty?" Clyde said.

"Oh yeah," Roland said, a sad smile forming on his rugged face.

Clyde replied, "What went wrong?"

"She asked for too much," Roland said. "I'm a simple guy. I like the way things are. The past is garbage. The future ain't got nothing to offer me. Why drag me into something I don't want to handle?"

"Sounds like she had a baby on the way," Clyde said.

Roland's anger flared, just as Clyde hoped it would. "What did you say?"

Clyde repeated himself, but louder.

Roland looked like he wanted to tear out Clyde's throat.

Clyde said, "From what I hear, you weren't man enough to handle the responsibility."

Roland punched Clyde in the jaw. Clyde's head snapped to the side. Roland pushed out of his seat and punched Clyde again. This time, Clyde let himself fall. He hit the hardwood floor.

The bartender shouted. "Both of you out!"

Roland loomed over Clyde. "You know nothing about me."

"I know about Lydia McCormick," Clyde replied.

Eyes widening, Roland took a step back.

Clyde wiped the blood from his lip. Sitting upright, he said to the bartender. "Call the cops."

Roland said, "You mother f—"

"Run, Roland. Rollers are coming," Clyde interrupted.

Boiling with rage, Roland dashed out the door.

The bartender asked, "You still want me to call the cops?"

"I do, and hurry up," Clyde replied.

Roland was arrested a few blocks down the road. Clyde explained what happened to the officer. The bartender was his witness. Clyde never fought back. All the blame fell on Roland. He would have a nasty fine, but even more so, Sarah would get a chance to question him. The ball was in her court. Clyde hoped she could make the shot.

22

THE TOOTH

Clyde sat at home. Despite his wounds, he felt accomplished. Pathfinder rested her head on his lap. He scratched her behind the ears and enjoyed the soft couch cushion. A day had passed since Roland had been brought into the station.

Sarah came over that evening. She brought a six-pack of tall boys. They cracked them open on the newly-finished front porch. Clyde needed to paint it. He was thinking of a nice coat of white paint. Pastor Murr had power tools he could use to make nice wood trimmings around the upper lip.

Sarah said, "Sebastian is as silent as the grave."

"And Roland?" Clyde asked.

"Denies all accusations. He'll have a court date in a few days for assault charges. He claims you egged him on." Sarah replied.

Clyde cringed. "We're just going around and around in circles with this guy. What if you sent pictures of his lockbox?"

"I want to wait for the forensic report."

"Yeah, and it's taking forever," Clyde replied.

"I've been calling them every day. They hate me, but they said that they'll get results back soon."

The answer frustrated Clyde.

Sarah said, "I have some good news though. I talked to Elizabeth's parents. They confirmed the rumor about Hawkins. He did bribe them to keep quiet about the prostitute."

"How does that help us?" Clyde asked.

"It goes to show Hawkins may have a role in the killings. Roland was selling to him after all."

"But Sebastian won't talk?"

"Not a word," Sarah replied. "Besides, there is a good chance that he doesn't know Hawkins is the buyer. Roland was the one who instigated the deal."

Clyde slouched back in his seat.

"Relax," Sarah said. "The wheels of justice are meant to be slow."

Clyde replied, "I'm aware. But knowing he's guilty and being unable to do anything is frustrating."

Sarah put her hand on his knee and gave him a pitying smile. "You've done enough, Clyde. I can do the rest from here."

"I'm not going to leave this half-finished," Clyde said.

"There will be other cases," Sarah answered. She sipped her beer, keeping her eyes on the front lawn. "I actually dug into your past a little bit."

Clyde's shoulders tensed up. "Why did you do that?"

"You've been such a help with my case, I thought I'd give you a hand with yours," Sarah replied.

Clyde set his jaw.

"Are you mad?" Sarah asked.

"No, I… I try not to think about it too much," Clyde replied, his palms sweating.

Sarah asked, "Is what happened to your parents the reason you don't open up?"

Clyde stayed quiet. He blinked, seeing his parents' bodies on the floor. He was tired of going back to that place. He always felt like a child when he did. Hopeless. Defenseless. Depressed weighed down on him.

Sarah said softly. "I'm sorry you had to go through that."

"It is what it is," Clyde said, trying to shrug it off. For a long time, he blamed God, fate, and even himself for what happened. Eventually, he came to the realization that evil existed in the world. Sometimes it wins. Sometimes it doesn't. Clyde felt helpless to change anything, but the Gift had opened his eyes up to many new possibilities. "We'll see what happens with Roland and this whole mess before I commit to digging into that."

"Well, just know that I have your back."

Clyde raised his beer. "And I have yours."

They clinked cans.

Sarah took a sip. She leaned over and pecked Clyde on the cheek.

He didn't show his response outwardly, but his heart raced. In his thirty years of life, he'd only been with one other woman. She was long out of the picture now. Relationships had been hard for him. Getting close to someone only to lose them left a bad taste in his mouth. His career consumed most of his time anyway. A female companion would only slow him down. Still, loneliness would creep on him at strange times. He was a man after all. He had urges. The goal was to master them instead of being enslaved by passions. Despite the self-control he practiced around Sarah, the curvature of her body, her soft lips, gorgeous freckles, and alluring eyes would stay in his thoughts long after she left.

"You could be my boyfriend if you want to," Sarah said.

Clyde chuckled lightly. "You sound like you're asking me out to middle school prom."

A wry smile formed on Sarah's face. "Well, that may or may not have been the line you used on me."

"And I remember you saying no," Clyde replied.

"I was a stupid girl back then," Sarah said.

Clyde smiled to himself. He stayed quiet, afraid if they continued in this conversation, it would end in a foolish place. It's not that he wasn't tempted. By gosh, after all his near-death experiences recently, he wanted some fun time. Nevertheless, love shouldn't be something small. It should mean something. He might've been a hopeless romantic, but he'd much rather have one woman whom he truly cared about than a thousand hotties who couldn't stand outside of the sheets.

After they finished the six-pack, Sarah hit the road. Clyde went inside, spent some time with Pathfinder, and reviewed Andrew's case file. He looked over the suspect list, glad to see Roland was his only real enemy. Clyde was still unsure if Chief Hawkins was involved in the killings. He put the file aside and faced the town map. Clyde had visited all the areas marked by his late uncle. He just had to get Roland and all this would be over.

A miracle happened the next day. Sarah called Clyde, telling him that Lydia McCormick's identity was confirmed. Better yet, they discovered that the skeleton was missing a tooth.

"The golden tooth found in Roland secret lockbox, perhaps?" Clyde asked, feeling his blood pumping.

Using Roland's past relationship with Lydia as a starting

point, Sarah was able to get warrants to search Roland's trailer and scrapyard. Hawkins wasn't happy, but let Sarah helm the case. In the meantime, Clyde stuck with Pastor Murr and painted the porch.

At the end of the long day, Sarah's search for Roland's lockbox was fruitless.

"Did you search the entire scrapyard?" Clyde asked, annoyed.

"Not every nook and cranny," Sarah said. "But the places where we thought the box was didn't turn up anything helpful."

"And the photos of Lydia under his bed?"

"Nada," Sarah replied. "Maybe your ghost friend was wrong."

Clyde set his jaw.

"Hey, are you still there?" Sarah asked.

"I'll find it myself," Clyde said.

"Clyde, wait—"

Clyde ended the call. He sent Murr home and got dressed in his uncle's clothes. He put on a ski mask and gloves. Night had already fallen over Hartwell. Clyde drove quickly. He couldn't see Roland walking free for another day. Why did he kill the others? He didn't know. His motive weren't certain, but acts were what held up in the court of law. Clyde arrived at the scrapyard first. He expected the police had thoroughly searched Roland's home. The police would probably try searching the scrapyard again. Clyde's goal was to find the tin box and leave it in a place where Sarah could find it. She'd get the arrest. Clyde would go home a happy man.

Clyde parked his minivan out front. He climbed the fence and dropped off on the other side. He rolled his ankle on impact and stifled a grunt. He could add the limp to a growing list of injuries. Using the flashlight on his phone, he reached the center of the scrapyard. There was a lawn chair Roland would sit in as he drank beer and shot glass bottles.

Clyde walked to the disabled van behind the seat and opened the sliding door. He shined his light inside. Judging by upturned furniture, the police had already searched the place. Clyde did his own investigation but had no luck finding the box.

He spent hours popping open trucks and searching under vehicles. He spent more time at the places the police were less likely to check. He climbed on top of crunched vehicles and felt the wobble beneath his feet. The search's endless toil reminded him of grad school. He'd work long hours, committing laws into memory until his eyes hurt. This search fatigued him. If he was a less patient man, he would've given up a long time ago.

Late into the night, he heard the rumble of a truck. He hid behind a stack of disabled cars. Headlights slashed through a gap between cars. The truck came to a stop at the large open center of the junkyard. Half-drunk and wobbling, Roland stepped out. He kept the truck running and held a revolver in his hand.

"Come out!" His slurred shout thundered. "I know you're here!"

He must've seen the van. Clyde expected him to be in the station. He must've paid bail. If the man was smart, he would've called the Clyde's car car renter or the police. His drunkenness had dumbed him down. Clyde just had to get out.

Slightly hunched, Clyde moved out of cover and intended to cross the street. The shadows concealed him.

Roland waddled away from his truck. He climbed up the side of the stack of tall junk cars and reached his hand into the broken, crushed window of the third vehicle up. He removed his hand, holding the tin box.

Clyde's heart rate spiked. If Roland left with that box, the evidence would be lost forever. As Roland climbed down, Clyde rushed to his truck. He grabbed a bent metal bar on the way over. The pain shot up his thigh as he jogged.

He reached the side of the truck by the time Roland turned back. The old drunk walked back to the truck, holding the box against his side. He walked around the front of the truck. Clyde moved around the back, staying out of sight. Roland got into the driver seat and closed the door.

Clyde peered over, seeing Roland shuffling around. He must've been putting his revolver under the seat. Clyde climbed over the tail and into the bed of the truck. He stayed as flat as he could. The truck started moving. Clyde assumed that Roland didn't see him.

Roland drove out of the gate. He parked, got out, locked it, and climbed back in. He drove by Clyde's minivan. Clyde stayed completely still. A few miles up the road, Roland parked the car. Wearing a flashlight on his head, he took the box and a bottle of lighter fluid before heading to the woods. Clyde climbed over the side of the truck. He landed on his feet and followed. Roland reached a rocky crag deep in the woods. Clyde had no clue where they were. He moved as quietly as he could, but didn't have light like Roland. A few twigs snapped under Clyde's step. He stayed quiet. Roland didn't notice.

Roland put the box and lighter fluid aside. He grabbed twigs and leaves and put them in a circle of rock. He slashed the lighter fluid on the kindling and used a lighter to ignite it, then opened the box. He leafed through his photos one last time before dropping them into the flame.

Clyde moved closer, staying about twenty feet from

Roland and lingering behind a tree. He felt overwhelming dread as he watched the photos blacken and curl in the dancing flame.

Roland lifted the golden tooth from the box. It reflected in the fire.

Clyde picked up a fat stick and tossed it away from him. The stick spun in the air before hitting a tree, startling Roland. As fast as lightning, he drew out his revolver from the back lip of his jeans and aimed it into the woods. "Who's there? I'll shoot!"

Clyde pulled out the camera on his phone. Roland aimed the flashlight his way. Clyde ducked, barely avoiding the stream of light. He turned the camera back to Roland. The man cursed. He turned over the box and dumped it into the fire. He shut the empty box and watched the flame for a moment.

"Screw it," he mumbled. Leaving the fire to die on its own, he walked back to the truck. When he was gone, Clyde removed himself from hiding. Still filming, he approached the small fire. Sucking a breath of air through his teeth, he raised his foot and rapidly stomped the flame. The heat bit at his heels. He winced, praying that the flame would die quickly. He succeeded after a few seconds. Keeping the camera rolling, he grabbed a stick and prodded the ash, revealing the darkened golden tooth and bracelet. He got low, making sure the flashlight on his camera captured both items.

Clyde called the police tip line. He got the officer working the graveyard shift and said he had information on the discovery of the recent skeletons. He sent the police the video. Using the GPS on his phone, he was able to direct them to the fire. Clyde started his way back home and was picked up by Sarah. She wasn't happy to be woken up but was too tired to complain. She brought Clyde back to his minivan.

A few days later, Roland was in court and Clyde was a witness. Unlike Lydia's case seven years ago, Roland didn't have a master lawyer. Without his supplier and buyer, his money train had run out. Clyde testified against him in the assault case. Roland got a five-hundred-dollar fine but no jail time. However, a state prosecutor came against him, claiming he murdered Lydia McCormick. Roland vehemently denied it. The trial went on for a few weeks. Clyde's video footage was used as evidence. The gold tooth matched Lydia's missing tooth. In the end, the judge deemed him guilty of the murders of Lydia McCormick and Glen Iving. Roland eventually confessed to killing Lydia, but not Glen.

He said, "I knew Glen's body was there, but I didn't pull the trigger."

No one believed him. No one but Clyde, who saw Lydia pass into the beyond, but not Glen.

23

WRAP UP

Clyde left the courthouse, unsatisfied. He wore a frown as he marched down the steps. News teams loaded the equipment into their vans. Curious locals scattered, thinking about the next big scandal to satisfy their minds.

Clyde yawned. Andrew's house was completed. All that was left to do was talk to a realtor. He rubbed the back of his neck and stopped in front of his repaired Cadillac. Small dents and chipped paint marked her black body, but she was running, and that's all that mattered to Clyde. Much like the car, Clyde's wounds had mostly healed. He had new scars and ruptured veins on the eye where Roland hit him. A small pain jolted up his leg every time he put too much weight on his right foot.

"Mr. Barker!"

Clyde stopped fumbling with his keys and twisted back. Hawkins, wearing his Chief of Police uniform, hiked down the steps and approached.

Clyde lowered his keys.

"You were just the person I wanted to see," Hawkins said.

There was something disingenuous about his friendly smile.

"Why is that?" Clyde asked.

Hawkins chuckled. "You've been quite the controversy around here. First with stopping Terry and now sending local man Roland Alcott to jail, I'd say you were sent to Hartwell to bring some much-needed justice."

Clyde shrugged. "I just got lucky."

Hawkins leaned in, still smiling, but speaking quietly. "Don't lie to me. Don't think for a minute I didn't see you."

"Doing what?" Clyde replied, loudly and sounding confused.

A few pedestrians turned his way.

Hawkins smiled and waved at them. The moment they passed, his expression darkened. "We need to have a nice chat, you and I."

"Regarding my heroism?" Clyde asked sarcastically.

A black Audi sedan rolled to a stop at the curb. The driver, a well-dressed man in a suit, got out and opened the back door. He stood beside it. His hands folded over each other on his belt buckle.

Hawkins put his hand on Clyde's back. "Please." He gestured to the door.

"You want to talk now?" Clyde asked.

"There's no time like the present," Hawkins replied.

Cautiously, Clyde sat in the back of the car.

Hawkins sat next to him.

The driver shut the door.

Hawkins took a breath. "So, what's your deal?"

"I don't have one," Clyde replied.

"Play dumb then," Hawkins replied.

The driver started driving.

Hawkins said, "I should be thanking you, Barker. You saved me from two treacherous scandals."

"Enlighten me," Clyde replied, seeing just how far Hawkins was willing to admit his villainy.

Hawkins smirked. He looked out of the tinted window. "I've been involved in something I wished I had no part in. Dealings I agreed to at a young age and was never able to escape. You see, my father has always been close to the mayor. The mayor also needed a trusted Chief of Police. Because of that, it was important that I behaved myself, more so than the rest of the mongrels in Hartwell."

"I didn't realize this town was so wealthy," Clyde replied.

Hawkins turned to him, dumbfounded by his response. "You can cut the charade."

"Meth and hookers line everyone's pockets. Is that what you're trying to tell me?"

"The former is greater than the latter," Hawkins admitted. "You seem shocked by my honesty. You knew about Roland. You knew about Sabastian. What else do you know?"

Clyde kept quiet.

Hawkins said, "It doesn't matter so much, I guess. You ruined my side gig. Though it was costly, I'm freer than I've ever been. For that, I want to reward you."

"That's why you brought me in here?" Clyde asked suspiciously.

"I'm not a mafioso, Mr. Barker. Dozens of witnesses saw us enter this car. Any harm to you will come right back to me," Hawkins explained. "All that to say, I'm willing to offer you a sum of money for all your services."

Clyde replied, "And to have me go away."

"Smart cookie," Hawkins said. "To keep our accountants happy, I'll write the check for your uncle's house and land. We can both go back to our lives a little less burdened."

Clyde replied, "I'm not interested in your money."

"I find that hard to believe. Your attorney practice is failing, you live in a studio apartment, and you can barely afford to repair your car," Hawkins said.

"You've done your homework," Clyde replied.

"I have friends all over Georgia," Hawkins said. "Good ol' boys. Our blood runs red, white, and blue."

"You and *your boys* can keep your money," Clyde replied.

"Then what will make you happy?" Hawkins asked, annoyed.

Clyde eyed him. "You know."

"I don't, really," Hawkins answered.

"Ask yourself something, Hawkins. Why have I done all that I have? I'm not getting paid. I'm no puppet. What's driving me?"

Hawkins grew more annoyed. "I'm not a psychologist."

"Think, Hawkins," Clyde replied.

Hawkins set his jaw. After a moment, the revelation came to him. "The Huntsman."

Clyde leaned back in his seat and crossed his arms. He waited for Hawkins to speak.

The Chief of Police said, "Terry Wells has already confessed."

"He killed Alana. He didn't kill the rest," Clyde said.

"And what sources do you have telling you that?" Hawkins asked.

Clyde ignored his question. "Glen Iving took part in the murders. I thought Roland did too, but I was wrong."

"What the hell are you talking about?"

Clyde said, "The Huntsman is still out there, and until I find out who he is, I'm not leaving Hartwell."

Hawkins looked at him like Clyde was a madman. "Glen was killed by Roland. The judge ruled that today."

Clyde rose his voice. "I don't care what the judge says. I care about the truth."

"I can't help with this," Hawkins replied.

"Can't or won't?"

"I don't know anything about those killings," Hawkins said.

"Except that Elizabeth Mara walked in on you with the prostitute and now both of them are dead." The instant the words left Clyde's mouth, he knew he made a mistake. All his evidence, though little, had been exposed to Hawkins. He had nothing to leverage anymore. He kept his poker face.

Hawkins glared. "You believe every rumor you hear around here?"

Clyde said, "You want me out of Hartwell for good, you tell me the truth about those killings."

Hawkins gestured to the driver. "Pull over up here."

The driver pulled up to the curbside.

Hawkins said to Clyde. "You should leave."

"That's mighty suspicious of you," Clyde replied.

Hawkins said, "I'm not going to entertain a madman. Get the hell out of my car."

Clyde stepped out. He was on a backroad flanked by farmland.

"Your killers are captured, Mr. Barker," Hawkins shouted. "You have nothing left here."

Clyde opened his mouth to speak, but Hawkins slammed his door. The Audi sped down the road, leaving Clyde alone in the Georgia countryside. He was but a few miles from town. He decided to jog back to his car.

Storm clouds grew in the distance. Clyde thought about his last lead. He reached the courthouse, got his vehicle, and drove back home. He made a call on his way back, keeping an eye on his rearview mirror. He felt anxious.

"Hello?" the woman answered.

"Hey, it's Clyde. I was wondering if I could come over?"

24

TEA TIME

Fat rain pelted the windshield. The wiper blades went haywire, barely combating the downpour. Torrents of rain flooded Hartwell in the greatest storm it had seen in years. Though usually a careful driver, Clyde squeezed the steering wheel with two hands. The veins bulged on the tops of his hand and up to his toned forearms. He had changed out of courtroom clothes in exchange for Andrew's pastel blue polo, white chinos, and cognac chukkas. A squiggly blood vessel connected from the white of his eye to his hazel iris. His look of anxious determination rested on his lips.

Pathfinder sat in the front seat, whimpering at the rain.

Clyde glanced at her. "We're in the thick of it now, girl."

Clyde drove down the tree-lined road. Violent winds battered the branches. A thin one snapped off and slapped Clyde's car. The white visage of the old plantation house appeared beyond the sheets of rain.

Clyde parked in the roundabout, opposite of the large pick-up truck.

"Looks like we're making a run for it," Clyde said.

He opened his door and stepped into the shower. Head down, he jogged around the front of the vehicle and let Pathfinder out. The dog dashed to the mansion's front door, escaping the rain.

Lightning struck behind the house. Thunder rumbled a second later. Clyde dashed under the porch. He had spent thirty seconds in the rain and was now dripping. In the distance of the wall-managed lawn, Glen Iving stood. Despite the storm raging all around, he stayed dry. The red mask hugged his face and extended past his neck. It had frayed ends. He held the Remington in both hands, not aiming anywhere in particular.

Clyde rang the doorbell.

Pathfinder shook her hair, showering Clyde's lower half.

"Thanks," he said dryly.

Cathy Barnes opened the door. Her lopsided smile grew over her semi-attractive face. She held a hand towel. "My, you're wet. Come on in. Wipe your shoes on the rug. Here."

She handed him the towel.

Clyde dried his hair.

Cathy closed the door behind him and petted Pathfinder. "Beautiful husky."

"She's my new best friend."

The smell of wet dog wafted off of the animal.

"My father only let me own terriers. He was very particular about what he wanted," Cathy said. "Please. We'll chat in the lounge."

Cathy led him to the back of the house. Grand photos lined the walls. Cathy sat on the armless couch under the large window. On the other side of the glass, her garden swayed, tossed to-and-fro by the wind.

Clyde sat in a velvet-upholstered chair. He felt the hardness of the wood under the thin cushioning.

"How is your cop friend?" Cathy asked.

"Sarah? She's good," Clyde replied.

"You two seem close," Cathy said.

"We knew each other when we were young," Clyde said. "We spent a whole summer together."

"Dating?" Cathy asked, flirtatiously.

"Just friends," Clyde said. "She was one of the people that could get me to come out of my shell after my parents passed."

"It's a hard thing to get over," Cathy said. "Despite how demanding mine were, I still miss them."

"Oh, I wanted to say that your tip about Glen paid off," Clyde said.

"What tip?"

"About him being in the lake," Clyde replied. "A female's body was found in there with him."

Cathy tensed up a moment. "Yes, I talked to your cop friend extensively about this a few weeks ago."

"What made you think he would be there?" Clyde asked.

"If I were to hide a body, that's where I'd do it," Cathy said jokingly.

Clyde mustered a fake laugh. He said, "I wonder how the victims' families must be feeling now that the murders are solved."

"It sounds like closure," Cathy replied. "Glen didn't have a great family life."

Clyde leaned forward on his seat. "You know, I have this theory about the whole killings thing."

"Do tell," Cathy replied.

"The Huntsman didn't work alone," Clyde said.

"What makes you think that?"

Clyde replied, "Glen was a quiet kid and socially challenged. You said yourself that he was stalking girls. But the thing is, Glen had an alibi that night, so it couldn't have been him."

"Because the real killer was Terry," Cathy corrected him.

Clyde said, "Terry lied. I knew after he was put away. The man is after a name. Serial killers are immortal."

Cathy's smile wavered. "So who do you think did it?"

Clyde replied, "Glen."

"Why?"

Clyde avoided her question. "Roland knew something. He claimed he never killed Glen, but somehow he knew where his body was dropped. The two of them only had one shared connection."

Clyde waited to see if Cathy would give him another tell. The conversation made her uncomfortable. Did she know that the person they shared in common was her? Roland was like an uncle to her. She'd said so herself. Glen was her best friend.

Cathy didn't take Clyde's bait.

He changed his tactics. "On the night of the killings, you claimed Glen was with you. What did you really do that night?"

"You think I covered for him?" Cathy asked.

Clyde raised a brow, waiting for her answer.

Cathy waved him off. "Please, Clyde."

"I'm after closure, Cathy. That's it."

Cathy replied, "You're a funny man, Clyde." She stood from the couch. "I'm going to heat up some tea. You want some?"

"Sure," Clyde replied.

Cathy left the room.

Clyde felt chills rise on his arm. Glen stood beside him. The man held his rifle, aiming it at Clyde. He spoke quietly. "Tell me the truth, man."

Glen was silent.

"Just say who killed you. That's all I'm asking," Clyde said.

The rifle barrel stayed pointed at Clyde's head.

"Are you protecting her?" Clyde asked. "If she's involved, you don't get to pass on until she's apprehended. Isn't twenty years free of consequence enough?"

"Who are you talking to?" Cathy replied, holding a tray and two cups of tea.

Clyde scratched his husky behind the ear. "My friend here."

Cathy placed the tray in front of him and sipped her piping hot tea.

Clyde lifted the little porcelain cup. Its pleasing aroma filled the room.

Cathy sat next to him, her arm resting against his. "You're right. I've not been completely honest."

Clyde listened intently as he sipped the tea.

Cathy sighed. "I didn't spend that whole night with Glen. He left early before dark."

Clyde's heart rate quickened. "Where did he go?"

Cathy had a serious look. "After those kids."

Clyde cursed. "You're serious."

"Deadly," Cathy replied coldly. "He had a look about him that night. It was a hunger. A lust. He talked about his need to hunt. I didn't understand fully, but I sensed he wasn't talking about animals. He asked me to promise him not to tell anyone that he was leaving that night. I agreed foolishly. He left. I didn't know what he wanted or why, but he came to me the next day and said to keep the promise or he'd hurt me," Cathy stopped herself. "I didn't want your cop friend to know. Clyde, I'm a victim here as much as those others."

Clyde said, "You have to confess."

"But the court already has their killer. Why does it matter?" Cathy asked.

"To give the victims closure," Clyde said.

"But they're gone, Clyde," Cathy said. "Glen is gone."

"Did you kill him?" Clyde asked.

"If you lived your life in fear for so long, what would you do?" Cathy asked, her tea cup shaking. She put it on the tray.

Clyde rubbed his hand over his mouth. "Roland worked for you. Did he help you hide the body?"

Cathy teared up. She sucked in her lips, keeping herself from crying.

Her silence spoke louder than any confession.

Clyde thought aloud, "He must've thought that the lake was a good spot to drop Lydia there thirteen years later." Clyde cursed again.

Cathy said, "I trust you, Clyde. Please, you have to keep this secret between us."

"The police need to know, Cathy." Clyde's heart raced faster. He started to sweat.

"I'd go to jail."

"The jury would side with you. They'd give you a light sentence," Clyde replied.

"But I don't deserve it!" Something about the way she said it sounded insincere.

Clyde said, "Something doesn't make sense. How did Glen know where to find them, and what was his motive?"

"He was insane," Cathy said.

"But you could've told the police that all those years ago. They'd take a pretty young girl's word over a drop-out any day."

"I was sixteen," Cathy replied.

"But you knew how dangerous he was, and still hung out with him," Clyde said.

"I don't understand what you're trying to say," Cathy replied.

Clyde said, "You know more than you're letting on."

Cathy slapped him in the face. "How dare you?" She stood up, her emotions turning from sorrowful to angry at the blink of an eye. "I open my heart to you and you accuse me?"

"Cathy, your story. It doesn't add up—" The room seemed to twist. Clyde blinked a few times. He felt sickened. He stood but lost his balance. He hit the ottoman before landing on the floor. "What is..."

Cathy stood over him. She looked deep into his eyes.

Chill bumps rose all across Clyde's skin in waves. His mouth dried. His muscles spasmed. He was losing control of his body. "What... What's did you do?"

Cathy gestured to the garden. "I have a lot of plants growing there. Some aren't for human consumption."

Pathfinder barked at Clyde.

He glanced at the tilted teacup.

Cathy sat on Clyde's lap. She brushed her hand over his face. "Such a waste. You were a handsome young man."

The dog barked viciously.

Darkness closed in on the sides of Clyde's vision. He fought to rise, but his body betrayed him. He opened his mouth to speak. Only a rattle escaped his lips. He had survived death once, but this seemed different...

The world turned darker and darker and darker. Then black.

Clyde's arm lifted. His body dragged on the floor.

Pathfinder barked.

"Quiet, girl," Cathy said, her voice distorted.

The dog snarled.

Snap!

"Ow!" Cathy shouted. "No biting! No biting!"

Clyde's shirt lifted as he was pulled. The skin of his back rubbed against the cold hardwood floor.

"I said stop it!" Cathy shouted. "No biting!"

A door opened.

The sound and smell of rain bombarded Clyde's numbed senses.

Cathy gasped. Clyde felt the rain against his arm, face, and then the rest of his body. His head bounced down the step at the porch.

A truck's tailgate opened.

"You're heavy," Cathy mumbled to herself, breathing heavily. She put Clyde's arm over her shoulder. Water cascaded down his face and parted lips. His body was like a heavy slab of meat. His weight was too much for Cathy and brought her to her knees.

She cursed loudly.

Pathfinder kept barking at her.

"Shut it, dog!" Cathy shouted. She gritted her teeth and stood, lifting Clyde with all her might. Her knees trembled. At the brink of falling, she slung Clyde's upper half on the car. His chin hit the tailgate. He bit his tongue. The taste of copper filled his mouth. His arms were extended past his head. The gate's corner pressed into his hip.

"Move!" Cathy shouted at the dog. She wrapped her arms around Clyde's shins and pushed him up.

"Gosh!" She heaved.

Clyde's cheek dragged on the ripped bottom of the truck. Rain and blood mixed beside his lips. His hips and thighs crossed over the gate. His feet extended out the back. Cathy grabbed each foot and pushed it in.

Pathfinder snapped at her.

Cathy cursed. She quickly closed the gate.

The dog snapped again. "Ow!"

She quickly got into the front seat and slammed the door. The truck moved below Clyde.

Rainwater puddled in the bed. It slashed into Clyde's lips. The water level rose and splashed his teeth. He was slowly drowning.

The truck accelerated.

The rainwater sloshed around Clyde. It drained out and started refilling at the next stop.

The poison disabled Clyde's body, but his mind raced. His phone was in his pocket. If he could only reach for it... the truck hit a bump. Clyde bounced, bruising his head. He had too many unanswered questions to die now. Who killed his parents? Why Cathy? How could he have this Gift, only to lose it now? There had to be more to life. Fate was on his side. Right? He doubted.

Cathy drove for a long while.

Rain completely soaked Clyde.

The ride became suddenly rocky. Cathy must've turned off-road.

Time passed. Clyde trembled. His body temperature had dropped immensely. The downpour continued.

The truck stopped.

The driver-side door opened.

The tailgate lowered.

Cathy coughed. She tugged on Clyde's foot. "How are you feeling? Still numb? Good."

She grabbed his ankle and pulled. It took a long moment, but Cathy got Clyde mostly out of the truck. He flopped into the puddle of mud. He tasted a twig in his mouth. Half of his face rested on the wet dirt. Rain pelted the other half. Cathy grabbed both his ankles. She dragged him like a plow, dropping him a few times to catch her breath.

Thunder cracked.

Clyde tasted dirt. His eyes opened. It was nearly dark. Tall trees stood all around him. The branches waved him goodbye. His fingers twitched.

"There we go," Cathy said, getting winded. She dropped Clyde's legs.

She walked over to him, grabbed his shoulder, and rolled him to his back. The canopy of leaves kept thirty percent of the rain from hitting him.

Cathy bushed her wet hair out of her face. Her wet clothes stuck to her skin like rags. Standing over Clyde, she grabbed his shirt and lifted his torso enough so his back could rest against a tree. Clyde's head drooped to one side. Two feet away, a roughly thirty-foot cliff dropped into the secret swimming hole Alana had shown him.

Cathy loomed over him. "This is a secret place only us locals know about. They won't find you here. They won't even have a reason to look. I'm sorry it had to come to this, Clyde. I liked you from the moment you arrived in Hartwell. You were just too nosy."

Cathy stretched, reaching high above her head and then touching her toes. She grabbed Clyde's shirt again. "Okay. Over you go."

Clyde's phone rang.

"Oh, come on," Cathy exclaimed. She patted down his pockets and fished out the smartphone. She read the screen. "*Pastor Murr.* I'm afraid God won't be getting you out of this one." She tossed the phone off the cliff. It plopped in the dark blue water. "You probably had your client list on there too. What a shame."

She turned back to Clyde. His eyes locked on hers.

Cathy opened her mouth to speak, but Clyde grabbed her throat with his right hand and squeezed.

Cathy tried to pull off his hand, but he was stronger.

Cathy's eyes went so wide the whites were visible around her irises.

Clyde attempted to lift his other hand, but could only get his finger to twitch. Desperate for breath, Cathy clawed at Clyde's face. Pain seared his handsome face as Cathy raked through his flesh. His left eye shut. He squeezed harder. Cathy clawed faster. Blood and rain poured down Clyde's cheeks. The pain became too much. Clyde pushed her to the side. Her heels slipped on the cliff's edge. Screaming, she grabbed Clyde's forearm and pulled him down with her.

They tumbled in the air for less than a second before crashing into the dark blue spring. The water enveloped them. Clyde drifted lower, unable to swim. Ribbons of blood drifted from his wounded flesh. Cathy put her feet against his torso and launched off of him, swimming as fast as she could. Clyde grabbed her ankle at the last possible moment.

Cathy looked down at him and shouted. A school of bubbles escaped her lips.

She kicked at him.

Gaining some function back in his left arm, Clyde took hold of her ankle, pulling her lower. She waved her arms. It helped her swim but not escape.

Despite the poison, Clyde's heart and lungs had been trained from years of running. Cathy was fit, but she was worn down from dragging Clyde's body. Clyde guessed it was a coin toss as to who would drown first. Unless his legs regained function, his watery doom confirmed his fate.

Clyde's foot moved slightly.

Cathy fought hard, kicking at Clyde's hands pulling her lower. Clyde descended deeper into the underwater cave. The surface ring looked like the size of a trampoline and was shrinking.

Cathy's fighting slowed. Her arms drifted above her head. Her body dragged.

Clyde focused his attention on his legs. He needed to kick. *God, if You're there. Help me out.* He right knee moved slightly. It still wasn't enough. He pushed himself harder. His body regained some function. He released Cathy. She drifted in the water, slowly rising.

Using his upper arm strength, he swam upward. His lungs felt ready to burst. He tried his best to breach the top. He was losing the fight. *Come on! Come on!* Bubbles escaped his mouth. Though the poison was losing effect, he was starting to drown.

Pushing himself to his absolute limit, he neared the surface. He started to black out. He lost momentum. He refused his watery tomb. Eyes closed, he found the rocky wall. His fingers left the water. He pulled himself up in one final attempt to escape. His head breached the surface. He gasped as if it were his first breath. He placed his forearms on the edge of the spring and spit water.

Rain fell on and around him. He rested his head on the cold mossy rock. Long scratches marked his face. The shallow wounds stung. His teeth chattered. He saw Elizabeth's shoes in front of him. He glanced up. All five victims towered over him. They seemed completely indifferent to his struggle.

Clyde took a deep breath. He held it and dove back under.

Barely having function in his legs, he swam down into the ice-cold water and wrapped an arm around Cathy. He held her close to his side and raced up to the top. He pulled her out of the water and presented her at the feet of the dead.

The rain died down to a sprinkle. Like a tadpole, Clyde dragged himself out of the spring. His energy was nearly completely sapped. He turned to Elizabeth. "What now?"

The blonde woman stared at him.

"Isn't this what you wanted?" Clyde shouted, at the end of his rope.

The dead were silent.

Clyde grunted. He pushed his palms against the cold stone. His arms wobbled. He got to his hands and knees. He pushed Cathy over. Her lips had turned purple. His hair stuck to her pale skin. He contemplated letting her die. He lowered his ear to her mouth. No breath. Nevertheless, her spirit hadn't appeared. Maybe there was a chance.

Clyde put one hand on top of the other at the center of her chest and started compressions. "One, two, three." He continued counting compressions for a minute. He lowered his ear to her mouth.

Nothing.

He pinched her nose and gave her mouth-to-mouth.

The dead watched in judgment.

He gave her two breaths and followed by thirty chest compressions.

No result.

"You're not going to get off that easy," he said and tried again.

In the middle of his compressions, Cathy spat out water.

"That's it," he said, and kept going.

Cathy turned her head to the side and coughed.

Clyde rested her head on a rock, allowing her to breathe easier. Her pulse and breath returned.

Someone shouted Clyde's name.

"Down here!" he yelled back.

Sarah appeared between two trees at the top of the cliff. "What are you doing down there?"

"I need an ambulance!" Clyde said.

"It's on the way!" Sarah ran off.

Clyde rested on his back.

A few minutes later, Clyde saw Sarah squeezing through the gulch. She avoided stepping into the water and reached the spring.

She approached Clyde, stepping through the ghosts as if they were nothing.

"Your face," she exclaimed.

Clyde said, "Cathy confessed."

"I see that," Sarah replied. "The police will be here soon."

"Sarah," Clyde said, "Thank you."

"For what? You did all the work," Sarah said.

"For believing in me," Clyde replied.

Sarah was taken back by his kind words. A small smile grew on her face. "I can't have you dying on me now. Hartwell needs its ghost whisperer."

Cathy groaned.

Sarah cuffed her. "Not taking any chances."

The police and paramedics arrived. They struggled to find the best way into the gulch. They lifted out Cathy first, putting her on the stretcher. Clyde needed one too. He trembled. The cold water had soaked into his bones. They put him in the back of the ambulance. Just like the showdown with Terry, he ended up in a hospital room and slept.

He awoke, seeing Sarah on a chair nearby. She was sleeping and snoring gently.

Clyde sneezed.

Sarah jolted awake.

"Hey," Clyde said softly.

"Hey," Sarah replied.

"You never said how you found me," Clyde said.

"I tracked your phone," Sarah replied. "I knew something was up after you got into Hawkins's car. A little while later, I got this feeling in my gut that I should check on you. Using your phone GPS, I saw the tread marks from Cathy's truck and followed them. She wasn't smart in covering her tracks."

Clyde said, "Give her time and she would've."

Sarah said, "Once she's up, I'm getting to the bottom of this."

Clyde replied, "Be careful. She's slippery."

Sarah said, "Don't you worry about me."

CATHY CONFESSED a few hours after waking up. She didn't pull the trigger during the Hartwell Massacre, but she convinced Glen to do so. As his only female friend, Glen was willing to do anything to win her affection. Cathy admitted to giving it to him at a price.

"Why, though?" Sarah asked.

Cathy's expression darkened. "Those kids were better than everyone. Better looking, more intelligent, and had a good friendship. Meanwhile, I'm stuck at home, berated constantly by my parents and never measuring up. All my *friends* liked me for my money. The moment I was born, I was forced to be the heiress to the estate, never allowed to leave this stupid town. Meanwhile, they get to go to college and make a difference in the world. I knew Elizabeth and her cronies were going camping. They bragged about it to everyone. I told Glen to scare them, but he went too far.

"I stuck with him for a few years, but I got sick of being around him. He was a major loose end. I convinced him to go out on the lake with me one night and told him to dress up how he did the night of the killing. He thought I was being kinky, but I did it because it would be easier to kill a monster instead of a man. The freak even brought the rifle with him. In our little canoe, I told him to look at the water while I got undressed. The moment he turned his back, I popped him in the back of the head. I tied bricks around his ankles and tossed him over, almost tipping myself."

"And Roland?" Sarah asked.

"He was watching from a distance," Cathy said. "Little did I know, he'd use the same spot to drop off another kill."

"Do you still have Glen's rifle?"

Cathy replied. "The last I saw it, it was in Roland's scrap-yard. It's long gone now."

Sarah asked, "Do you regret it?"

Cathy shook her head. "I was tired of being the one everyone pushed around. Now, I'm in control."

Sarah replied, "We'll see about that." She jotted down the confession.

"I am," Cathy replied. "You wouldn't have known any of this if I hadn't said it. Honestly, I'm surprised Clyde got as far as he did. I was perfect, even buying plane tickets and hotel reservations for the time of Glen's murder."

"Maybe there are greater forces at play," Sarah replied.

"What do you know about it?" Cathy asked.

Sarah shrugged.

CLYDE WAS RELEASED from the hospital and returned to Andrew's house. He had a bad cold and direct orders from the doctor to get more sleep. Without his phone, he'd lost the contact info of most of his clients.

"At least I have you, girl," he petted Pathfinder as he stepped in the front door. He sniffled. His nose was red and his eyes were baggy. Scabs marked his cheeks and nose. The doctor said there would be scarring.

All this for a couple of dead people. Clyde thought cynically. He grabbed a beer from the fridge and sat out back.

Pathfinder joined him. The lush property extended for acres in front of him.

"We're going to have to do something, girl," Clyde said as the husky rested at his feet. "My bank account isn't looking too hot."

Glen approached him from the side.

Clyde glanced up at him, using his hand to guard his eyes against the sun. "Here to shoot me?"

Glen stood still.

"She's gone," Clyde replied.

Glen turned the gun around and smashed the stock into Clyde's nose. He fell out of his seat, crashing into the dirt. Blood gushed from his nostrils. Pain pulsed through Clyde's face.

Glen rested the rifle on his shoulder and walked toward the woods. He passed between the trees and into eternity.

Clyde lifted his chair and sat himself back up. He shut his eyes, counted back from ten, and opened them. The pain was gone. "I'm starting to get the hang of this."

The husky tilted her head to one side.

"Thank you," Elizabeth said.

Elizabeth, Gena, Tommy, and John formed a half-circle around Clyde.

"I'm surprised you haven't gone yet," Clyde said.

She put her icy hand on Clyde's face and peered into his soul. "I'll see you again, Clyde."

"Hopefully not too soon."

Elizabeth was expressionless. She drew away from him and walked to the woods. The other three followed, blood still leaking from their wounds.

Clyde felt a weight lift off him. The case was closed. He could rest.

After taking a short nap, Clyde returned inside and booted up his computer. He typed Hartwell Police Department in the search bar and found the career tab on their webpage. His leg tapped anxiously. He hesitated filling out the application. He had not felt like a lawyer for weeks. Maybe it was time to change. Hawkins wouldn't be happy. *Screw it.*

After completing the application, he took Andrew's case file and braved the basement stairs. His sickness made his head throb and covered him in a cold sweat. He reached the safe, unlocked it using his parents' death date, and put it inside. He grabbed the second file. Heart racing, he opened it.

62392646R00176

Made in the USA
Middletown, DE
23 August 2019